THE
REIGN

ON EARTH AS IN HEAVEN

A NOVEL

By

Jeffrey McClain Jones

Book II in the Series

THE REIGN: On Earth as in Heaven

John 14:12 Publications

www. jeffreymcclainjones. com

Cover photos from Shutterstock.

To my son Joshua, a man of whom I am very proud.

CHAPTER ONE

Joshua Stippleman squinted at the single-story house, its paint peeling and most of its windows covered with plywood. In its best day it would have been considered a cottage, had it been situated among wild trees and fields or along a lakeshore. Instead, it stood surrounded by ragged asphalt, a strange sight to him. The roads of his childhood were pristine and smoothed to perfection.

He evaluated the little house while he waited for his inner GPS to adjust for the instant transport to this barren place. Next to him, waiting patiently for her student, stood Theresa. As usual, she wore the costume of a nineteenth-century farm wife, with her dark, rough, cloth dress and her sunbonnet hanging down her back amidst her shining brown hair. Since his eighteenth year, Joshua had stood beneath the windfall of wisdom from this woman who had died before his birth.

On this day, Theresa served primarily as his means of transportation, instantly carrying him from his home in Chicago. Joshua and his mentor had arrived at the edge of the rebel zone. In his father's youth, this land was known as the Yukon Territory of Canada. Time travelers from a hundred and thirty years in the past wouldn't have recognized these urban fringes of subdued geography as the site of that remote Canadian wilderness.

The paint-chipped door of the sad house opened, and a dark-skinned boy smiled at Theresa and Joshua. He spoke to Theresa in Urdu, his face animated and joyful. He motioned behind him and a serious filter fell over his demeanor. Apparently, Theresa asked the boy to use English at this point, for Joshua's sake.

Nodding to Joshua, the boy continued. "They have all settled down to playing." He gestured over his shoulder again, toward the dark interior of the house.

Even under the anonymity of the foreign language, Joshua had known the subject of the consultation. And he knew who "they" were. They were the reason for this trip. The who were his mission.

"This is Shirish." Theresa introduced the boy to Joshua. She didn't, however, complete the circle, because they all knew that Shirish recognized Joshua. Joshua was used to meeting people who didn't need caller I.D., and he was also used to being recognized.

"How many are there?" Joshua followed Shirish into an empty living room, which appeared to have been swept thoroughly that day.

"Seven. Two boys and five girls, the usual ratio."

Joshua nodded and said no more as they turned to their right, toward a well-lit room with two low tables and small chairs. They were occupied by children intent on coloring, gluing or animating small plastic figures or vehicles. One little boy, with a pale, pink face, freckles and straight, brown hair, looked up from his paper and crayons and fixed his eyes on Joshua.

Returning the interest, Joshua smiled slightly and raised his eyebrows to say, "Well, what do you think?"

The boy stared a moment longer and then returned to his coloring with a bit more intensity. Joshua continued to watch him, opening his spirit to the emotions emanating from the little refugee. Like a fan drawing out warm air from a house, Joshua collected an impression from all the children. His brief survey of their feelings avoided clinical precision. He merely attempted to take the temperature of their souls, not yet attempting to make a diagnosis.

Again, his attention turned back to the little boy who had made that eye contact. "Oliver" came to Joshua's mind. He glanced at Theresa, who read his mind like a monitor on a computer, and he received a nodded confirmation from her that he had discovered the boy's name. He followed that name to the identity and the soul of the boy on which it had been embossed. An impression rose to Joshua's mind—a boy always curious, always questioning, and frequently frustrating the efforts of adults to bend and contain his spirit.

Oliver looked up at Joshua again and seemed to sense the invasion of his story by this man whom he would probably have known was a mortal like himself. But he seemed particularly curious about this mortal man.

Joshua walked to one of the little chairs, pulled it a bit nearer to Oliver and sat down, careful not to land on it any more forcefully than

Theresa had landed him on the ground outside. When he settle in, Theresa withdrew into the empty living room.

Shirish remained standing in the doorway, away from the children. He watched Joshua with obvious curiosity.

Others of the little people who were seated at the table glanced at Joshua, like rabbits checking where the human stood, in preparation for escape, if necessary.

Oliver's stout hands gripped the crayons tightly, bearing down to turn the green grass from grainy to solid. His other hand clutched a brown and a yellow crayon just as tightly. Then, suddenly, he stopped coloring and looked at Joshua.

"I knew they wouldn't really eat us. The aliens, I mean." He tightened one side of his mouth. Not a grin or a grimace but a thinking pose.

"When did you know?" Joshua noted that half of the other children had stopped what they were doing. He sensed that two of those others hadn't yet discovered Oliver's level of certainty that they were out of danger.

Oliver hesitated. "I don't know. It just feels like I could always tell." His voice faded like a boy used to being corrected for such speculations.

Joshua nodded. "Good. That knowing came from the image of God planted inside you. You did well to listen to that."

Oliver stared through Joshua. "Image of God?"

Joshua smiled. "It's that part of you that people were always so afraid of."

He watched this explanation tumble into Oliver's heart like a half a dozen surprise birthday gifts, all perfectly selected, all wonderfully made. Those riches clearly overwhelmed the boy's capacity to receive, starting a giddy sort of laughter that began in his nose and spiraled down his throat and into his belly. As his chuckling became cackling, and cackling turned to snorting, all the other children stopped their activities.

Shirish allowed tears to drip down his cheeks. Joshua smiled at him briefly, glad to see how much the immortal was emotionally invested in these little refugees.

Oliver laughed cathartically for two full minutes, until a smaller girl, with long, dark hair and serious eyebrows, stood and slipped up behind Oliver's chair. She placed a hand on his shoulder, as if to comfort him in his hysteria. And then she began to weep.

Joshua reached out and took the girl's left hand, hanging loosely at her side, and held it gently while she wept. Slowly, she turned toward Joshua and looked into his eyes, her pretense of comforting Oliver gone, and her longing to be cared for opened wide. She appeared to read his eyes—eyes that he didn't turn away under her close scrutiny. Joshua's smile stretched full length. She smiled back through her tears.

"My name is Joshua." He was nearly eye-level with the girl.

"I'm Ginny. You aren't one of them." Ginny glanced at Shirish.

Joshua knew that she meant that he wasn't immortal like Shirish or Theresa. He also knew that she was still uncertain about what she thought of the immortals.

"I'm just like you."

"But you can see things. You know things." She clearly thought she was posing a problem.

"You can see things and hear things too. I'll show you, if you want."

Ginny tilted her head. The other children all attended to this conversation. They monitored Ginny as they had monitored Oliver, their souls flocking like birds.

"Show me." Ginny's voice cracked, but her eyes stayed firmly on Joshua's.

Joshua smiled and placed his left hand in the middle of Ginny's chest, still holding her hand with his right. "Just listen."

Ginny stood still. She looked toward the corners of her eyes, away from Joshua. Joshua prayed silently. Ginny's eyes closed. But he could see that they had begun to scroll back and forth. A smile approached the edges of her face. To the other children it might have looked as if she wore invisible headphones that Joshua had put on her ears.

"Oh! Oh, I do hear. I hear music." Her eyes opened, fully round.

"Those are some very happy people, dancing and singing around the throne of the great and mighty King—the King that loves everyone, including little girls who dream of being pilots."

Ginny launched her eyebrows higher. She turned to Joshua like a friend half-resenting her secret being told—only half, though. Then she shifted to curiosity again. "Does *he* know that I want to be a pilot?"

Joshua slowly removed his hand from her little chest, nodding. "Oh yes, he knows. He's the one who told me about it."

"You know him?"

"Yes, Ginny, I know him and love him. And you can too."

CHAPTER TWO

If the aliens were even real, Ginny guessed that they were probably good. Which was why the nervous and deceitful people around her all hated them. That's what she was thinking. That's what she hoped was true. And that was before she heard about Oliver.

She knew about a boy who had a dad who drank too much liquor before she knew the boy's name was Oliver. The angry woman that lived with the drunken man was no mother that Ginny would ever want. Not even as a replacement for *her* mother. who couldn't even look at Ginny these days.

Her mother ... well, that was another thing all together.

Oliver's mother was a stewardess or something. She wore a uniform and looked like a doll when she left for work most days. If his mother turned out to be a robot, Ginny wouldn't have been surprised. Most of the moms and dads she knew could be mistaken for robots. Except the drunk ones, of course.

When she met Oliver, he told her that he was going away. He was going to find the aliens and see if they were real, to see if they were better than the people in the city, better than the grownups, that is. The kids were mostly okay.

"Why are you leaving now?" She was in front of her house trying to make the remote-controlled flying saucer stay in the air. She let it fall so she could hear Oliver's answer better.

"My dad hasn't come home in two days. And my mom is traveling for work."

She later heard that Oliver had tried to leave the city that weekend. She heard that when the cops showed up and asked people questions. It was her friend Patrick who told her what was happening.

Patrick was no older than she, but he was taller. That made him think that he could tell her things all the time. Ginny didn't mind him always thinking he knew more. He was sore at his parents, just as she was at hers. Who could blame him? He lived with his grandparents and they were really old and always mad.

Anyway. Oliver didn't get to leave the city that time. And his dad did come back, and then his mom. So Ginny had thought he might change his mind about leaving the city. But he didn't.

"I think we can call on the aliens and they will just come get us." Oliver was sitting on Ginny's stoop when he said this. He looked sad. But he seemed pretty sure about what he was saying about the aliens. She knew he was serous because he said he didn't want to fly her flying saucer even for a little while.

Ginny was worried about Oliver. What if the aliens really did kill children and eat them? That would be awful for Oliver, even worse than a drunk dad and gone-away mom.

Her grandma interrupted. "Come in and eat, Ginny." She said it like it was punishment.

Ginny sighed and left Oliver on the stoop. Just before she closed the door behind her, she said something that felt really dangerous.

"If you contact them, Oliver, make sure me and Patrick can be there when they come for you." And she went in to eat her dinner before her grandma got more upset.

Her grandma wasn't as old as Patrick's. And she wasn't so mad. But she was busy all the time. That was probably why she was always in a hurry for Ginny to do stuff. "Go to bed now. Eat supper now. Go to school now." *Now* was never a good time when her grandmother said it. *Now* always went with doing stuff that she *had* to do, not stuff she *wanted* to do.

That night, Ginny was in bed when a stick scratched at her window. She knew it was something because there was no tree by her window. There were hardly any trees on her block. Oliver had a tree in his yard. It was mostly dead. But it had sticks on it.

"Come with me to the shed behind your house. I think the aliens are gonna come and get me tonight." Oliver whispered this to her when she opened her window to see about the stick.

Ginny could hear the streaming video from the other room. It was loud. But her grandma was probably asleep in front of the screen. Ginny pulled on her shorts and a light jacket and climbed out the window with her sneakers in her hands. She wanted to bring the sneakers in case she had to run away from the aliens. If they really did come because Oliver wanted them to.

"What about Patrick?" She whispered as loud as she could. But she found the answer before Oliver could give it. Patrick stepped out from behind the shed.

"Hi, Ginny. I think Oliver is right. I think the aliens aren't like what they tell us in school. I don't think Mrs. Broder even *knows* what they're like. She just reads it out of a book."

There was Patrick, telling her what she already knew again. But she didn't stop him, or even say, "I know." She just nodded.

"So what do we do?"

"You wanna come with me?"

"Where are you going?"

"I'm gonna let the aliens take me away."

"How do you know they'll take you?"

"I figured it out. Remember Jimmy Carlsen?"

"Yeah. Did he go with the aliens?"

"Of course, he did. That's what they said on the news."

"But that got everyone mad." Ginny was remembering it all now. Everyone in the neighborhood started locking their doors and windows after that. No one knew when the aliens would come and get some kid and take them away.

"Jimmy's parents were mean. His mom yelled at him all the time, no matter what he did."

"Yeah. So?"

"Well. The aliens only take kids away if they *wanna* go. Jimmy wanted to go. I remember he always said he wanted to fly around the world to get away from his parents."

"So they'll come to get you because your mom is so ... so quiet all the time, and your dad drinks liquor so much?"

"And they might take you guys 'cause your grandmas are so mad all the time."

"I think my grandma is just too busy." Ginny didn't really want to argue about that part. She thought Oliver might be right. She had heard of another girl who got abducted. The news said it was because the aliens were so evil, but she remembered that girl's parents were hardly ever around. Maybe that was the real reason.

"You ever hear of someone with real good parents that got abducted?" Oliver was still explaining his idea.

Patrick shook his head. "I hardly ever heard of anyone getting abducted. But never anyone with really good parents or grandparents."

"I don't think they tell us every time someone gets taken away. It might scare us if they did." Oliver sounded pretty sure, like he had been thinking about this a lot.

"Okay. So, what do we do?"

"I heard of this thing they used to do before the wars. I seen it on a movie a couple of times. It's called praying. You just talk to this invisible person, sorta like a great big alien. And this alien sends you what you ask for, if you're really good or really need some help."

"I heard of that." Patrick looked like he was working hard to remember what he had heard.

"So, how do you do it?"

"Like this." Oliver put his hands together like he was clapping, only he just kept his hands together. Then he looked up at the sky.

Ginny looked up there but could only see some stars through a hole in the night clouds. Maybe the aliens were from the stars. So maybe that made sense.

"Oh, great King of the aliens. Please come and rescue us kids from our bad families. At least show us that you're real." And then Oliver waited a bit. "And please don't send any of those ones that eat children, if there really is that kind."

Ginny was sure that she heard a man laughing then. It was sudden but not as scary as she might have thought it would be.

"Did you hear that?" Patrick sounded a bit scared.

"Is that one of your neighbors?" Oliver was looking around at the apartments nearby. Then he stopped still, with his neck twisted. Some kids were laughing now.

"We're not aliens. We're kids just like you."

And that was when these two girls stepped out from the other side of the shed. One of them held up a candle that made her face glow yellow. The strange thing about that candle was that the wind didn't blow it out, or even make it flutter.

"Did you come because I p-prayed?" Oliver still held his hands together like that, but he was letting them fall more toward the ground now.

"Yes, we did. The King heard you. And he sent us to take you to a safe place outside the walls."

"I tried to get outside the walls. They caught me."

"We can take you there in a second. Boom. Right from here to there." The girl with the candle smiled big when she said this.

The smaller girl, with dark hair, giggled. “And it won’t hurt at all.”

This was all so different from anything Ginny had ever seen before that she kept thinking she should be scared. But it was hard to be scared of those happy girls.

Patrick took Ginny’s hand and she could tell that he wasn’t scared either. And that helped her know that it was okay to not run away from the new girls.

“Okay. I wanna go. Take me.” Oliver held out one hand to the taller girl with the candle. He was looking at that candle as if he had noticed how weird it was that it didn’t blow out or anything.

The girl with the candle smiled, took Oliver’s hand and looked at her friend. The smaller girl reached out her hands to Patrick and Ginny. They each took the hand offered, though they didn’t say they were gonna do it. They just did it.

And that’s how they got to the house outside the walls.

Really. That’s how it happened.

CHAPTER THREE

At that safe house outside the rebel city, two other girls rose from their seats, the two oldest. One was tall and slender with golden skin, black hair, and almond-shaped eyes, and the other pale and blonde. Joshua looked at them and smiled broadly again.

"Wendy and Katie?" He confirmed what he thought he knew about these two delicate, young ladies.

They both nodded, then the blonde girl asked, "Are you here to take care of us?"

Though that question lacked precision, Joshua knew what she meant. "I am here to welcome you, and to help you shake off the heavy pieces that are stuck to you, after the trouble you've seen in your life."

Katie nodded and breathed a sigh, as if Joshua had named a sickness that she had been suffering, without knowing what to call it. To Katie, that sickness was as obvious as if it were a bleeding cut in the middle of her forehead. Joshua saw it and knew that Katie was constantly aware of it.

But her cut had never been literal, Joshua could tell. She had none of the soul-marks of the physically abused. Her scars were deeper, because her wounds were from neglect and spite. Katie bore the wounds of a child rejected by her parent. She had tested them by rejecting their lifestyles, or perhaps their philosophies. Whatever it was, it was a test. And they had failed. They had failed her, and she knew it.

He had heard the story of the way Katie and her friend Wendy had escaped their boarding school. In the world managed by immortals and ruled by the King, two young girls had survived on their own for several weeks in alleys and abandoned buildings. When the two girls began to discuss what they knew about the world outside the city, about the aliens and the King, their openness prompted their rescue.

Before Joshua could say more to Katie, another girl, still seated at the table, challenged him. "If you're not one of the aliens, then why do you help them? Are you their slave?"

Joshua shifted his attention from Katie and Wendy, releasing Ginny's hand, and casting a curious look at a stout, little girl with dark brown skin, big dark eyes, and hair tight in two pigtails. She spoke in a way that conjured the word "sassy." This little girl's name was Tanya.

"You sound just like your mother." Joshua winked at her.

Tanya looked hard at Joshua. "You know my mother?"

Joshua shook his head. "No. I just heard the King tell me that you sound just like her. She likes to challenge people, to poke holes in their stories—when you can get her to talk, that is." This latter note called to mind sullen, drug-induced stupors in which her mother had blanked out day after day, leaving Tanya to fend for herself or to find refuge with a neighbor.

Looking at Joshua, Tanya puckered her lips and lowered her straight eyebrows. Instead of challenging him further, she relaxed and smiled placidly at the cars she was playing with.

During that one long afternoon, Joshua spoke with the seven survivors together and individually. Each one accompanied Joshua on a walk, or just sat with him on the stoop outside. As he expected, each of the children cried more in that afternoon than they had in the past year, no matter how sad or tortured their lives had been. This was his gift. With him, children opened emotional gates that they had chained and locked early in their short lives. He saw enough of the interior of each child, with supernatural eyes, to find their place of deepest pain. He also cared enough with his purely human heart to go delicately and persistently.

Toward the end of the afternoon, as he returned from his walk with Melanie, a seven-year-old known to everyone as Mel, he stopped at the front door to check on her emotional status. Mel pushed her mousy brown hair off her face and looked up at him. She returned his smile, a bit less shyly than when they started their walk.

She spoke in a voice distorted by vocal cords damaged when her father attempted to choke her. "Are the others like you?" When Joshua hesitated to answer, she added, "I mean the other regular people, not the angel ones."

Joshua addressed the real question. "You'll find that life outside the walls is free and peaceful. More than that, we'll arrange for you to have a family that will take good care of you and will love you for the rest of your life." He paused briefly. "There's something I want to do for you first."

Mel looked at him, as if wondering whether this, too, would hurt, the way it had hurt when he started to heal her heart.

"This won't hurt at all. I want to heal your throat, your voice."

Raising her eyebrows like someone who had just heard a good riddle, she said nothing, but stood still, waiting.

Joshua gently reached down to her warm, and slightly damp neck. He didn't say anything but stood that way for half a minute. He felt Mel swallow hard. Then she laughed.

"Hey, I'm back! Oh, that sounds good as new. Hey! Ho! Ha! Ha!"

Impulsively, she turned and lunged at Joshua, jumping into his arms. He held her off the ground for just two seconds, before he felt her defenses going back online. When her feet again touched the ground, he held her at arm's length, crouching to meet her at eye-level.

Shy again, she said, "Thank you. Thank you for everything."

That moment was what Joshua thought of as "The payoff." His life was full of everything he needed, and he wanted nothing more from his work than to witness that breakthrough moment of unrestrained joy. His sympathetic spirit experienced the full spectrum of that joy and gained strength from it.

Back inside the house, Joshua prepared the children for the next stage of their rescue, introducing them to two of the immortals they hadn't yet met. Michael Teller was a tall man of African descent in his mortal life. His youthful, athletic build contrasted with his long mortal life, which ended at a hundred and five years. Accompanying Michael, Denise Holman greeted the children with a winning smile and sparkling eyes. A bit over five feet tall, pale-skinned and with short-coiffed brown hair, Denise asserted authority with no effort.

Oliver was impressed by Michael's muscular presence. "So, why don't you guys just stop the people from hurting kids like us? You could conquer them easy."

"Well, Oliver, you're right. It wouldn't be much of a fight if it came to that. For one thing, we can't be killed." Michael grinned. "But that's not what we're about. How would you feel about someone that was forced to be your friend, someone that just played with you 'cause he knew that somebody would beat him up if he didn't?"

When Oliver scowled, as if unmoved by Michael's reply, Joshua interjected. "The King will make everything right in the end. Until then, his saints will keep people from injuring and killing children. And we will keep rescuing the ones that aren't being treated right. You just have to learn to trust the way his kingdom works."

Ginny spoke up. "We've seen how mean people can get." She turned toward Oliver. "That's all we know about. We don't know about people being good and treating each other good."

Joshua remembered his father's argument in favor of the immortals ruling the Earth, back in the early days. Rodney had noted that mortal humans hadn't done a great job managing the planet, so surrendering control to alien invaders might not be such a bad idea.

Denise and Michael had finalized their communications with mortals who were on a waiting list for rescued children. They had confirmed placement for all seven of these refugees. With Shirish, they would coordinate the kids' transportation to locations around the hemisphere—regular transportation in a bus and three different airplanes. Ginny laughed at the prospect of flying in an airplane. But not all the children celebrated the journey away from the only life they had known. Joshua worked to assure these, promising to visit each of them in their new home.

When Theresa arrived to carry Joshua back to Chicago, he hugged each of the children and said goodbye, relishing this part of the job less than the moments of healing and gratitude. His work required releasing these wounded souls into the hands of the King. He harbored no illusion of being their savior. He had enough faith in their true rescuer to have hope for their assorted futures, without personally shepherding each of them every step of the way. He would see them again, and that was enough.

CHAPTER FOUR

Walking out the front door of the little rescue house with Theresa, Joshua expected instant transport back home. But Theresa had a different trip in mind.

"You should do some research, while you're all the way up here."

Joshua decided not to call her on that phrase "all the way up here." He knew she could transport him anywhere in the blink of an eye. But he could tell that she had an important lesson waiting for him. He focused on that prospect. "All right, lead the way."

Theresa held out her hand, as she did when preparing to transport Joshua and herself. Joshua took her hand, facing her. When he landed, with the usual disorienting surge in his adrenal system, he turned from the familiar sight of Theresa's pleasant face to the strange cityscape of the walled fortress that he had seen from the scarred ground outside.

Towering buildings of concrete and glass loomed all around him, yet the street on which they stood glared an accusation of neglect and abuse. Long cracks and mismatched patches marred the surface in every direction. Within a few seconds, Joshua could tell that they stood behind an office building on one side and a parking garage on the other. A few old structures like these had survived in cities governed by the King. But these massive concrete buildings were new, part of the rebel style of urban construction. While standing there taking in his unfamiliar environment, a huge, roaring vehicle ended Joshua's gawking. In a moment, as the heavy machine rounded a slight bend, he could see that it completely filled the alleyway in which he stood, an alleyway that allowed no space for pedestrians.

Theresa still held Joshua's hand. Gripping it tightly, she pulled him toward a door, evident only by a thin line marking its perimeter, no handles or hinges in sight. Theresa pressed on the door and it slid to one side, allowing them entrance into a cool, metallic interior. In that moment, Joshua couldn't tell whether his escort simply knew the working mechanism of the door, or if she had overridden it with supernatural power. Before he could even begin to ask her, voices in the corridor stifled his curiosity. Theresa strode purposefully toward the voices, her face resolute but unconcerned.

When they rounded a bend in the corridor, they faced two uniformed men. Joshua told himself to relax against the primal fight-or-flight instincts bursting inside him. And the two men stopped still, frozen just at the point where they began to speak to him and his guide. Theresa pushed past the stunned men, Joshua close behind, his wrist still firmly in her hand. They wound through three more turns before Theresa persuaded another electronic door to yield and led Joshua into the daylight that filtered down between fifty-story buildings.

On the street, Joshua suddenly noticed that the plain, black dress that Theresa usually wore had changed to a more modern, tailored suit a generation newer than the generic pants and shirt that he wore. She had done nothing to transform Joshua's clothes, apparently confident that he wouldn't stand out as glaringly as an Amish woman from a previous century. The pair of infiltrators now elicited only passing glances. Rows of video screens and speakers blaring professional voices diverted a large measure of the attention that might have fallen on the two strangers.

Around the globe, dozens of these megacities had grown up, like massive grey mushrooms in formerly remote regions such as the Yukon Territory. What had begun as hidden survivalist communities had evolved into giant enclaves of mortal engineering, surpassing all previous human cities in scale, conformity and technology. In fact, the peace imposed by the Reign of the King had provided the platform for unprecedented human accomplishment by the enemies of that Reign.

Joshua thought of the ancient tale of the Tower of Babel whenever he saw news coverage of the walled cities. The survivors of the last great mortal war, who rejected the final advent of the King of creation, had begun to use their freedom to erect the mechanisms of their own salvation, with the same folly as that ancient tower. This time, however, God was deferring intervention against the counterproductive efforts. The King was allowing the weeds of human hubris to grow up in the midst of the peaceful garden that now flourished on the Earth.

Propaganda poured through the streets. Slick video screens caroled the sorts of self-deception required to choose the walled city over loyalty to the King. The compensating architectural style—which some loyal subjects of the King had facetiously labeled Post-human Grandiosity—testified to the residents' deep denial. That the rebel culture offered so many easy targets for outside critics, begged the question of how thinking people could choose the walled cities over the King.

Theresa nodded toward a café or bar at the near corner of the next intersection. Joshua followed her unspoken suggestion and walked with her through the café's open entryway. The King's subjugation of the sort of insects that had annoyed outdoor diners for millennia clearly operated even in the rebel zones.

The interior of the establishment gleamed with chrome and glass, and with more video screens. Above the bar, one of those screens displayed a couple wrapped in each other's arms, glowering at a microphone into which they recounted the abduction of their little girl. They impugned the aliens who robbed them of their parental rights and said nothing about any kind of neglect or abuse of that little girl, which Joshua knew would have been the cause of the "abduction." The interviewer offered no curiosity in that direction, instead launching into an editorial tirade.

"So, we see, once again, that we face a heartless enemy that dares to violate our natural familial rights, pretending to offer a better life to our children, better than their parents are sacrificially providing them ..." The indictment ran on.

Joshua knew that many of the rebels devoted themselves to their children. When those children offered no resistance to the consumer society of the rebels, that parent-child relationship provided the context in which that TV editorial made sense. What Joshua didn't know was the extent to which the listening audience could see the disconnect between the claimed parental rights and the failure of many parents to genuinely care for their children, above their own gratification. The news report made way for a hair-coloring advertisement, filled with barely clad women flaunting impossibly luxurious hair. Next a beverage commercial linked sexual virility with their fizzy product.

The barista addressed Joshua and Theresa in a syrupy tone, as they stood staring at the video screen. "What can I get you two?" A slight woman, with a shaved head—except for a long braid starting at the top of her crown and winding once around her neck—the barista wore a silky blouse that billowed loosely away from her torso, revealing as much of her as anyone cared to see.

Joshua focused on her soul and bypassed her display of erotic availability. Though the barista wore that revealing clothing, she would have shied away from him if she had known how much of her soul Joshua could see.

"Two sonic cocktails." Theresa accessed some knowledge of life behind the walls that Joshua hadn't bothered to acquire.

When the young woman turned away to mix the drinks, Joshua grinned at Theresa, impressed by her undercover persona. He looked more closely at her modern—but still modest—costume. She appeared to be a bit younger than he, though she was born decades before him. Would they appear to be a couple to the small crowd in the bar? Perhaps.

Focused again on the barista, a question came to Joshua's mind, as she stood the two tall, thin glasses in front of them. "How long have you worked here? I haven't seen you here before."

The barista nodded. "I've just been here a couple weeks. I'm new in town." The loneliness the woman emanated rode on an insinuating tone. But Joshua bypassed that insinuation.

"How do you like the big city?"

She shrugged. "It's not so big. New Brunswick City is where I'm from." She referred to the largest rebel city in North America. "I just hope I can make the kind of contacts I had there." She spoke wistfully. "My brother promised me this city rocked."

A very thin, young man with spiky, black hair, highlighted florescent green, sauntered up to the bar. Joshua could tell that the newcomer was trying to look more sober than he was. He slid along the chrome surface toward Theresa, perhaps feeling that Joshua was already in the process of being hooked away from her. Joshua glanced past Theresa and absorbed a wave of panic from the inebriated young man. Loneliness was something Joshua had expected to find. But the young man's undertow of sheer terror at being alone turned Joshua's stomach. He took a broad breath to cover the internal shock.

The barista looked at the young man. "What are you up to, Roger?"

Joshua picked up an added surge of hostility from her, as if she had designs on both Joshua and Theresa. Joshua asked another question, ignoring the interruption. "So, your brother lives here? What about your parents?"

The barista looked at Roger, who leaned slightly on Theresa and very heavily on the bar. "Parents? Ha! I got free from them years ago. I don't know where they are and don't need to know." She only glanced at Joshua after finishing this answer, as if she sensed a gap between herself and this stranger.

Before Joshua could begin to engage with the barista's response, a commercial appeared on most of the video screens in the bar. There, in vivid full-motion color, flowed a huge crowd of people in a stadium, dancing to music that sounded like an imitation of the worship music around the throne in Jerusalem. As Joshua stared at the video spectacle, the camera panned the heaving, sweating crowd of apparently delirious, if not deliriously joyful, young people.

He could feel Theresa monitoring his response. He tried to control his breathing, which had grown swift and shallow. He had met hundreds of the escaping children, and hundreds more of the adults abandoning the rebellion, but had spent little time inside the high-tech, low-hope cities. Meeting a survivor of a disaster pales in comparison with watching the ones still trapped in the collapsed buildings.

Joshua released his gut reaction. "Such a joke, to try to imitate the worship around the throne, when they have nothing at all to worship."

A woman who appeared to be nearly Joshua's age had just entered the bar and stood to his left. She had artificially curly blond hair and an artificial tan. She stared open-mouthed at Joshua's acidic comment. The barista and her drunken customer did the same.

"What are you talking about?" The barista broke the stunned silence.

Joshua looked into her soul. "Remember that little china doll you got from your grandmother, the one that meant everything to you when you were six years old? That was the last time you allowed yourself to be really devoted to anything. You grew out of any feeling of worship because no one offered you anything to win your devotion after that doll fell out the window."

The hard-edged barista, whom Joshua now knew was named Candice, placed a glass on the bar harder than she probably intended. She staggered, planting both hands flat on the chrome surface.

"How ... how do you know about that?" She breathed erratically. "Who are you?"

The woman who had just entered the bar said, "Oh, I know."

Roger, considering Joshua and Theresa without the benefit of all his faculties, closed his mouth long enough to swallow, before turning away and vomiting on the floor between fake leather stools.

The barista swore viciously, her anger at Roger apparently subduing her shock at Joshua's insight into her life.

Theresa touched Joshua's arm, her signal that they had to leave before attracting more attention. He moved with her toward the door, shaking his head at his sad discovery in this one shiny bar, in this one concrete city—knowing that he could easily multiply it by a hundred million.

The newly arrived customer had her mobile device in her hand. She was recording Theresa and Joshua as they left the building. He watched as Theresa nodded toward that device, guessing that she was erasing that video.

Theresa touched Joshua's arm once more and swept them both out of the walled city, known as Humanity City, and back to the unwalled city still known as Chicago.

Roiling with emotions from his face-to-face encounter with the unrepentant rebels, Joshua barely noticed the usual disorientation from his blink between distant locations. He was busy being frustrated at himself for losing control in front of the inmates of Humanity City.

He stood outside his apartment building studying Theresa's placid face. Her sympathy for his emotional ricochets was written on that face, while he sensed no similar frustration within her.

Theresa glistened a mother's empathy from her dark brown eyes, her head tipped slightly to the right, a smile approaching her lips. The only difference in her appearance now from when Joshua first met her was the displaced bonnet she had worn on top of her head in her mortal life. She stood now before him in her usual costume, having switched from her modern disguise during their instant transport.

"That was a hard lesson."

Joshua nodded. "I missed the warning. I see now that you sent it. I just failed to receive it."

"Really, you think I telegraphed that?"

"Telegraphed?" Joshua tried to remember that ancient technology.

"An old English saying,"

Joshua sighed. "I guess it makes me more grateful that those children got out when they did." He looked away from her, remembering each of them. "I'm assuming that you pulled me into that place because those people are a representative of the ones that don't escape."

Theresa nodded. "The ones who have no *desire* to escape."

"No desire. That's what twisted my insides. I could feel their numbed hearts, their lack of real desire, as if wanting those shiny new things and the new drugs, was itself a drug that soothed their God-given urge to be free."

Theresa's face had turned more serious. "The way they've redefined freedom is as the ability to get new toys and new stimulants. That prevents them from seeing what they're missing." She shook her head. "Free? They are free already. What more could they want?"

"I'm having a hard time believing that they have a real chance to choose."

"That's why we rescue them when they're still young, but old enough to choose. Maybe it's the age at which the King counts the turning point that bothers you."

Dissatisfied with this explanation, he nodded just the same. "Maybe that's it. But I've seen inside the hearts of so many of the rescued children. I've seen the first calluses forming already. How could that be what's bothering me?"

Theresa patted his left shoulder as she stood facing him. "Is it so much harder to read your own heart than someone else's?"

Joshua watched a ladybug slowly flying past Theresa's head, catching the late afternoon sun with its blur of tiny wings. He returned to the question of freedom. "I think I'm feeling doubt that God made them truly free, given how prone they are to choosing slavery."

Theresa waited a second. "But bondage has to be an option, if freedom is real."

"Of course." Joshua's face turned downward as his thoughts grew heavy. "The question is how his children, created in his image, could be so easily deceived."

"Self-deception is the hardest kind. Generational inheritance of self-deception is doubly so."

Joshua chuckled, despite the gravity of the discussion. "Farm wife." He admired the inherent irony of Theresa, as he had so many times over the past eighty years.

Theresa feigned feeling insulted. "Don't underestimate how much you can learn about people by feeding pigs."

Joshua raised his hands slightly. "Ah, yes, there's that." And he laughed with her.

"Get something to eat and have some fun tonight."

"Yes, Mom."

"Oh, and you might call your mother while you're thinking of it."

Grinning, Joshua surrendered to the wisdom of his teacher, grateful for the kindness that accompanied his lessons.

"Hey, you get some rest too. You're looking pretty worn out, old girl."

Theresa just smiled slyly, and then vanished.

Joshua shook his head. "Wish I could do that."

CHAPTER FIVE

"Wish you could do what?" Franny had found her neighbor talking to himself. Not so unusual, actually.

"Hi, Franny."

"Theresa just left?"

"Yes. And I'm under orders to eat, drink and be merry. Are you up for a night out?"

Franny planted her feet close together, clasping her thin briefcase in front of her with hands crossed at the bottom of it. She weighed Joshua's invitation. "You know, you're worse than those guys who buy me dinner and then disappear after they get what they want in bed. You disappear *before* bed. You expect me to put up with this much longer?"

She saw him hesitate, as if starting a mental inventory of alternative dinner companions.

But he apparently wasn't giving up so easily. "Well, you know, I'd just ruin you for all those other guys. They wouldn't be able to compete."

"Umhmm."

Franny and Joshua had each lived in this apartment building for nearly ten years, Joshua slightly longer than Franny. They had dated on and off since she moved in. If you could call it that. His ideas about intimacy without sex seemed as alien as the folks in Jerusalem. Something she could never grasp, and something disjointed from her other relationships.

"I sense that you're not buying what I'm selling."

Franny was aware of his ability to read her feelings, which helped her to relax and wait as Joshua completed his internal surveillance.

She sighed. "Sure, I'll buy your offer of a night out. I was gonna be bored and lonely tonight anyway, so I may as well be bored and lonely with you."

"Ha. Not much of an endorsement. But you know I love a challenge. I'm going to make sure you have a grand time tonight, so much so that you end the evening with absolutely no regrets."

"Umhmm."

Franny led the way into the building as they discussed the logistics of the evening, before each of them headed home to change clothes. Joshua convinced her to eat at a restaurant run by immortals, where they would hear a band consisting of both mortals and immortals, one of the former being a young man that Joshua had helped to rescue from the rebels. This personal connection convinced Franny to accompany him into a place so full of immortals.

Alone in her apartment in the renovated nineteenth-century building, Franny dropped her briefcase on the counter in her kitchen. She pulled her lunch bag out and left it lying empty and ready for next week. It was a weekend. She may as well start out with a night on the town. Tomorrow she could contact another guy she knew. Someone with standards and expectations different from Joshua's.

It wasn't that she didn't like being with Joshua. It just wasn't enough. Not that *he* wasn't enough, just that his limits seemed impossible and unhuman. She shook her head at this thought and strode to her bedroom. She would dress the way she always dressed for a date. Joshua would just have to figure out how to deal with that.

Twenty minutes later, dressed in a breezy, thin cotton dress of pale lavender—one intended to entice interested males—she greeted Joshua downstairs. He wore a shiny, dark purple shirt and straight, black slacks—a definite upgrade. She grinned at him and shook her head slowly.

He spoke first. "You look smashing, as usual. Love those curls." He gently bounced the entwined loops of golden hair that fell just short of her bare shoulders.

"Thank you. You look pretty good yourself, for a man of your age." She giggled lightly.

"Yeah, rapidly approaching middle age."

Franny took hold of his left arm and focused on the first gray hairs around his ear. "Approaching?"

The streets of Chicago had been paved with long-lasting organic material in a variety of colors over the past several decades. The planners further assured the longevity of the pavement by limiting the use of heavy vehicles inside the city. Neighborhoods generally contained everything needed to sustain human life, with food-producing gardens and even small farms salted over the whole city. There were a variety of employment opportunities close to residential areas. Long commutes had become part of an abandoned history, just like combustion engines.

Franny and Joshua boarded the light rail line, which hummed on a cushion of air toward downtown, breaking out of their neighborhood for the sake of entertainment. The train's well-lit compartments had just surpassed the light outside, as the sun set behind the apartment buildings and tall trees. She and Joshua settled side by side into a cushioned seat, with a clear view of the scenery during their surging ride toward dinner and music.

"How was your work today?" Joshua glanced at her.

She smiled. "It was good, especially the part where the nudists came in to buy wrapping paper."

"'Edenists' is what they call themselves, if you don't mind." Joshua corrected her with a grin.

Franny rolled her eyes. "Well, whatever they call themselves, nude is what they were, and it was too weird for me. My coworkers were either gawking or straining themselves, trying not to laugh. It was an older couple, and let's just say they weren't in the best physical condition."

"And you? What did you do?"

"I had to wait on them, to help them get the paper they wanted, and to take their money. I was perfectly professional."

"Umhmm." He imitated Franny's skeptical sound. "But what I'm wondering is, where did they carry their money?"

"They had little pouches." She shook her head at her regrettable wording, as Joshua started to laugh out loud. She raised her voice to recover. "They had like small shoulder bags made of some cloth." She lowered her voice as his laughter faded. "Actually, I thought her bag was pretty nice, and I told her so."

Joshua was still chuckling. "Well, you couldn't tell her you liked her blouse or pants."

Franny just rolled her eyes at him.

"Is this the first time you've had to wait on Edenists?" Joshua turned a little more serious.

"Yes. I've seen them on the streets before, and wandered into one of their neighborhoods by accident, but they've never come into the shop like that."

"And for wrapping paper, no less. You must've wanted to suggest they wrap themselves."

Franny laughed. "That's exactly what I was thinking."

Joshua did his usual probing about Franny's work at the shop, which she managed. He asked a few questions about the people working for her. She returned some curiosity about Joshua's work but preferred to stay only vaguely acquainted with what he did, as if he were a secret government agent from the days before the Reign.

When a call vibrated her communication device, Franny tipped her head apologetically. Joshua waved a "go ahead" and tapped his own device to start a call.

Her call was from Grayson, one of her employees.

"Hello, what's going on?"

"It's those aliens, again. They want to give us some of their ceramic tiles to sell. No charge of course."

Franny snorted. "You worry about accounting too much. Besides, I created a category for these free acquisitions. Just take what they're offering. No questions."

"No questions? But aren't a lot of people gonna ask questions when they see we're selling this stuff?"

"You *do* know that they're not really aliens, right?"

She could hear Grayson's deep intake and hearty sigh. "Of course, I know. But that doesn't mean I wanna be seen as one of their employees."

"Well, you're my employee right now, so you can cover yourself with that. You're just doing your job." Being the boss didn't usually mean being this bossy. "Don't worry about it, Grayson. Almost everyone is tangled up with them these days. It's unavoidable. And if someone complains, send them to me."

"Yeah. I know. Okay. Just venting, I guess. I see that free acquisition category now on the display. Okay. Have a good evening."

"I plan on it." She had skipped a step in here somewhere. "Hey. Those ceramic tiles, they're the ones with the deep color layers and mesmerizing detail?"

"Yeah. Those are the ones." He sounded tired.

"You should be going home by now."

"I should. But those aliens knew I was still here after hours. They just popped right into the shop. It doesn't do any good to lock up at closing."

"Okay, Grayson."

"Right. Venting over now."

"Over and out."

"Yeah."

After Franny hung up her call, she could hear Joshua ending his.

"Goodbye, Mom." He leaned back and looked out the window.

"How's your mom?"

"She's well. She's going to watch some of her great-great-grandchildren while their parents go out tonight."

Franny smiled. "Still going strong, with great-great-grandchildren."

Joshua nodded, his eyes falling to the floor. "I need to visit the farm soon."

"Yes, you do." It seemed to her like he was always working. She didn't doubt that he needed a break.

The train slowed and Joshua nodded toward the door. Franny rose to her feet with him and stepped up to the silent, sliding doors just as the train stopped. A man stood with them and smiled, glancing at the ceiling of the train.

"Fascinated by the trains?" Joshua was apparently fascinated by the man.

The stranger replied with a merry grin. "Just enjoying my work."

Joshua looked from the stranger to the sleek hardware around them. As he stepped off the train, he looked back again. "Good job."

The man nodded humbly. "Thank you." He was still grinning as Franny turned to walk away.

"You know him?"

"I only know *about* him." Joshua had that far off look in his eyes, as if he were traveling internally even as they were walking off the train platform.

They stepped out of the lush train station, past a mix of large plants from around the world. Franny followed Joshua onto the street, which smelled of flowers. That smell reminded Franny of a visit from her mother, years ago, when her mom had marveled at the contrast between the big cities of her childhood and the streets of the new Chicago. "They sure didn't smell like flowers back then," her mother had said.

That memory evaporated, however, when Franny stepped through a rectangle of sunlight and her eyes adjusted. Two North American mountain lions lounged on the pale blue sidewalk, catching the last amber rays of sun angling between buildings. She stared at the radiant color of the cougars' sun-soaked fur against the pleasing color of the pavement. Franny loved her gift shop because of the many ways she could explore style, design and color. She was distracted by a thought toward those tiles Grayson had called about, and then returned to admiring the animals who were looking at her now.

When she knelt next to the big male cougar and stroked his silky fur, she felt that same warmth from the sun that had attracted the big cats here. Joshua stepped back and took several photos of Franny and the mountain lions with the mobile camera embedded with his phone. When she stood to rejoin him, he was projecting the pictures on the pavement at his feet.

"You know, I didn't say you could take pictures."

"Yeah, but I got permission from the lions. I'll just delete that pesky human later."

Franny stood with her arms crossed in front of her, trying to scowl a rebuke at him.

He smiled at her. "You're beautiful when you're mad. Too bad you're just faking it."

She socked him in the arm, to punctuate the conversation.

"Hey, watch out. The immortals have swooped down and rescued people from lighter touches than that." Joshua gave her his lopsided grin before grabbing her hand and leading her past the mountain lions, toward the restaurant.

When they reached the front of the restaurant, called The Great Break Grill, she saw that it was quite crowded. Joshua stepped up to the hostess, however. "Table for two, please."

The lithe, young hostess raised her dark eyes from the electronic seating book in front of her and looked impressed. "Well, we do have a table for two that just opened up."

Joshua grinned simply, ignoring Franny's laser gaze. Had he done something to make that coincidental opening happen? She never knew how much the immortals intervened in such things, and Joshua's connections with them seemed much more extensive than she could quantify.

Then the hostess seemed to remember something. "Oh, Mr. Stippleman, there's someone here who would really like to see you."

Joshua smiled knowingly, but Franny lacked his advance knowledge of such things. She was, however, used to people recognizing him when they went out.

"Don't you ever want to be surprised?" Franny asked, as the hostess slipped away.

"Sure, all the time. I can plug my ears and cover my eyes whenever I want."

The hostess appeared again out of the crowd, towing a young man. Apparently, she hadn't told him who he was going to see, because the towing turned to stepping out of the way when that young man saw Joshua and rushed to hug him.

Joshua stood to catch that hug, and Franny raised a hand to prop him up. It was instinct. Joshua was much bigger than she, so she wasn't really going to provide much of a brace. And Joshua had a significant size advantage over the brown-haired, young man who had lunged into that embrace anyway.

"Nicolas, how are you?" Joshua's voice expanded with obvious pleasure.

Nicolas spoke through a grin just short of hilarious laughter. "I'm great, as you surely know. I was just thinking of you today, thanking God for you again and again."

Though she had stood next to these ecstatic reunions before, Franny was shaking her head again, at business as usual around Joshua. She studied the menu posted on the wall, only half aware of Joshua catching up on the news of Nicolas's life. She guessed that her dinner companion abbreviated that review with her in mind. That was one advantage of dating a guy as intuitive as Joshua. He knew when she was even a little bit annoyed.

Deftly, Joshua pulled away from Nicolas and patted the young man on the cheek. When Nicolas turned to go back into the restaurant, Joshua wrapped his right arm around Franny's waist. She followed absently as the hostess led them to their table, where Joshua held Franny's chair for her. She smirked at his old-fashioned manners.

Immediately, a young man landed next to their table, after zipping through the crowded restaurant. "Hello, my name is Carlos. Welcome to the Great Break Grill." His face was lively. He bowed and addressed Franny. "Would you like me to order for you, or do you want to order for yourself?"

This forthright offer froze Franny momentarily.

Joshua intervened. "I think we will order for ourselves tonight, Carlos."

Carlos nodded graciously and produced a glass pitcher of water from thin air. "Ice water?"

"Yes, please." Joshua glanced at Franny. "We'll take a minute." He lifted a menu from the table.

Again, Carlos nodded and then swept away toward the kitchen.

Franny watched him go. "Why doesn't he just walk like a normal ... like a normal mortal?"

Joshua looked at her sympathetically. "They're not trying to make us more aware of our limitations, or even disrespecting us. They were mortal humans once. I think you and I would experiment with the laws of physics like that, if we could."

Franny took a deep breath, relaxing a bit. "I need some wine." She said that under her breath.

Joshua smiled, though not wholeheartedly. He wasn't a fan of her drinking. This was one of the ongoing tensions in their relationship.

"Sure, let's order some wine." Was that resignation in his voice?

Carlos reappeared at the side of the table, this time simply winding his way through the dining room. Only the timing of this approach seemed remarkable.

"Might I suggest an African wine?" Carlos showed them an electronic wine list which they had neglected on the table.

"African?" Franny said. "Really? That's good?"

"The very best these days. Very fruity, very delicious, and a bit less alcohol content."

Franny hesitated here, but then nodded. When Carlos asked if they each wanted a glass instead of a whole bottle, Joshua agreed.

"I would have said the whole bottle. But I know what you think about my drinking."

"Have I been judgmental?"

Franny shrugged. "Maybe not. Maybe it's just me judging myself."

Up to this point, they had heard only recorded music drifting behind the noises of conversation and silverware. Now the live entertainers took up their place in the far corner of the room in which Joshua and Franny sat. A very large man with dark brown skin, a shaved head, and a gold earring sat down at the piano. Behind him stood a tall, blonde woman holding an upright bass. Two thin, young men with pale faces and assorted whiskers situated themselves and their electric guitars behind microphones toward the center of the stage. One of these was Joshua's friend Nicolas. A woman, whom Franny guessed was Brazilian, lifted a microphone from its stand and strode regally to the front of the stage. She made no introduction. Instead, she simply started singing in a deep and mellow voice that climbed the scales until it sparkled into a versatile soprano. Along the way, she clearly articulated words in at least three languages, as far as Franny could tell. The way her voice wound in and out of the piano tones, the bass tones and the guitars, defied human limitations.

Franny watched Joshua beaming his delight at the music. He seemed truly relaxed. And that was before the wine had arrived.

Carlos delivered their wine and Joshua broke from his reverie to toast Franny. With her glass in hand—as good as the waiter had claimed—and the music rising and falling around them, she settled in like a child burrowing deep into a pile of pillows.

Walking home from the train that night, both hands wrapped around Joshua's left arm, she smiled sleepily. She felt like a girl on her way home from a fair. Keeping the impending separation from Joshua out at the edge or her awareness preserved that peace.

She could sense his effort to tap his last ounce of energy as they stood outside her apartment door. Despite his exhausted state, he maintained his path toward his own bed.

"I love you, Franny." He blinked heavily. "And I don't have to spend the night to feel it or show it."

A warm energy emanated from him, perhaps from his words, or from something deeper. And she accepted it as an offer of contentment, even if it was only temporary.

Franny kissed him on the cheek and then pushed through her front door as he headed for the stairs. Inside, she dropped her clothes on the floor and slid between smooth, fresh sheets. Alone again.

CHAPTER SIX

Theresa checked Joshua's status around midnight, pleased that he had taken her advice and gone out for the evening. She also celebrated that Franny had enjoyed the evening, free from much of her usual frustration with Joshua's limitations on their relationship.

"You are good to us all day and all night." She addressed her Lord. In return, she received his affirmation of her praise, warming her heart with his affection. She smiled like she was falling in love for the first time, even as her hands concentrated on forming clay into the shape of a mother deer and her faun. The two figures represented a small fragment of a huge bas-relief she was creating in Paris, near the center of that renewed city. As she sculpted, she listened to a choir of small singers, who hovered in the night sky above her.

As her joy escalated, Theresa's immortal body followed her ecstatic soul, and she transported instantly to the royal city. She soared inside a whirl of worshippers, a few hundred yards from the throne. She could see the King's physical manifestation perfectly from over a quarter mile. She could see the sparkling love in his noble eyes, and could feel the magnitude of his power as he energized her worship dance, along with the celebrations of hundreds of millions around her.

Amid an uninhibited vertical flight she caught sight of a thin girl who looked much like herself. Theresa swooped in and grasped the waif-like darling, twirling her as they rose above the throne. "Hannah!" She shouted as she spun in worship with her youngest daughter from her former life.

Hannah chortled and struggled, wrestling with her mother and embracing her in turn. "Let's grab Jack." Instantly, they were three instead of two, and Hannah's older brother Jack had grasped them both by the hand and launched the little family high above the Earth's atmosphere. They paused for a three-way hug in the cool, clear stratosphere, and then began to sink back toward the throne. They parted with satisfied laughter.

No loss of joy followed that departure, only hope and fulfillment. All was well with Theresa and her children. Neither did her longing to see friends or family ever produced any anxiety in the moments *before* they met.

She made a rocket-fast flight into the moonlight shadows of an oasis in the Egyptian desert.

Two young men and a small girl welcomed Theresa when she landed a few feet away. They embraced her with strength and passion, and they all laughed together at the beauty of the night. The two young men began to sing a song in Arabic and Theresa harmonized expertly, though she had never heard their song before.

Her dear friend Kim, whom she had known now for eighty years, wrapped both arms around Theresa's waist as they walked the perimeter of the oasis. Kim hummed contently as the others sang, and Theresa felt the vibration of her friend's low voice in her chest. Like a leaf settling to its rest among the colors on the forest floor, Theresa stayed with her three friends for the remainder of the night, holding each other, singing and telling stories.

Kim told the most intricate and glorious stories, which inevitably launched Theresa into ecstatic worship of the King, who was always the hero of those tales. At the end of one of Kim's narratives, one of the young men called to a friend who managed the weather in that region, and a sudden rain shower doused the oasis, just before dawn. Theresa lay back on the sand and allowed the temperate rain to patter over her whole body. As she lay looking up at Kim, she could see her small friend weeping joyfully, her tears mixing with streams of rain.

"If they could only know this joy." Theresa shouted intercession for mortals whom she knew or would someday know. And her three friends echoed her prayer. That prayer for the joy of their Lord to pour down on every mortal soul reflected the longing of the King himself. And this chorus of petitions lasted through the sunrise and into the first light of day.

When the King released them from this labor, two of her friends said goodbye and transported away. Only one of the young men, Aarif, remained to feel the warmth of that new day with her. This oasis was his primary responsibility. After checking on some of the plants around the growing edge of the oasis, even Aarif said goodbye, transporting to the throne for worship.

Alone in the morning desert light, Theresa felt the urge to paint a picture. She stored that desire away in her soul for later, like a deposit of future pleasure. Her responsibilities among the mortals limited her freedom to follow every urge. But she lost none of the joy those longings promised. She would paint later.

Now she transported to a small town on the southern coast of what used to be Spain, near the city of Valencia. There, in a small house painted white, with a red tile roof, she met one of her students. Similar to her work with Joshua when he was a teen, Theresa mentored a young woman named Osana, who had a special ability to see into the future.

Theresa greeted Osana's father, Rodrigo, at the front door. The stout man preferred that the tutor enter and depart from the house in the manner of mortals. Theresa always honored his preference.

Not surprised by the scheduled arrival of her tutor, Osana waited in the center of the little entranceway, behind her father. As soon as Don Rodrigo excused himself, the two women embraced and began to speak rapidly. Osana led Theresa back out the front door, toward their usual walk by the sea.

For three hours, Theresa conversed in rapid Spanish with her eager student. The petite sixteen-year-old ardently investigated everything Theresa could tell her about mortals becoming immortal when they died. Not satisfied with general principals or abstract ideas, Osana fixed her dark eyes on Theresa and insisted on specific examples of people who had made that transition. How had they changed, after passing from their mortal life to immortal? Where did they go?

Osana endured the lectures on the nature of the human spirit, and the immortality embedded in all humans. But she also found satisfaction for her curiosity. Theresa knew that her student pursued this curiosity less for herself than for her grandmother, who had been born before the Reign and was now over 140 years old, growing less lively every time Theresa inquired.

When their time together stepped toward the end, they discussed Osana's studies at the University in Valencia, and made plans for a trip to Madrid, for which they had been preparing over the course of several weeks. There, Osana would spend two weeks living with a family, helping around the house during the day, and meeting with the father and eldest daughter at night, to encourage each other in learning about the prophetic gifts at which they all excelled.

Finally, Theresa excused herself, saying goodbye to Osana at the front door of her house, with a kiss and hug before launching into the sky.

CHAPTER SEVEN

With the sun now climbing high on a bright cloudless morning, Theresa stopped in Wales to pass some time with one of the oldest men in the British Isles—Evan Bowen, a gnarled, farmer born sixty-five years before the Reign. As mortals count such things, Theresa had no responsibility for taking care of Evan. But she considered greeting the old gent a high calling, as much part of her work on the Earth as mentoring Joshua and Osana.

Theresa landed behind a hillock, before walking the dirt path to Evan's barn, where he was tending to the medical needs of several sheep.

"Hello there." Theresa called from outside the low, rustic barn, careful not to surprise the old man.

"Hello, yourself." A scratchy bellow sounded from the open barn door.

"How are ya', Evan?" Theresa saw her friend step into the triangle of light on the rough wood floor next to the doorway.

"Fair to middlin', I'd say, old girl. No complaints." Evan stood barely five and a half feet tall if he forced himself to stand up straight, but he rarely made that effort anymore. "Are ya here to sample that cheese I was tellin' ya about?" Evan cocked his head a bit to the right to look up into Theresa's eyes.

She smiled and nodded. "Of course. I flew all the way from Spain for a taste."

"Ah, yes, playin' at bein' an angel again, are ya?"

Theresa laughed. "Lead the way, my friend."

Evan emerged from the barn and waved weakly for her to follow around the side of the house. He headed for his kitchen door with a distinctly lopsided waddle.

Theresa had repeatedly offered to heal his misaligned back and lengthen one leg. Evan had generally stared at her, as if to calculate the cost of such miraculous surgery, and then shook his head. "Some o' your folks took away the pain of it years ago, and that's enough for me. Besides, what would ya be doin' next, making me handsome and young like you?" He flirted, even as he defended good old natural mortality.

Inside the low and cozy cottage, built centuries before the Reign, Theresa could smell fresh-baked bread. Evan's great-granddaughter lived a few miles away and came by to cook and clean for the old man.

"I had Marianne make us some bread to complement the cheese." Evan stepped onto the smooth stone floor and sniffed the fragrance of the fresh bread. "Can't smell the cheese so much. It's not that kinda cheese." He said that last part under his breath.

"Any way I can help?" Theresa was monitoring Evan's labored movements.

"No, no, you just take a seat there by the stove. There's still a nip in the air." He focused on an assortment of knives on his countertop. "Or maybe you lot don't get cold anymore." He muttered now. "I keep forgettin'."

Theresa sat in one of the two heavy rocking chairs by the wood-burning stove. "I enjoy the warmth of the fire. Thank you."

Though she could have eased his movements with a word, or the least little touch of her hand, Theresa respected Evan's reserve, and settled for watching her old friend without intervening. In her old life as a farm wife, watching the toddling old man would have driven her to distraction. But she wasn't subject to the guilt and fear that badgered her during her mortal life. She rested in the knowledge that she could do nothing against Evan's stubborn will.

In her peaceful inner space, a song was born, and she began to hum as she watched Evan. Any close observer would have seen the slight easing of his mobility and the slacking of his breathing, at the sound of that tune. The accompanying relaxation seemed to brighten his smile and lightened his conversation during the half hour visit that followed. During that time, Theresa sampled the hard Welsh cheese and the warm, homey bread.

Like most of her visits to Evan's farm, she listened to the cares and memories of her friend, offering small responses and warm smiles. And, as usual, Evan welcomed her attention and unleashed a few smiles of his own.

After the bread and cheese on her plate, and the tea in her cup, had disappeared, Theresa thanked her host. "Evan, it was wonderful to see you, and the cheese is just as marvelous as you boasted." She stood from her chair.

Evan rocked his own chair back and then forward to boost himself to his feet. Theresa extended a hand to help him land this maneuver. Assisting with the dishes only as long as Evan would tolerate the attempt, Theresa finally embraced her old friend and said goodbye. Her easy immortal steps evaded the plodding wobbles of the old man as they made their way toward the garden door.

There, amidst the verdant green of Evan's kitchen garden, Theresa waved and winked at the old man. As she rounded the hillock out front, her expansive hearing caught what he said to himself as she passed out of sight.

"Goodbye, old girl. It won't be long now."

CHAPTER EIGHT

Joshua stood by his dining room window, which welcomed the morning sun and offered him a sparkling view of the courtyard of his building. From there, he could also see part of Franny's dining room and detected some movement beneath the half-drawn blinds one floor down and across the corner. He held a cup of coffee in one hand and smiled at memories of the evening before. Those memories tumbled aside, as if before a sudden gust of wind, however, when Theresa warned of her approach.

She usually sent this warning to avoid startling him, without resorting to landing outside his apartment and knocking, like a mere mortal. She respected his privacy, always checking that he was alone and landing only in his living room or dining room. His ability to sense most of her thoughts and feelings further rendered her supernatural approach anticlimactic.

Turning just in time to see Theresa appear next to his china cabinet, Joshua greeted her with a grin. He could sense her pleasure at his relaxation and his time with Franny. Theresa hadn't lost her feminine affinity for romance, though she herself had no need for such relationships.

"You really should eat something." Theresa cast her eyes toward his coffee and spoke in her most motherly tone.

Joshua nodded. "Toast and jam?"

"Better than coffee alone."

While Joshua scuffed to the kitchen on calloused bare feet, Theresa took his place by the window. She joined him in the kitchen as Joshua was slipping two pieces of rye bread into his toaster oven. He tapped a button and the orange-red glow rose quickly to begin warming the bread. Theresa opened the shiny black refrigerator and pulled out the butter, without looking. Joshua knew this wasn't a trick meant to impress him, rather a sign of her comfort in his place. She didn't dull her powers in order to protect his ego. By now, he was quite familiar with the immortal life Theresa led, whether with him or without him.

"How is Osana?" Joshua lifted a heavy butter knife from a drawer beneath the granite countertop.

"She has seen her grandmother's death in the future." Theresa spoke nonchalantly. "And that leads her to wonder about what lies ahead for her beloved *abuela*."

"You assured her?" Joshua took the butter dish from Theresa's hand.

"Of course. She is young, still prone to wander into the future, longing to comprehend what lies ahead."

Joshua nodded. He rubbed sleep from one of his eyes. He looked her full in the face now. "So why did you drop by today? I have my meeting in Minneapolis and I'm going there by old-fashioned bullet train."

Theresa smiled affectionately. "You know how much I love to see you first thing in the morning." She regarded him in that warm, enveloping way.

Joshua reflected Theresa's affection. "Well, I would know even better, if you would let me read your heart more completely."

At that moment, just before the toaster dinged and he returned to the process of waking up and getting out the door, Joshua strained against that familiar urge to wrap his arms around her, to hold her next to him for however long he could. Theresa obviously recognized the emotional restraint. She turned away and wandered into the living room, where he heard her greet Gwendolyn, his cat. A minute later, Joshua followed her, taking a seat on the smooth gray couch and propping his feet on the coffee table, which bore several stacks of books.

"Soft piano music." Joshua spoke to his digital music system, before he bit into his toast. Obediently, the system queued up a dozen songs composed in the last fifty years and began to play at low volume.

Theresa sat in a burgundy chaise lounge with her bare feet up and the white cat in her lap, stark against her black dress.

"Why don't you tell me I ought to get a wife, maybe marry Franny, when you see me straining against my physical urges?" Joshua spoke with his mouth half-full.

Theresa took a deep breath, released it, and stroked Gwendolyn from ears to tail, watching the long Persian cat hairs drift toward the floor. "You know that I've never doubted your ability to carry out your commitment to celibacy. Even when you struggled and failed many years ago, I knew this was your way in the world, the opening in the universe through which you would travel and encounter the King most fully. The only thing I wonder is whether you might find another mortal who shares your commitment, as I have my brothers and sisters, who know how to love and be loved without vows and rings and sexual attachment."

Joshua inhaled deeply. Since that time, over sixty years ago, when he yielded to sexual temptation for one disruptive weekend, he and Theresa had spoken little of his calling to remain single.

Joshua purged his mouth of toast crumbs with a long sip of coffee. "Well, if you're going to talk like that, I'm going to become like those mournful folks longing for death, so they can be like the immortals."

"I didn't say it to make you jealous, but to start you looking more intentionally for companions that match you more closely. Being the pioneering rebel suited you well for the first fifty years or so."

Joshua checked Theresa's face for irony, and found it there, as she teased him toward his goal. What most surprised him about Theresa's serious intention, behind her taunting, was the implication that he had outlived his role as youthful iconoclast by half his life. He found refuge in the fact that his was the first generation born under the Reign. He had to be excused for not knowing how to regard age in relation to an indefinite life expectancy. But maybe fifty years of advanced adolescence was enough.

"Since I have yet figured out how to read all your thoughts, you will have to tell me now whether you have someone in mind."

Theresa lifted the cat from her lap and stood from her seat with the grace of an elite gymnast, before placing Gwendolyn on the end of the chaise. She smiled at Joshua as she reached full height and swept cat hairs off her dress without looking.

"Do you remember that girl who told you the story about the mortal woman who could fly like the immortals?"

Joshua nodded, trying to collect the details of that memory, without losing the context of Theresa's question.

"You remember that you concluded that the girl really believed the story, but you assumed that she was confusing two experiences into one?"

"Yes. Wait. It's true?" This was half question and half realization.

Their conversation took on elevated significance, as Joshua realized the purpose of Theresa's unscheduled visit, and then flipped through the prospect that his mentor was acting as matchmaker, for the second time in their long association.

"When can I meet her?"

Theresa smiled wryly. "You can meet her when you believe that you can fly without me."

With that, the small Amish woman vanished.

"Ha!" Joshua shouted to the empty space in front of him. Gwendolyn looked at him, obviously wishing to express something. That cattish rebuke left him grateful that he couldn't read *her* mind.

CHAPTER NINE

The day after Joshua returned from his trip to Minneapolis, Theresa met him early, outside his apartment. She lounged on a bench next to a flourishing little flower garden. She often waited there for Joshua to get ready for the day, especially a day that would require some superhuman transportation.

Joshua squinted in the early sunshine that angled into the eastward-facing courtyard. In contrast, Theresa's eyes resembled those of an indolent cat focused on resisting sleep, more than keeping out the bright light. But that resemblance was only apparent and not real. No matter what she did overnight—and Joshua couldn't even venture to guess what—she never needed sleep. He knew that what appeared to be sleepy contentment was only contentment.

"Ready to fly away with me, young man?"

"Ha. I'll bet you say that to all the guys."

As if she had planned this cue, Theresa launched into a story. "Did I ever tell you about my first boyfriend?" The question served only as a rhetorical instrument. Of course, Theresa knew everything she had told Joshua for the past eighty-two years.

"Not that I recall." Joshua wandered into the shade cast by one side of the apartment building, as Theresa joined him on the walk out of the courtyard.

"Hmm." Theresa seemed to savor the memory, if not actually savoring the old boyfriend. "His name was Mark. He lived on the other side of the valley, far from my father's farm. But we went to the same school, and I sat behind him in the row of desks when I was twelve years old."

"You started early." They stood now on the sidewalk parallel to the street.

Theresa seemed in no hurry to transport.

"Oh, yes. He was two years older, but still in the same grade, because he had missed school for the harvests and such." She tossed her head slightly to gather a stray hair, allowing the wind to settle it into its place. “Later he left the community and even became a colonel in the army during the Middle Eastern wars, promoted for heroism. But, when I knew him at school, he seemed quite shy, which was one of the things I loved about him, along with his wonderful dark hair, which I admired every day.”

Her tone escalated slightly. “He appeared to be shy because he was always thinking about things, always imagining things, and this kept him from speaking up or responding quickly when someone asked him a question. Patrick reminds me of Mark.”

The second boy rescued the previous week, along with Oliver and the five girls, was Patrick. Though he had spoken the least of the seven refugees, Joshua had sensed a depth of thought in Patrick that invited him to explore the seven-year-old’s catacomb of longings and dreams. Such an emotional exploration excited Joshua, the way others felt about climbing a mountain or diving into the depths of the ocean. Though Joshua had already begun reading Patrick’s inner life, Theresa provided him confirmation with her little story. Her observation would encourage him to delve deeper than Patrick might offer at first, when they arrived at his new home.

“A colonel in the army, huh?”

Theresa grasped Joshua’s hand. “I’ll spare you the story of our first kiss.”

With that, the pair of travelers left Chicago’s sunshine and landed in a tree-shaded neighborhood in Fayetteville, Arkansas. Joshua had to wait a moment while his eyes adjusted to a darker street, only sparsely dappled with sun streams. He also had to adjust to standing on a slope that cut sideways across the stoops and stairs of the bungalows on either side of the street. He and Theresa faced a gray clapboard house, with white trim and red brick pillars supporting the friendly porch, with its two-seater swing and matching white rocking chairs. It wasn’t a large house, probably three bedrooms and some basement space.

Joshua immediately sensed the peace resident in that little home. More than fulfilling a job requirement, Joshua’s assessment of the homes for the children he served was a sort of christening, like the launching of a ship in generations past. It represented a blessing on what the new parents provided the children, as well as a blessing on what lay ahead for the new family. Without the sort of detailed instruments for assessment that social workers would have used before the Reign, Joshua simply sensed the value of this home situation.

Theresa remained behind, as Joshua climbed the few concrete stairs up the front walk toward the bungalow. He stepped onto the expertly painted wooden porch and followed the gentle rumble of his feet with a sharp knock on the door. A smiling woman, old enough to have survived the war before the Reign, answered the door. When she saw Joshua, she called over her shoulder.

CHAPTER TEN

"Justin, Talia, the man is here from the rescuers."

Patrick heard his new grandmother at the front door. She had answered the doorbell.

"Martha? Is it?"

"Yes. And you are Joshua?"

"Yes." Joshua was hanging onto Martha's hand when Patrick stalked down the stairway. He expected that Joshua was looking into her heart as he had done with the kids in the rescue house.

A stir of jealousy in Patrick's heart made him wonder—*was he jealous of the old woman or of Joshua? What would it be like to read people's hearts like that?*

Talia came out from the kitchen. She was tall with pale golden skin and dark, straight hair down to her shoulders. She approached the front door with her head tilted to the right, eying the visitor curiously.

"Talia." She wiped her right hand on a dish towel before offering it to Joshua.

Joshua greeted her and then looked over her shoulder at Justin. He was about the same height as Talia. He slowed down and let Patrick slip into the line forming at the front door.

Patrick was trying to slow his breathing but didn't really know how to do that. He felt himself blush when he knew that Joshua would be reading all his worry and fear.

Reaching over Patrick, Justin shook Joshua's hand. "Mr. Stippleman, so glad to see you."

"Just Joshua, please." Joshua took Justin's hand and hung on for an extra second or so.

Looking up at Joshua from among the tall adults, Patrick felt himself rise, as if lifted by the eyes of the man smiling back at him. That smile wasn't quite all there, as if he were holding something back. Maybe Joshua could tell that Patrick hadn't quite found this house to be a home for him. What would he do about that?

The first answer came in the handshake. Some warm feelings crossed from Joshua's hand to Patrick's. And Patrick noticed that his own hand was sweaty when he felt that warmth. Then he found a sort of message waiting for him, a silent message. He didn't know if he could open it. Did he trust this kind of silent message?

"Perhaps I should take Patrick with me?" Joshua still hung onto Patrick's hand, but he was talking to the grownups.

Take me with him? Take me away?

Patrick twisted his neck so he could see the faces of the adults, one at a time.

Talia seemed to think Joshua was saying something else. "Perhaps just for a tour of the house."

Was she right? Was that what Joshua meant? Disappointment and relief spun past like they were on a merry-go-round. Patrick wanted to be with Joshua. But he did like living in this house. He did like Talia and Justin.

When Patrick looked again at Joshua, the tall man seemed to be waiting for Patrick to decide something. He just nodded. Not really knowing what he was supposed to decide.

Joshua nodded too.

Patrick tried to settle the questions. "I could show you my room." His words came out hollow, as if his voice was broken.

Joshua looked at Talia and then Justin, sending them some kind of signal about not worrying. Patrick got distracted by how he could know what Joshua was sending with his silent thoughts. But Joshua grasped his shoulder and that woke him up again.

"Your room, then." Joshua was accepting the invitation. And maybe he was settling what it was he was offering, and what Patrick had accepted.

Patrick checked with his adopted parents briefly before leading Joshua up the stairs. White curtains at each end of the upper hallway puffed and arched with the wind. Like the hallway, Patrick's room had lots of morning sun. Patrick continued to lead the way past the large sign Talia had made, "Patrick's Place."

He stood inside the doorway, raising one hand, demonstrating that they had arrived. It was goofy to do that. But he really didn't know what he was supposed to be doing. He must have had those questions showing right on his face.

Joshua answered one of the big ones. "I wasn't trying to trick anyone with what I said down there. I was just testing out the idea of you leaving here and finding another home. I can read people's feelings, as

I explained when we first met. I needed to read how each of you felt about you being here."

Patrick might have asked about the result of the test, but he thought he knew the answer already. He had read the results himself, really. He had felt a sort of ripping feeling about him leaving, even though he was interested in being with Joshua and doing what he wanted. Maybe the ripping feeling was from the grownups as much as inside himself.

He really wanted to hear the answer to a simpler question. "Are they as nice as they seem? Are they gonna change when you and the immortals stop watching?"

Joshua smiled at Patrick standing there in the doorway of his room. "In fact, I think they *will* change. But that's just because they're nicer than you've seen so far. They're being careful not to scare you with too much goodness." He tipped his head toward the stairway. "When you all settle in, you'll find them to be even better than they've been already."

Joshua paused for a breath or two. "And the immortals will never stop watching. They hear everything God tells them, and God sees everything that happens. So, you see, they will never stop watching."

Looking up at Joshua, Patrick tipped his head to the side. "What about you? Will you keep watching?"

Joshua nodded gently. "I will know if there is any trouble at all. I get such news from the best of sources."

He stepped a bit closer where he could see the whole bedroom. Patrick made way and shared the view, surveying his new place along with his visitor, feeling a bit less like a visitor himself all of a sudden.

Probably finishing his answer to the last question, Joshua said, "I'll come and visit you a few times in the next couple of months, and many times after that. You can talk to me about any troubles you're having when I visit. So, make yourself a list, in your head or on your computer, and we'll talk about whatever you need."

Patrick looked at the shiny, new computer on his desk and raised his eyebrows. He hadn't thought that he would have such an important task to perform on that little machine.

He thought a minute about that new computer and then let go of another bothering question. "You think these people give toys at Christmas?"

Joshua laughed a little. "It's true. Families in the world outside the walls really do give boys and girls toys at Christmas, celebrating the King's birth."

His questions were multiplying. "I still miss my grandparents sometimes. Is it crazy to miss people that were always so mean?"

Joshua shook his head and rested a hand on Patrick's shoulder. "No. They are your family, and you'll always be connected to them in here." He pointed to Patrick's heart.

"I won't ever see them again, will I?"

"I don't know. You can't be sure about all that could happen in the next few hundred years of your life."

A few hundred years? Was that real?

When they returned downstairs, the adults sent Patrick outside to play with the neighbor kids, who were climbing and laughing next door. Joshua was in there for half an hour or so. It looked like Talia was wiping away a tear, even though she was still smiling when Patrick spied on them from next door.

Joshua must have seen him, because he came over to say goodbye.

"I'll see you soon, Patrick." It was as if he were ignoring the other kids. That made Patrick feel good, actually.

He waved as Joshua turned toward the street. Patrick could tell that Joshua was still watching when the kids ran to a hiding place in the bushes. He was pretty curious himself just how Joshua would leave. He was really hoping he wouldn't just walk away.

In the middle of the street, Joshua reached one hand up and rotated it above his head with a sort of flash of his fingers, like a magician making a rabbit appear. Suddenly there was that lady that was with Joshua at the rescue house, the little lady with the black dress and that hat-thing hanging around her neck. Patrick didn't know if she ever actually wore that hat-thing.

The kids around him all made excited sounds. But Joshua didn't look at them. Patrick was thinking, though, that Joshua had a sort of joking look on his face.

Someone bumped Patrick and he got prickled by the bush. That made him look away for a moment. But another gasp from the kids swung him back to watch the pair on the street. Joshua had raised both hands above his head. Which was when they launched into the sky, Joshua and that little woman, as if they were both rockets or maybe just one rocket.

The kids all ran out from under the bushes to look up at the sky. Patrick stumbled but got out in time to see Joshua and the woman getting smaller and smaller and then turn toward the sun.

"I'm gonna do that someday." If anyone heard him say that. None of them laughed.

CHAPTER ELEVEN

Joshua and Theresa landed beneath a hybrid fruit tree that cast its waving shade over a patch of pavement made of smooth, pinkish stones. The walkway was designed to massage the feet of walkers wearing moccasins. They stood at the outskirts of a blossoming Kansas village founded about forty years before, once the rebels had abandoned that sparsely populated region. Joshua squinted into the rising sunlight, turning toward the west to make it easier on his eyes. There he spied the sign welcoming visitors to New Hope Village and directing them to the various sections of the community. Ahead and to the right lay the marketplace. To the left, the residential area. Joshua followed Theresa toward the low, square homes spread along smooth roads and pebbly sidewalks.

Though he had heard much about these cooperative settlements sprouting in rural areas around the country, Joshua had rarely visited one. After five or six experimental decades, the independent villages had established themselves as a trend with a long future. Many of the pioneers of this movement, away from the cities and off private farms, honored their Native American ancestry, or at least looked there for inspiration. Surrounding the residential area of the settlement, the land grew grain and fruit trees, tended communally by the people of New Hope.

While the cultural influences of the past, from Lakota ancestors and others, united this community, the organizers grew and maintained their movement with the latest communication, horticultural, and marketing technologies. The combination of old and new adhered productively, under the guidance and energy of immortals, who assisted where desired.

Joshua read the inscription on the arch at the end of the residential street they were entering. “Let me learn the lessons you have hidden in every leaf and rock. Chief Yellow Lark.”

Theresa interrupted his contemplation. “We will get to meet the tutor that is being assigned to Oliver on this visit.” Joshua wondered if this comment was prompted by that quotation.

This was the first Joshua had heard of a tutor for Oliver. But, instead of loitering around the surprise, he added together what he knew of Oliver, with the way the immortals had worked with him when he was a child. The intuitive gifts and strength of will he had sampled in Oliver would understandably attract the same sort of attention as his own gifts and lineage had attracted. That Oliver lived with mortals devoted to the service of the King, also invited intimate involvement from the immortals. Just like their King, the immortals asserted themselves most generously where they were most welcomed.

"Is the tutor someone you know?" Joshua was sensing a particular intensity of feeling from Theresa.

She laughed. "I can't hide it from you, can I?"

Assessing her, as they walked, Joshua pressed the question. "Who is it?"

Theresa glanced at Joshua and then kept her eyes forward as she explained. "It is Gerald Tompkins."

"Gerald?" Joshua asked.

"Yes, Edward's brother, the leader of the resistance in Canada, before his martyrdom."

Joshua nodded. Though he knew only historical bits about this famous family, he could tell that Theresa was excited at the prospect.

"You're anxious to meet him."

Theresa nodded. "I'm excited to meet him. I have been instructed to take part in the meetings with all of you."

To Joshua, this meant that the situation into which he now walked would be quite different from the one he had left at Patrick's house. Theresa very rarely took part in any parent or child meetings. But, then, very rarely had an immortal tutor been appointed to a child before Joshua's first home visit.

Stopping at the stoop of a pale pink house, Theresa smiled more broadly than usual. Joshua could sense her anticipation, yet her excitement lacked any hint of anxiety. He envied that combination.

The little house had open-air vents all around, beneath the slanted roof, in the manner of modern buildings in the temperate climate. Red and white flowers, of a species Joshua didn't recognize, tossed their heads in the breeze off the open plains. Joshua knocked on the white door, which appeared to be hand-carved out of oak. The door opened to a smiling round face, a man apparently in his early forties. He had short-cropped, dark hair, and wore a white linen shirt and white linen pants. The stout greeter stepped forward and grabbed Theresa in a bear hug, lifting her off the ground. To Joshua's surprise, she giggled like a schoolgirl.

Setting Theresa back on her feet with a merry kiss on her cheek, the man looked up at Joshua. He said something to Theresa in rapid French. She smiled and giggled again. This new facet to her personality provoked Joshua to laugh aloud, ignoring the apparent comment on his size made by the jolly little man.

"I'm Gerald!" The greeter bellowed, grasping Joshua's hand and shaking it vigorously.

Without any premeditation, Joshua connected to the wide-open soul of the former resistance leader and martyr. The word that amplified most clearly out of the complex impression Joshua gathered was "Rescued." Immediately, he knew that Gerald embodied a constant living experience of gratitude at being rescued by the King. In the sparkling gray-blue eyes fixed on him, Joshua saw a mirror of what God intended for his own soul. He laughed to the point of tears at that revelation.

As he wiped tears from both his cheeks, Joshua could see a short woman with prematurely gray hair in the dim interior of the house behind Gerald. She was wiping her cheeks in the same way he was. He smiled at her and then knew her name to be Destiny, Oliver's new mother. In the early years, Joshua had studied computer files to gather this sort of information. However, as his intuitive insight became sharper, he had discovered that learning the names and nature of the people as he met them better prepared him for a genuine and deep connection—as if the computer file had been more of an obstacle than a means for valuable introductions.

Destiny reacted to Joshua much the same way Gerald had greeted Theresa. She took two quick steps out to the porch and leapt at Joshua, wrapping her short, strong arms around his neck. Joshua received the embrace full-force, locking his arms around the woman he had never met before. Connected via that embrace, Joshua read a sort of internal file on Destiny, which contained all that the King wanted him to know about Oliver's new parent. This organic download explained the early presence of the male mentor.

She would be raising Oliver as a single mother. She had no husband. In addition to Gerald, however, Oliver's new life included a half dozen mortals committed to assisting with his upbringing. One of these stood now where Destiny had stood a second before—Destiny's sister Harmony. Joshua wasn't so serious about his task to forego a smile at the names of the two women, obviously given them by free-spirited parents born before the Reign. That these two women had gravitated to one of these new communal villages would surprise no one.

When Destiny finally released her hold on Joshua, he could sense that someone approached him from behind. He turned to find a very old man with gray hair flowing well past his shoulders. The contours of his wizened face also left no room for surprise when Joshua heard him introduced as Chief Calling Bird, one of the leaders of the village movement in Kansas and Nebraska. When Destiny introduced the Chief, Joshua and Calling Bird bypassed the usual modern handshake and instead grasped each other's forearm in the manner of native tribes from the distant past. The two men locked eyes and stood that way for a full minute without spoken words. Again, Joshua received a data dump directly from Calling Bird's soul, and he knew that the communication flowed both ways.

After breaking his connection with Calling Bird, Joshua looked at Gerald and knew that *he* had brought these people together, including Oliver. Gerald's God-given ability to discern the hearts of mortals had sifted through the options for supporting Oliver and Destiny. And he had appointed himself tutor in order to serve as one of the surrogate fathers.

Destiny called out to Oliver, looking up as she did so, as if she expected him to drop from the roof. Instead, he came running around the side of the house, followed by a slightly smaller girl with strawberry blonde hair and freckles. They were both rosy and sweaty from some game they had been playing around the yard. Joshua had noticed the beginnings of a footpath, worn in the short green grass, which testified to Oliver's habit of rounding the house in this way, and doing so along with either pursuers or prey.

When he saw Joshua and the other adults gathered with him, Oliver checked his run and left his playful face behind. His hair clung to his face in blades, like dark grass. He swept his hand across his forehead unconsciously, used to having longer hair, as when Joshua first met him.

To Joshua, Oliver immediately seemed more at home than their first meeting would have implied possible. A clear path to the boy's heart seemed to have opened in this new setting. Joshua could see that the immortals had done their work well, selecting the right home, as well as providing the support that home needed. Joshua smiled broadly at this picture of hope and restoration. He held out his hand and Oliver took it, attempting to look grownup in the way he performed that ritual.

Joshua made no comment about that pretense. "Hello, my friend. You look happy."

"Are you reading my mind, or just going by what I look like?" The curious Oliver clearly lay just beneath the happy, sweaty surface.

A slight motion of Destiny's eyebrows alerted Joshua to tune into her response to Oliver's challenge. Joshua surmised that Oliver had camouflaged from Destiny his inquisitive and adversarial tendencies. This alteration to fit the space in which he had landed didn't seem dishonest. But it did seem calculated.

Joshua answered Oliver. "I'm not reading your mind so much as sampling your soul, like the way you're always testing the temperature of the people around you."

For an instant, Oliver seemed to examine what Joshua had said, and then he blushed. He released Joshua's hand and responded nonchalantly. "So that's what that is."

He was playing at being an objective observer. But he finally let that go and simply smiled, as if unwilling to keep up the ruse.

Harmony spoke into the pause between Oliver and Joshua. "Let's all go inside. We have homemade bread and some fruit."

As the company turned toward the door, to follow Harmony's invitation, a full-grown bobcat bounded into the house, following Oliver's path. Joshua stopped to watch as Oliver squatted to greet his friend.

"Hey, Bobby, what took you so long?" Oliver held the big cat's face in his hands and give him a good scratching behind the ears.

Joshua spoke quietly to Theresa who had stayed behind with him. "Another part of the team."

Inside the simple and airy house, Theresa and Joshua ate homemade bread full of grains, nuts and bits of dried fruit. They also sampled some of the fresh fruits raised in the community—hybrid apples crossbred with pears, and peaches crossed with cherries, as well as a species of banana suited to the local climate. As they ate, Joshua circulated among the adults, asking them questions and listening to their stories, both biographical and anecdotal.

His basic evaluation of the home had already been settled, but he attempted to dig deeper, to look for where he could help, and to anticipate future issues for Oliver. He discovered no ticking timebombs and no obvious needs. That didn't end his responsibilities for Oliver, however. Life still added complexity and discouragements, even under the Reign, especially as a boy became a teenager and then a man. Add to that the multiplying factor of interacting with the immortals, and Joshua sensed that he would have some work to do here in the years ahead.

After a brief, informal interview with Harmony, Joshua noticed Theresa speaking animatedly with Gerald. He smiled and wondered at her apparent hero worship of the old martyr. He knew better than to judge her for it. On most days, he envied the immortals. But occasionally they seemed just as human as he. At those times he sensed the closeness of the doorway from his present life into the next. A brief thought in that direction gave him a shiver even in the warmth of midday.

Retreating from his mental wandering, Joshua noticed Oliver looking at him inquisitively. "Is something the matter?" Oliver tipped his head forty-five degrees to the right.

Joshua smiled and laughed at himself, then answered honestly, careful not to do the adult thing and pretend that the boy hadn't witnessed what was obvious to them both. "Sometimes I think about how great it will be to be immortal." He glanced toward Theresa and Gerald.

Oliver followed his glance and nodded. "So, it's true? We really get to be like them someday?"

Joshua took a step to his right, sat down on a long couch against the wall, and motioned for Oliver to join him. Oliver plopped down, keeping his question alive with that inquisitive look, the look Joshua most associated with Oliver.

"It *is* true. You and I have an opportunity to join the eternal ones when we die. We can have a long and meaningful life and then die and have an even more wonderful life like them."

Oliver pursued the topic like a thirsty horse smelling water. "We just have to do what the King wants us to do?"

"In a way, that's true. But you should understand that what he wants from us, more than anything else, is to be with us and talk with us. It's not about doing lots of stuff. It's about being his friend."

Oliver considered this answer, even taking a moment to briefly measure a few of the adults in the room before he replied. "I guess that makes sense. The people I've met outside Humanity City are pretty friendly and not so bossy."

After Joshua had spoken to everyone who would be close to Oliver, he waited for Theresa to end a conversation with Destiny. He stood on the grass near the front stoop. Oliver, his friend Melany, and the bobcat chased and rolled around nearby.

Joshua's heart and mind turned then to the condition of more fractured and tentative survivors, in full contrast to Oliver's idyllic situation. At first, he assumed this was just a bad habit, emerging from a weary pocket in his heart, the sort of regret that arises when one remembers dissatisfaction in the face of its opposite. But then he recognized an impulse that amounted to a sort of poke from the Spirit of the King, alerting him to pay attention to the juxtaposition.

When Theresa joined him on the grass, she spoke first. "Are you ready to go and visit Mirabelle?"

Joshua turned resigned eyes toward her. "So you got the message, too."

"Umhmm." Theresa adjusted the collar on her simple black dress. "He wanted you to enjoy seeing Oliver before we went to see the ones that need you most."

"The ones that need Him most."

Theresa looked him in the eyes. "He chose you. You are needed there."

Joshua said nothing, instead tracking the flight of a monarch butterfly from its place in the shade of a small fruit tree into the bright sunlight. He stretched his hand toward Theresa without looking, and she took it gently. The butterfly and the sound of the children playing disappeared, and Joshua and Theresa arrived in front of a very large Bertan house, under an elm tree that was older than the Reign.

He knew this street in Lincoln, Nebraska, very well. He had taken hundreds of walks over the smooth new sidewalks with many dozens of children over the past forty years. Here stood the house known as Mirabelle. It had been named for the first little girl who arrived there, from an abusive home in a rebel community. That was back when Joshua was still new to this work.

CHAPTER TWELVE

Unlike Oliver and Patrick, the children living at Mirabelle hadn't sought a way out of their lives, hadn't prayed for rescue. The hardest hit among them didn't know they needed rescue. And those in between didn't think rescue was possible.

To a sympathetic soul like Joshua's, this house represented the front lines of the war that remained confined inside minds and hearts. This was a place where reading the souls of others included enduring horror stories—memories designed to destroy a human spirit, crimes perpetrated by those who boasted of their humanity the most loudly.

Most of his visits to Mirabelle occurred like this, with no advance warning. A perfected saint wouldn't have needed this precaution. But Joshua still knew the burn of anxious anticipation. He had learned to appreciate bypassing this part of the visit, preferring the jolt of adrenalin instead of smoldering dread. Though Joshua thought of himself as carrying on a constant open dialogue with the King, he usually prayed very specifically and intensely, as he walked up the front steps to the broad, dark gray porch.

As usual, Theresa wouldn't accompany Joshua inside the front door. She stopped on the porch and surveyed her student. Her face radiated joyful pride better than even the best of mortal mothers. He knew she harbored no fears or worries for him. Attuned to the heart of God, his immortal mentor could see the end of things, as well as the beginning. Joshua recharged his own confidence from that peace in her eyes.

"I'll see you in a few hours. I will be praying for you as you meet with them."

Like supercharged nutrition during a marathon, this assurance boosted Joshua's emotional energy still higher.

"Thank you." He trusted that Theresa knew his heart and could read the depth of his gratitude without more words.

When he rang the bell by pressing the little, yellow button next to the screen door, Joshua began to settle himself into listening mode, attempting to assess the emotional temperature of the entire house. So focused on listening with his soul, he missed the sound of footsteps approaching the door over the polished oak floors inside. He was startled slightly when a medium-sized woman with straight, black hair and golden-brown skin opened the door.

Shari Verma smiled at him. "Hello, Joshua." Her slight accent betrayed her birth on the other side of the globe. Though he had never asked her, Joshua had wondered—and then settled the question himself—about why she had traveled so far to find a place to help troubled children. His years of experience had revealed how individuals fit together to form the most effective teams. Joshua's frequent flyer miles attested to the fact that the person most fit for a job may not live nearby.

"You were expecting me?"

"Of course. Thomas met with me this morning."

Thomas was to Shari what Theresa was to Joshua—mentor and messenger.

Joshua tuned into Shari, drilling through the usual outer shell that she projected to the world. Deeper inside her personal atmosphere, Joshua found more of the same steady, peaceful soul. But he could detect a grit of concern wearing at a tender spot in her heart. He stopped in the entryway, sensing an opportunity to help her.

"It's getting to you just a bit, isn't it?"

Shari took a deep breath. "I know it's not personal. I know it's not about me. But it still hurts when they run away."

Joshua nodded. "Is it possible that you're actually feeling God's hurt and not just yours? It's really God and the King that they're running away from."

Shari's always-animated face—dark eyes and nimble eyebrows, large smile and shining teeth—stuck in place, locked on inner discovery. Like Joshua, she carried her heart out front, where she could connect deeply with the children. He knew her great capacity to love and accept even those who wanted no part of her. Her heart stood open to all, like the sky sparkling overhead on a clear night. In this posture, she stood ready to judge herself for any sign of rejecting those the King sent her.

"It's always okay to mourn a loss."

Shari released a pent-up breath and visibly shook off a bond of self-condemnation.

"Ha!" She blurted it.

Joshua laughed with her. They hugged briefly. Shari joked. "When are you going to marry me and move in here?"

From their years of frequent contact and from reading her heart now, Joshua knew she was teasing. But he gave a serious answer.

"Then you would depend on me, and you don't want to do that." He maintained a friendly grin. "You're not that kind of light in the darkness."

Shari shook her head loosely, as if it had become unhinged. "Whoa! Yeah, I would probably have my head spinning all the time and never get anything done, with insights like that."

They laughed together again, and Joshua hugged her once more, from the side this time. He was waiting for his instructions, the reason for his visit.

Settling back into her role as the director of this halfway house for rescued children, Shari stepped away from him and slowly turned up the hallway.

"Bonnie is a new girl that needs something, and I don't know what it is. Thomas wouldn't tell me. He said that you will know. Then there's Richie. He's still here and he needs another walk with you. His anger still feels dangerous to me, dangerous to himself." She stopped at the staircase leading up. "After those two, just do what you think best, as usual."

"Richie ran away again?"

"Yes. This time, they let him get all the way to New Brunswick City before they brought him back, with his cooperation, I think. He wouldn't tell me, and the immortals didn't fill me in on the whole story."

"I guess they figure he's getting old enough now for them to respect his privacy a bit more."

"He's eleven, a very old eleven years."

Most of the children stayed at Mirabelle for a matter of weeks or months, until they accepted their rescue and a placement in a new home. Very few of the children that were moved to homes ran away to the rebel cities. But among long-term residents of Mirabelle, runaways were more common. Richie had attempted it three times now, over the course of a year. Generally, the immortals wouldn't allow a child of his age to return to his abusive home, though Joshua hadn't discovered an exact age at which the King defined the transition from dependent to accountable. A sixteen-year-old had been returned to Mirabelle against her will once. But knowing her very personally, Joshua understood why. Her connection with the reality and meaning of her sexual misuse remained fractured, as did her entire personality. That girl's case was an extreme one, at a time when the lies and accusation inflicted on the minds of the abused came only from human enemies.

Forcefully returning the children to this refuge, of course, involved no violence. Rather the immortals used the same sort of transporting that Joshua had voluntarily experienced hundreds of times. Many of the children surrendered to the inevitable. They discovered the futility of trying to run away. Finding their geography changed instantly, from some far field to their comfortable bedroom at Mirabelle, convinced most of them. The genuine charm and warmth of the halfway house persuaded almost all of the children eventually, even some who missed their old homes yielded to the house's appeal.

Joshua followed Shari to one of the playrooms to meet with the new girl, Bonnie. When they approached the room, a young woman with long, russet braids spotted them through the window in the door and rose from her seat atop a little indoor slide. As she approached the door, Joshua could see that she was nearly as tall as he was, over six feet. She moved gracefully, like an athlete, reaching the door in three long strides.

"I'll be just a minute, Bonnie." She spoke over her shoulder, as she opened the door and stepped out into the hall. The young woman stood where Bonnie could see her but stepped a few feet away from the door.

"We can talk here." Shari knew the status of each of the nearby rooms.

"Hi, I'm Greta." The young woman reached her hand toward Joshua.

He could tell she was pushing herself beyond a nervous boundary in taking this initiative.

"Joshua." He took her hand with a smile.

"It's such an honor ..." Greta stopped abruptly. "I promised myself I wouldn't gush."

Joshua breathed a small chuckle. "Sounds good to me. How long have you been at Mirabelle, Greta?"

She looked at Shari, as if needing help to remember. "About four months, I'd say. They're still giving me the easier cases."

Joshua nodded. He hesitated a moment and then followed an inner prompting. "Do you sense that Bonnie's is an easy case?" He glanced briefly through the window.

Greta's eyes sought Shari again. Shari's pleasant but neutral facial cues probably told Greta that she was on her own. She took a deep breath and began a brief summary of Bonnie's history.

"She was subject to repeated attempts at sexual abuse by an older brother and the brother's friend, and the parents didn't intervene. They were too inebriated most of the time. She says she doesn't understand why she's here and won't acknowledge that her brother tried to do anything bad to her. She is relatively undisturbed by being away from her parents. That's partly, I think, because she was often sent to stay to be with an aunt or a grandmother. For someone who doesn't acknowledge attempted abuse, however, she seems relatively uninterested in being returned home."

Joshua filled a small pause. "What do you think?"

Greta allowed a confused crunch to her eyebrows. "If you're asking me whether I can tell how deep the pain goes, and what it will take to get Bonnie through it, I have to say honestly, that I don't know." Then, after Joshua didn't fill her next pause, she said, "If pressed, I would wonder whether the wound isn't a lot deeper and more complex than she lets on." She looked at Joshua, as if reading *him*. "And maybe she's not really such an easy case, at that." Greta finished in a tone that implied that she had just learned something from her own answer.

Joshua smiled. Shari looked at the floor, trying to conceal a smile.

Instead of punctuating the lesson, Joshua returned to Greta's comfort zone, for more information. "How old was the brother when this began?"

"Twelve." Greta seemed still unsettled by her earlier discovery.

Joshua pressed on. "And how old is he now?"

"Thirteen. The immortals never let these things go on for long."

"I'd like to see their report." Joshua decided to avoid pressing the young social worker for details about the attempted abuse.

In some cases, Joshua relied solely on supernatural revelation to tell him as much about the experiential details of the case as he needed to know. But he was treading on Greta's home turf in order to increase her comfort with his help. He knew she needed that extra assistance.

She pulled her personal data device from her front pocket, as Joshua retrieved his. With a few touches on the screen she sent the report to his device. For a minute, he turned and looked at the report projected on the white wall across from the playroom.

Without looking up, he spoke to Greta. "You should go back inside. She's getting uncomfortable in there alone, with us out here talking."

Greta nodded without saying anything and turned back to the room. Her voice rose in a reassuring greeting as she stepped through the door, its closing cutting off her exact words after the first few syllables.

When Joshua turned around, he saw that Bonnie's face confirmed what he had sensed. She looked stern, her version of looking frightened. Small for her age, especially by standards of children living under the Reign, Bonnie reminded Joshua of a lemur. Long arms and legs and a pointy nose between large brown eyes made her look like a pink relative of Madagascar's primates. As he set aside this whimsical observation, he sensed that Bonnie was restraining herself from climbing into Greta's lap and wrapping those long arms around the young woman's neck. As social workers go, Greta didn't seem the coziest person Joshua had met at Mirabelle, implying that Bonnie's urge to be held by Greta originated in her own sense of need more than in what the tall woman was offering.

Joshua knocked on the window, stuffing his mobile device into his pocket. When Greta signaled for him to enter, he glanced at Shari and smiled his temporary farewell as he opened the door and stepped into the room. Bonnie's attention locked on Joshua immediately. This helped him read her feelings more clearly. She seemed more opaque than most people. Either she had boarded up the windows of her soul, or someone else had.

"Hi, Bonnie." Joshua spoke meekly.

Greta stood up and motioned to Joshua. "This is Mr. Stippleman, Bonnie. He's here to help us."

Smiling first at Greta, Joshua turned to Bonnie. "You can call me Joshua, if that's easier." He lowered himself onto a purple couch designed for children, no hard edges anywhere, and a long way down for a tall grownup.

As soon as he settled in, he could sense that Bonnie's desire to be held had turned toward him, as he suspected it would. But Joshua knew that other forces in the little girl's soul would resist that desire. He offered a moderate next step.

"Do you want to come sit over here with me?"

Without saying a word, Bonnie put down the two foam blocks she was holding and walked to the couch. She sat next to Joshua, neither as far from him as possible nor up against him. In that position, Joshua asked her basic questions about herself, from how old she was to what was her favorite ice cream. When Greta started to look for a place to sit, Joshua motioned with his hand toward the other end of the couch but said nothing. A bit confused, perhaps, Greta decided to sit on the floor and lean on the couch, at eye level with Bonnie and very close to the little girl. This satisfied Joshua's intentions.

"How do you feel about being away from your mommy and daddy?"

"Um, I've been away from them before. I don't mind. I'll see them when I get home."

Joshua sensed that she suspected that she might not be going home any time soon, whether any of the rescuers had implied that in what they said or not.

"Were you scared when the people came to take you away from your house?"

Bonnie thought about it a moment. "Well, first I saw this boy, not much bigger than me. And he wasn't scary at all. But then there were others." She hesitated again. "I don't remember if I was scared of them."

"Do you remember who came next?"

"Um, not really." Bonnie apparently felt no concern that she couldn't remember this detail.

That traumatic event happened just two days before this meeting. From this, Joshua could tell more about how much Bonnie was closed off from her emotional memories. He sensed that her desire to be held was part of her desire to reconnect with her emotions, both positive and negative.

"How would you feel about sitting on my lap?"

Bonnie looked at him like someone evaluating a leap across a wide puddle, and then glanced at Greta. Joshua could tell that Greta was restraining her discomfort with the idea. Bonnie decided to risk it. Joshua helped her situate her fifty pounds on one of his legs and put his left arm around her for support.

"Do you want to tell me anything about your big brother?" Joshua asked gently.

From her new perch, Bonnie had to turn her head to evaluate this question. When she looked away to think a moment, Joshua nodded for Greta to move closer. Greta suddenly seemed to understand what he was doing, and she smoothly slid closer, so that she could easily touch

Bonnie. The effect of this human envelope delayed Bonnie's answer to Joshua's last question.

During a slow and patient exchange between Joshua and Bonnie, Greta gradually grew into her part as silent mother-replacement.

Joshua stayed with Bonnie and Greta for over an hour that first day, before sensing that Bonnie was full, like an over-satisfied diner at a Thanksgiving feast. Helping her to climb off his lap, his pant leg creased from their combined warmth, Joshua assured Bonnie that this was only the beginning.

"I'll be back to see you every week. In the meantime, you can make new friends here, and find out more about Miss Greta. I have a feeling that you'll be amazed at the things she's seen in her life."

Greta looked doubtfully at Joshua but brightened her face for Bonnie's scrutiny.

Joshua found Shari in her office, just closing a conversation with her mentor, Thomas. Joshua arrived just in time to see Thomas disappear.

"Don't ya love those exits?"

Shari smiled at him, looking up from her desk. "Thomas said things went well with Bonnie. He also said Richie is ready for you now. He's out back with one of our workers, Donald. I think you've met him."

"Yes, I have. Donald is the guy you use to keep people from making a break for it."

"Richie's still confused."

Nodding, Joshua turned to leave, but stopped at the door. "You ever wonder if it's not really confusion, but rather just plain old self-preservation?"

Shari looked perplexed, but Joshua didn't stick around to ease that condition.

CHAPTER THIRTEEN

In the back yard of Mirabelle, fenced in by eight-foot wooden slats tightly arranged around the whole perimeter, Richie sat on top of the swing set, looking down at his jailor. That Donald guy was huge, but he didn't try to reach Richie up there.

"Young Mr. Phelan." Joshua was stepping out of the house. "So, we meet again. I thought you'd be outta here by now."

Richie slowly adjusted his gaze from Donald to Joshua. "I tried to leave again. But they just keep bringing me back here." He didn't want to say anything about the mess he found back at home before agreeing to be brought back. But maybe Joshua knew all about that.

"Yeah, they just can't get enough of you here." He clapped the big guy on the shoulder. "I got him, Donald. Thanks."

Donald took a break from guard duty and went into the house.

Taking one of the hard rubber swings, Joshua pulled it back far enough that he could lean on it and look up at Richie, using the swing as a sort of back brace. He looked around. "Wish I had one of these when I was a kid."

"I guess you never got 'rescued' when you were a kid."

"Yeah, that's true. So, why did you run this time?"

"I miss my mom." Richie wished he could say it without the crack in his voice.

"I can understand that. She was on a radio show up there telling about your wonderful life at her house and how the cruel aliens grabbed you away to brainwash you 'or something worse.' That last bit was a direct quote. I wonder what 'something worse' is in her mind."

Richie snickered. "She's always thinking about sex, so that would be my guess." He sat up straighter. This wasn't the most comfortable seat. "Too bad it was radio. If it was TV, she coulda found a new boyfriend—or twenty—when they saw how beautiful she is."

"Is she really beautiful?"

Richie shrugged. "All those men always said she was."

"You don't miss all the men."

"Course not. None of 'em was my dad. And most of 'em got no right to be *anybody's* dad."

"Yeah. That's why the immortals grabbed you in the beginning. That guy was trying to be your dad in a really bad way."

Richie shivered. He checked out some of the other play equipment in the yard for a second. "Why does she wanna be with all those creepy guys?"

Joshua stood up straight now. "Ever go to a soccer game?"

Richie scowled. He couldn't guess why Joshua was bringing that up. "Yeah, my uncle took me once. My real uncle, before he moved away."

"You liked it?"

"Yeah, it was cool to see how far they could kick it, and right to their own man all the way across the field."

"Did you wanna play soccer after you saw that game? Did you try to copy them?"

"Umhmm."

"You see, it's like that with your mom, and a bunch of other people in the walled cities. They've heard that there's this King ruling outside their walls and they sorta know how magnificent he is, and how much in love with him his followers are, and how fantastic the immortals are. And she just tries to imitate what he offers the best way she's found, with drugs and drinking and sex. And she looks for the creepy guys, 'cause she knows that this is all just playing and not the real thing. She doesn't want anyone who'll stick around and try it for real. She knows that won't work. So the creepy guys are best."

It was a complicated explanation, but somehow Richie knew that what Joshua was saying was true.

"But why can't the immortals just go grab her, then, and get her outta there?"

Joshua looked at the ground and shook his head a moment. Then he looked at Richie again. "I've thought the same thing. But they won't force anyone to come out who's over a certain age. God has always been that way. He never forces us to go his way, once we're old enough to choose for ourselves, no matter how bad a job we do at it."

Richie thought for a while. "What if they took me back there and I tried to talk her into coming out with me?"

"That's just too much to put on you, my friend. That's just too much for a boy to carry on behalf of his mom. And it didn't work this time, did it?"

Richie swallowed hard. "You could come with me. She would believe *you*. She would trust *you*."

Joshua stood still like he was really thinking about this. That was a surprise. Richie didn't think anyone would agree that he had a good idea.

"Richie, if you'll stop running away, I'll look into the possibility of you and me going into the city to try and talk her out."

Richie jumped off the swing set and ran to hug Joshua. He surprised *himself* that time.

CHAPTER FOURTEEN

"The only real lasting risk is to Richie's battered heart." Joshua spoke into his mobile device as he rode the train from Chicago to Iowa.

"You mean you're prepared to get killed, or nearly killed, and put back together again, like that time with the biker gang?"

Joshua winced at the painful memory. Immortal aid often arrived too late to prevent all the pain consequent to the actions of well-meaning mortals. He wasn't in Heaven yet.

He answered seriously. "I'm prepared to take the risk of my own health. My only hesitation is risking the rise and fall of hopes in a boy so emotionally sore as Richie."

Speaking from his office in Minneapolis, Joshua's mortal supervisor, Ray Martinez, waited a moment before commenting. Like Joshua, Ray relied on input from the King and his Father.

"I share your concern, Joshua. What does Theresa say?"

Joshua watched the lush landscape passing the train windows, catching sight of a woman driving a large tractor over a field of black soil that was being carved into rows, ready for planting.

"She leaves the decision to me, of course, and offers no insight into the future that would help me know whether it's worth the risk for Richie. She only says that he is stronger than most of the children they've rescued, and that this opportunity is better than most I might have considered."

"Umhmm. Basically, she's confirming what we figured out already."

"Yeah. I'm thinking we have to conclude that the lack of a warning against attempting this is an encouraging sign. I'm inclined to go ahead."

"That sounds reasonable to me. Let's talk about support resources."

For the next twenty minutes, they reviewed the logistics of a trip into New Brunswick City with Richie. That he had reacted well enough to instant transport by the immortals in the past, when it was against his will, simplified the travel. Though the parameters for providing other forms of assistance weren't perfectly clear to Joshua, he knew that he could count on transportation and protection from the immortals.

After agreeing on timing and support staff particulars, Joshua and Ray said their goodbyes. Joshua decided to wait to tell Richie in person about his plan but had agreed that Ray should inform the staff at Mirabelle as soon as possible. Joshua spent no time or energy on wondering how Greta, Shari, or Donald would react. But he prayed for their wisdom and understanding in the matter. Then, having just crossed the Mississippi river. he turned his attention back to the verdant, blossoming landscape of the Iowa countryside. At over 200 miles per hour, he could absorb only distant vistas of farms and wild hillsides, past the constant blur of closer objects and creatures.

Joshua stretched his legs and glanced around the car. He could see only about a dozen passengers. He had consciously chosen to leave himself some physical distance from them, making it easier to avoid tuning into anyone's feelings. Though it would be short, he was on vacation now.

He had begun spending more and more time away from the farm when he had graduated from high school and then started his training with Theresa. That was eighty-two years ago, a long lifetime to his grandparents' generation, grandparents whom he had never met.

As his calling became clearer to Joshua and his mentor, he travelled around the world to learn from mortals who were just beginning to practice therapy with the aid of subconscious communication and the King's spiritual empowerment. Previous generations had dreamed of such things, but the atmosphere of the Reign made it a practical reality to those gifted for such work. By the time Joshua reached his twenties, mortals had discovered that the power of the Reign extended to them, as the King's influence circled the globe. The vacuum of opposing spirits allowed willing pioneers like Joshua to see clearly what had only been through a fog before and to hear clearly where there had only been static.

Enthusiastic converts of the King, his parents had encouraged what their son pursued but they remained spectators to a large extent. Joshua had met very few survivors of the world before the Reign who excelled at hearing the voice of God in their minds, or at communicating the power of the King to others by words or touch. The generation gap between the world before and the world after opened like a great gorge, bridged by very few. His parents had always made the effort to support him, even if they couldn't fully fathom how he did what he did.

Joshua hadn't been home for most of a year, a rare source of regret for him. Joshua still lived in linear time and couldn't transport himself anywhere without a train or plane ticket. And he still stored an occasional regret inside, at least short-term.

Somerville, Iowa, had grown into one of the larger towns in the state, having dodged many of the losses larger cities had suffered through the last war. After a transfer in Des Moines, Joshua was able to take a train right into the heart of his hometown. He stepped onto the multi-colored train platform around eleven o'clock in the morning, the sun casting bright bars across the fresh paint through skylights in the platform roof, a roof whose purpose included protecting the rare nighttime traveler from regularly scheduled rains.

Joshua was back home. It was a great feeling.

CHAPTER FIFTEEN

There on the platform Tina watched Daniel's half-brother grinning at them as if he had just won a prize. Obviously, he hadn't stayed away so long because he didn't like coming home.

"Hey, Daniel." Joshua spread his arms for hug.

Though only fifteen years younger than Daniel, Joshua appeared more than a generation younger, with very little gray in his light hair and none of the deep lines that Tina saw on Daniel's face when he relaxed his smile. Joshua seemed in perfect health, though maybe a bit too slim.

Daniel looked up at Joshua, who was about six inches taller. "You look good, kid, especially for a guy coming home to celebrate his hundredth birthday."

Before Joshua answered, he adjusted his attention toward Tina, who was still standing back. He broke free from Daniel and grabbed Tina in his long arms. In that moment she wondered how she looked to her brother-in-law. Surely she had aged like Daniel and seemed an old girl compared to someone born after the King returned.

"It's so good to see you, Joshua. We've been missing you awfully."

Daniel joined them, wrapping an arm around her waist. He nodded his agreement. Then he looked at the small bag Joshua was carrying.

"Travelling light, I see. Not a very long visit then?"

"A few days."

They all turned together toward the parking lot.

"How are the girls?"

"Great!" Daniel said.

"They're doing fine. Debora is living in Des Moines now, not so far away." Tina offered a fuller report.

"Debora?"

"She's a grandma now," Daniel said, as if that explained his daughter's transformation from Debbie to Debora.

Joshua nodded.

"And Rebecca is in Bavaria with her husband and his sister, working on preserving historical documents from before the Reign." Tina stopped by the car as Joshua loaded his bag into the back seat. She slipped in next to that bag.

"I've seen some of their work. Their digital versions of news reports and various books and films are really fascinating." He took the seat next to Daniel, up front.

On the way out to the farm in the self-driving electric car, Joshua asked Daniel and Tina about their shops that sold food developed by the immortals. He seemed proud of their expansion to several towns around Iowa. He also asked Daniel about his robots.

"You know, I sorta lost interest this past year, or at least finished losing interest. We still have some android employees, but that's more business than hobby now." Daniel looked at Tina here.

"Is the whole business pulling more of your attention, then?"

Tina answered. "No. Between the two of us, we're pretty much on top of things, and we have plenty of competent workers. So really we're moving toward a sort of half-time retirement."

"We spend a lot more time enjoying the Jerusalem worship these days," Daniel said.

"We're even planning a trip. We've never been there in person. I always envied you and Dad for that." She grinned at Joshua when he turned to look at her. He always seemed to be measuring, or maybe digging deeper than most people did.

"When are you going?"

"In June."

"You two seem so happy together."

She and Daniel looked at each other again. Somehow Joshua's observation added a spark in her heart. Tina was well over a hundred years old, as was Daniel. And they had been together for most of the Reign. Over that time, she had often wondered what it would be like to live the adventurous life Joshua lived. She envied his obvious satisfaction with his life. She had some satisfaction in her life. But the spark Joshua sent into her heart felt like he was sharing some of what he had with her.

That spark, nevertheless, lit a small fire of concern for Joshua.

"So, is there anyone special for *you* these days?"

"Nothing like what you two have." He didn't look sad, but maybe resigned.

She watched him as the car turned into the driveway. Then they all looked to the house where Emma stood on the porch awaiting their arrival.

CHAPTER SIXTEEN

Emma had lost a couple of inches in height, but still stood relatively straight. Her hair had become uniformly gray in the past few years, the color of early morning fog. She wore it in a braid down her back. Her eyes were still sure to capture the attention of people who met her, and she still offered that delicately scrolled smile, with fine curves at the corner of her mouth.

Joshua jumped from the car as soon as it stopped and met his mother with an elevating hug and kisses on both of her cheeks. They both laughed as they said their hellos.

"Hey, what d'you think you're doin' there with my wife?"

Joshua spun toward that crusty voice as Rodney strode from the open door of the barn, pulling gloves off and grinning at his son.

Joshua stood with his hands around his mother's waist, grinning right back at the wiry old man. "Hey Dad!" He let go and took two long steps toward Rodney. They hugged and laughed together for a few seconds.

"It's been too long." Joshua spoke through a tight throat, patting Rodney on the back. They both turned toward the rest of the family, waiting now by the front porch. Emma stood with her arms crossed and one hand over her mouth, covering a smile and perhaps ready to catch some tears.

The little crowd chatted about the trip and the last time Joshua had celebrated his birthday on the farm. When they had all passed through the front door into the living room, Joshua stopped in surprise. A shiny, four-foot-tall robot on wheels stood to one side, lights blinking, waiting for a command.

Joshua looked at Daniel. "I see you converted the old guy."

"What old guy?" Rodney interrupted with a guffaw. Then he turned serious. "We got him 'cause I can't hardly bend over any more, I'm so stiff and sore most of the time." Rodney massaged his lower back weakly.

Without hesitation, Joshua stepped next to his dad and placed his hand just above Rodney's. "Right about here?"

"Yep, that's where it usually grabs me."

"Hang on a second."

The other three stopped to watch.

Rodney stood up a bit straighter, his head turned toward Joshua and his eyes cast toward the action behind him. "Hey." He pivoted his surprised gaze on Emma. "Hey, that feels good. Oh, hey, that feels real good." Then he bent halfway to the floor, hesitated and pressed deeper, until he nearly touched his toes. Standing up straight, Rodney turned toward Joshua. "I didn't know you could do that." He shared the news with the others. "He healed me." He chuckled at Joshua. "I guess hanging around those immortals is rubbing off on you more all the time."

Joshua just smiled.

Rodney addressed the waiting robot. "Ha! I hope you have other prospects. I'm not gonna be needin' your services for a while now." He gave the voice command to power down the rolling computer and looked around at his family, gregariously satisfied with himself.

"How long has this sorta thing been goin' on?" Rodney gestured toward his back.

Joshua looked at his old dad, allowing himself another pulse of regret at having seen so little of him lately. "I started trying stuff like that about eighty years ago." He allowed a look of chagrin to grow on his face.

"Eighty years? Oh, my," said Emma.

"You've always been healthy when I've seen you, so I didn't have any reason to offer healing before."

"So, can you heal anything?" Rodney gestured for his son to take a seat in the living room.

Joshua pursed his lips. "Anything I've tried lately. It wasn't always like that, though."

Everyone but Emma took a seat. "I'll bring in some drinks." She shuffled quickly toward the kitchen. Tina offered to help, but Emma waved her off.

Joshua noted his mother's limited range of movement and planned to corner her later.

"You say anything you've tried. Are there things you don't try?"

Joshua settled himself into a comfy wingback chair and tipped his head slightly. "Well, you know how it is with the immortals coming to the rescue all the time, and most people visiting the clinics for any non-emergency stuff." He paused here to look at his stubborn father, who had apparently neglected his back for some time. "So. it's not like there's a lot of need for healing people."

"Remember that plane crash when you were a kid?" Rodney referred to a video stream the family had seen when Joshua was a teen.

Breathing a little laugh, Joshua said, "Yeah. I haven't heard of a plane crash for decades." He turned more serious. "Mostly, I find my healing useful with people who don't trust the immortals. I know people who still go to mortal doctors for health care, as rare as they are these days. And, of course, I meet people fresh out of the rebel zones, where those doctors aren't so rare."

"How good is healthcare up there?" Daniel had propped an elbow on the arm of the couch and leaned his chin on his knuckles.

Joshua sighed. "Not bad, compared to the way it was before the Reign. But their life expectancy is shorter than ours, and their health is generally worse."

Emma returned with a tray filled with glasses and plates. Rodney hopped up to help her settle the tray on the coffee table in the middle of the room. He looked around briefly as if to see if anyone noticed how easily he had gotten out of his rocking chair. Joshua had noticed.

"I heard they're having bigger families to try and take over more of the world." Daniel got up to take a glass, before Emma could hand it to him. He had always been an ardent fan of his mother's strawberry lemonade.

Joshua looked at his older brother thoughtfully. "I don't know how conscious that process is on a personal level, and most of my interaction with the rebels is on a *very* personal level."

Tina had planted herself next to Daniel. "That must be an opportunity to do some healing then. I mean the children you're dealing with are abused, right?"

This stirred a story from Joshua's memory, when combined with Rodney's question about what sort of things he could or couldn't heal. He considered for a moment whether his story was too startling for the early part of his visit, but he sensed that it would help his family to appreciate something about his life.

"Yes, it's true, they are abused, in one way or another. And sometimes it's really horrendous what they go through." He nodded toward Rodney. "Your question about what sort of things I can heal reminds me of one of those children, a boy who was seven years old. So many of the worst stories we hear come from the children of addicts and alcoholics." He looked at his family for an intensity-level check, and then continued. "Denny was one of those kids. His dad was always drinking and, when it got out of control, his dad would get all emotional about the King and whether he was doing right for his family by keeping them in New Brunswick City. And then, one time, in a sort of fit, he decided that killing his son would be the best thing for him, so the boy could join the immortals and be with the King."

Joshua sipped his strawberry lemonade and took a deep breath, reliving his part in the story. "When I met Denny at Mirabelle, the halfway house in Nebraska, he was just recovering. The immortals had rescued him just in time to save his life, but not before his father had severed his hand with a butcher knife. Denny had tried to defend himself." Here Joshua edited the fact that the hand had only been partially severed, cleaning up the story for his audience. "When they pulled him out, they sealed up the wound and stopped the pain but didn't immediately restore his hand."

All his listeners made a surprised sound at this point, as if releasing their breath in unison. Joshua stopped and took their emotional temperature again. He smiled sympathetically at his mother, who was starting to tear up.

"You see, Denny experienced the loss of his hand, and that experience left an intense imprint on him, of course. To simply restore it immediately would've caused a sort of emotional confusion. So, they left the wound healed, minus the hand. In a way, that loss finalized Denny's willingness to give up on his father and accept placement with a new family. Restoring the hand immediately would have reinforced the denial that comes after such a trauma. So, when I met with Denny, we had to deal with the loss of his hand for a couple of days, along with the loss of his family.

"Then came the time when the immortals determined that he was ready to receive his hand back. They also determined that it was a healing outside my faith boundaries, I guess, 'cause they sent this little girl to do it. She appeared even younger than Denny, a little wisp of a girl with golden hair, huge eyes and a gorgeous smile. She was one of those immortals that I struggle not to worship, she was such perfection."

Looking at Rodney, Joshua read his father's thoughts. "I know, I thought of Olivia too. But this girl's name was Natasha, a little Russian girl."

Joshua could tell that his insight into his dad's thoughts jolted Rodney. He sensed some intimidation as a result. Joshua paused to smile lovingly at his father.

"I'll never forget the sight of that hand growing out of Denny's arm. I may not have had enough faith to do that miracle myself. But seeing it sure did stretch my boundaries between impossible and possible. And there's no sight better than that smile on Denny's face when he got his missing hand back."

He sat up to grab a piece of nut bread and drop it on one of the small plates on the tray. "I still see Denny once in a while. That boy has more faith in God's power to heal than any mortal I know."

His own statement tripped an idea for Joshua. He suddenly realized that Denny would be a good addition to their mission into New Brunswick City, to try to rescue Richie's mother. He silently stored that notion for later consideration, breathing a brief "Thank you" to the King for opening his mind to the idea.

The conversation turned to lighter topics and eventually moved out to the back patio, which Rodney had built twenty years before. Emma had surrounded it with an assortment of exotic plants that found the new Iowa climate hospitable. As the afternoon lengthened, Tina pulled out her guitar and played some songs they all knew. She led with her strong alto voice, as their singing marked the turn from afternoon to evening, and the breezes cooled and calmed. They told stories from their lives, often stories in which the immortals surprised and thrilled with amazing powers and compelling compassion.

Rodney told stories about his old friend Baxter Slattery, twice President of the new American Republic, and a dear family friend. Baxter had died recently, which was what prompted Rodney's memorializing.

"Have you seen him since he joined the immortals?" Daniel was sitting in a cushioned outdoor chair, with a leg crossed horizontal to the ground.

Rodney shook his head. "Nope. Seems to me completely unpredictable what happens to a person when they cross over, except that they don't ever seem to go on with life as it was before they died."

Tina looked at Joshua. "What do you think? Do you know of anyone who lives the same life as an immortal that they did as a mortal?"

Joshua shook his head slowly. He was stretched out on a chaise lounge, sunk into a relaxation worthy of an old hound dog. "I can imagine it happening though, as we allow ourselves to conform to life with the immortals and get used to all the King offers us."

"It's like we're evolving to adapt to this new environment," Rodney said.

Joshua felt himself elevated out of his relaxed state and noticed his mother walking gingerly again. He sat up and stopped her. "Hey Mom, could you wait just a minute?"

Emma stopped to look a question at Joshua.

"Tina? You wanna give me a hand?"

Now it was Tina's turn to look at him with confusion on her face.

"Is it your hips that are bothering you?" Joshua was fairly confident of the answer.

Emma waived a hand weakly at him. "Oh, it's nothing serious. Just the sorta thing you expect when you get old."

"Do you take any medicine for it?"

"Sometimes, when it hurts more."

"Well, what if we could give you a dose of something that would take the pain away permanently?"

Emma paused and seemed to ponder that.

"Go on, dear," Rodney said. "You could use a little miracle. You know you could."

Emma smiled at Rodney. She stood compliantly next to Joshua.

He looked at Tina. "Could you put your hand on her opposite hip?"

Tina hesitated a second, then she reached toward Emma from her seat.

Joshua put one hand on the hip nearest him and looked up at his mother for just a few seconds before she reacted.

"Oh, I feel heat." Her voice skipped.

"So do I." Tina sounded even more surprised.

Joshua concentrated for a moment. "Just a little longer, I think. Okay, now how does it feel?"

Emma flexed a little from side to side. She smiled again, a bit dizzy perhaps. Joshua dropped his hand, and Tina followed his example. Emma stepped away, turned and stepped back, taking normal-length strides.

She shook her head and chuckled. "Now I feel embarrassed that I didn't go to the clinic to get it healed before. That feels great!"

Tina stood up abruptly and grabbed Emma in an impulsive embrace. "That's amazing!"

Joshua smiled at Tina. Part of his goal was to encourage her to give healing a try.

"And you helped," Daniel said to Tina.

Emma thanked Tina and Joshua, but Tina demurred. "I was just there for show."

"Yes, we just hired her for her looks," Daniel said.

"You felt the heat, didn't you?" Joshua challenged her.

"Yeah, but that didn't come from me."

"Ultimately it comes from God, of course. But we can carry it. You really did help."

Tina still looked skeptical.

"You chose Tina for a reason, didn't you?" Rodney had a calculating squint to his eyes.

"I did. I sensed that she has a healing gift that she hasn't developed. Everyone can heal, but some are more gifted than others. I could have asked any of you to help."

Tina pursed her lips, perhaps impressed, if still a little unconvinced.

Daniel and Tina stayed at the farm that night and Joshua slept in his old bedroom, which he had last shared with his brother James. Emma had long ago turned the room into her crafts-and-projects room. But they kept a spare bed in place for family visits. Daniel and Tina got the guest room with the queen-sized bed.

Joshua slept well, full of warm memories of childhood, even if the room didn't look the same as he remembered.

CHAPTER SEVENTEEN

The next day was Joshua's one hundredth birthday. Descendants of Rodney and Emma, as well as family friends, would be converging on the farm all day. The first to arrive was James. He landed his flying car on the driveway in time for breakfast.

"I love the early morning for flying." James stood on the driveway, removing his helmet. The car sat with its wings vertical and the doors open.

Joshua just smiled at his little brother, not surprised by his chosen means of transportation. James had tested all kinds of boundaries as early as he could, including the limits of gravity. He had set the Stippleman record for visits to the healing clinic during his teens.

James introduced Joshua to his new wife, Dianne, who stowed her own helmet in the front seat and tossed her long, red hair before shaking Joshua's hand. Without trying, Joshua sensed defensiveness from Dianne, as if she feared something about him. He had to force himself not to react.

"Good to finally meet you, Dianne. We seem to have been missing each other in all of the coming and going at the farm."

Joshua had grown used to those defensive walls erected by the rescued children, or even by casual acquaintances who knew about his gifts. Whether understanding his limits or not, people often feared the loss of privacy with Joshua, as if he were rummaging around in their bedroom drawers when they met him. He sensed this kind of concern from Dianne. In response, he smiled politely and resigned to keeping his distance.

Breakfast in the dining room, with seven people at the table, stirred more memories of childhood for Joshua. He enjoyed the gift of visiting the home in which he grew up, with so much of his family. Over breakfast, his mom confirmed that Miranda wouldn't be there. She worked with her husband in China, where they had studied art and now owned a studio in Nanjing, selling their artwork locally and over the Internet.

Everyone seated at the table owned at least one print by Miranda Chambers. When they finished their morning feast, Rodney queued up a video link to Miranda in the living room.

Joshua's smile stayed locked in place throughout the call. His sister wished him well and offered blessings, along with one of her prints, which she would be sending to his place in Chicago. They all oohed and aahed over the portrait of a young girl petting a tiger.

Two years younger than Joshua, Miranda looked healthy and happy on the video feed. Her husband, Roger, offered his greetings, and then they sang the birthday song that had been a tradition in Joshua's family. Playing an acoustic guitar custom-made for her by one of the immortals in China, Miranda's voice brought tears to Joshua. Tina pushed through the emotion to lead the family members watching on the farm, with voices distorted by the weight of nostalgia. Before they closed the connection, Miranda told Joshua that two of her sons would be arriving later for the celebration, along with some of their family.

"I love you, Sis," Joshua said.

"Love you, too." Miranda held a big, damp smile. And the life-sized image of Joshua's oldest sister blinked off, leaving a dark viewing surface and a swirl of melancholy.

For Joshua, that one hundredth birthday swept in and out of that same melancholy and joy for the next twelve hours. His little sister Betsy arrived before lunchtime with a new boyfriend and two of her grown daughters, followed by Daniel's and Tina's daughter Debora, accompanied by her husband Donald. And, as Miranda promised, her sons Niles and Kevin, with their spouses, joined the family for lunch served outside on the shaded patio.

Others began to arrive after lunch. The neighbors and old family friends included a half dozen high school classmates who still lived in the area. Among them was Claudia, Joshua's first serious girlfriend. Appearing only as one among the many new faces attached to old names and voices, Joshua didn't meet her one-on-one until the shadows outside had grown long.

Standing on the edge of the patio, enjoying a slight westerly breeze and a glass of iced tea, Joshua welcomed a break from reunion and reminiscence. Claudia found him there. She stood just short of six feet, her once-blonde hair now dark brown. She smiled at Joshua as if wanting to say much more than she knew how. Her deep blue eyes hinted at feelings beyond her control, and Joshua read deeper still, behind those eyes, to a story about loss and regret, and dreams of redemption with an old love.

"Claudia." He offered a tight grin. "It was great of you to come to my party." They exchanged an awkward hug.

"I jumped at the chance as soon as I heard."

As if reading the approaching relational storm from afar, Theresa joined the two tall adults at the edge of the patio. She seemed to materialize out of the twilight. Then she signaled her intention to rescue him.

Joshua followed her silent prompt and put his arm around her. "Claudia, this is Theresa. We've been together since right after high school."

Claudia regarded the petite woman in that plain Amish dress. Joshua could read how his apparently intimate relationship with this perfected and ageless woman intimidated his old flame, just as Theresa certainly knew it would.

With weak and unfinished sentences, Claudia excused herself. Joshua knew she wouldn't be back. She had stretched beyond her heart's natural reach and wouldn't risk that pain again.

Theresa consoled Joshua. "This is for the best. She would have been disappointed later, if not sooner."

Joshua nodded and gave Theresa a rare kiss on the cheek. "Thank you, dear teacher. As usual, you are right."

For the rest of the evening, and into the late hours, Joshua engaged in storytelling, or relaxing and listening to someone playing guitar, singing along for a song or two.

His most startling discovery that evening came from his old high school friend, Lon Taggert. For twenty minutes, Joshua and Lon talked on the front porch, where half a dozen people had retreated to catch the southerly breeze that hinted of rain.

In high school, Lon had been the target of considerable teasing. Full grown, he barely reached five feet eight inches tall, yet he had some of the largest feet in school. Thus, he won the name Frodo from provocateurs, who insisted that he was at least half hobbit.

Compounding his physical oddities, which included an unusually heavy forehead and brow, Lon tended to latch onto myths and mysteries that others considered bizarre. Joshua knew that some considered his friendship with Lon to be charity. But, to Joshua, it was no such thing. Beneath the things that made him a popular kid, Joshua longed for deeper truths and superhuman reality as much as Lon did.

At Joshua's birthday party, they each discovered how the other had *not* grown out of his adolescent fascination with the outer limits of rational knowledge. Lon asked a dozen insightful questions about Joshua's work with survivors from the rebel cities. He listened intently to the ways mortals like Joshua used the powers of the King to help and heal. And Lon seemed truly pleased with what Joshua was doing with his life, free from the fears that most people juggled when they heard about Joshua's gifts.

Part of Lon's comfort with Joshua's lifestyle came from his own close acquaintances with immortals. One of his surprises was that he had once spent an entire year in Jerusalem, as close to the throne as he could be. The immortals had fed him and encouraged him, sustaining his life physically and emotionally as he struggled to stay in the presence of the King, beyond the limits of most mortals.

"So that's when I knew what I was meant to do." Lon sipped his beer. "The King told me without words, sort of implanting the idea in my heart. And I started leading tours to Jerusalem for mortals from all over the world." Lon grinned. "Pretty amazing, thinking of us being born to do this stuff, like we were set aside for it before we even imagined such things."

Joshua nodded. He had often wondered at this very notion, quizzing Theresa about free will and destiny from every angle. "I've finally figured out that I don't need to understand destiny. That way I enjoy it more."

"Ha. That's exactly right."

Looking into the living room, at Daniel in animated conversation with one of the immortals who had accompanied Theresa to this celebration, Lon said, "Did he tell you that he and Tina are going with me in June?"

Joshua followed Lon's gaze toward Daniel and grinned. "He said they were finally going, but he didn't say it was with you."

"He might not have remembered that we were friends in school."

Standing up from his seat on the porch railing, Joshua reached a hand to Lon. Lon grasped it firmly.

"We're still friends, my man, still friends."

Conversations with Simon, his first mentor, with Devin, the immortal who announced Joshua's birth, and with Hyo and Young, still stationed there in Somerville, closed the long and satisfying party.

Goodbyes faded in the cool, night air as most of the guests left. The family members who remained found their sleeping accommodations in the house, and the farm finally fell silent, except for the occasional coyote checking in with others from near and far.

CHAPTER EIGHTEEN

The day after his birthday party, Joshua took more time to catch up with Betsy and James and the remaining family members until midday. Then he rode into town with Emma and Rodney to catch the train back to Chicago.

"I'm preparing for a mission that seems like the sort of adventure I always imagined you would enjoy."

"Mission?" Emma was sitting in the back seat. "That sounds like your father's territory. I'm just a farm wife." She grinned.

"I know more than one adventurous farm wife."

Rodney looked at him and smiled slightly. "Yep, I believe you do. So, what are you up to now?"

"A rescue mission."

"But I thought that's what you did all the time."

"Not like this. I'm taking a few people into New Brunswick City to try to talk a boy's mother into leaving with us."

"Oh, my." He could hear Emma's motherly concern.

Rodney's eyes faded toward the horizon, as if imagining what the rescue entailed.

Joshua could see a plan developing in his father's head. "No guns, of course."

"Mmm, too bad." Rodney chuckled.

"Do you think she'll agree to come out?" Emma was clearly concerned.

Joshua hesitated a moment, checking his current expectations. "It seems unlikely. But I have a feeling that we're going to see more than one unlikely outcome from this trip."

"How often do mortals go into those cities to bring people out?" Rodney asked.

"Well, considering the billions of rebels, I guess it's pretty rare. I only know of a handful of attempts on this side of the world. But then, I would mostly know about the ones that succeeded."

"The immortals will protect you, won't they?" Emma asked.

Joshua nodded reassuringly, blocking out the scenario he had included in his meeting with Ray. "The immortals won't take part in the effort to persuade her, of course, but they will get us there and will intervene if we need saving."

Joshua's was aware, of course, of his mother's personal experience with the immortals not acting to prevent injury, or even death.

Rodney hit a button that disengaged the auto-drive and took control of the vehicle. "I still don't trust these things completely." He maneuvered into a parking place next to the station.

Joshua caught a wince of concern on his mother's face and tried to guess whether it was his father's driving or his mission to New Brunswick City that was making her anxious. When the vehicle settled to a stop and her face relaxed, he had his answer.

Then she surprised him with a question. "Joshua, do you imagine that you will be one of the first of us to simply walk from mortality into immortality, and not miss a beat in between?"

Rodney turned with Joshua to look at Emma in the back seat.

Joshua loved his mother with his eyes, and a small smile. But he aimed his answer in a slightly different direction from what either of his parents probably expected. "I plan to live on in this mortal body for another hundred years, or more. Don't worry, Mother. I will visit you more often from now on."

She nodded slightly. "Well, not for another hundred years you won't. We won't be staying here much longer."

They climbed out of the car without saying any more. Joshua retrieved his bag from the back seat, hesitated in front of his mother for a moment, and hugged her. He turned and hugged his father as well.

"I love you two." He studied his father and his mother in turn. Then he hugged them both together. "Thanks so much for the birthday."

"You should send a message to Tina," Emma said. "She made most of it happen. She thinks about you often and wanted to do something special for you."

Joshua absorbed that little revelation and thanked his mother for telling him.

Rodney and Emma stood arm-in-arm by the car, watching Joshua walk toward the stairs to the train platform, where the electric train sat waiting for departure. On the platform, Joshua turned toward his parents, who were squinting into the sun. He waved once, smiling and letting tears flow unchecked down his cheeks.

CHAPTER NINETEEN

Two days later, Joshua sat in the back yard of Mirabelle, white clouds obscuring the sun every minute or two, shadow and sunlight taking turns on the swing set. Having heard Joshua's description of his plan for the trip to rescue his mother, Richie used his feet to move the swing, first back and forth, then side to side.

"We all have to face it sometime or other, and maybe even every day—that we can't change someone else's mind for them. You have to go into this knowing that your part is to *try* to bring her out. But it's her part to decide whether to accept the offer."

Richie's placid face, his dark eyes large and childlike, was as serious as any eleven-year-old ever should be. Internally, Joshua detected the rattling of fears that Richie was trying to settle into solid and unshakable places in his soul.

The next day, Joshua met with Michelle Hanneman, a woman who had escaped from New Brunswick City when she was a teenager. Ray and one of his assistants had both recommended Michelle. She had been on two rescue missions in the past. Joshua's only previous contact with Michelle had been around the rescue of a teenage girl whom she had talked into leaving the walled city. Michelle had remained present for all of Joshua's meetings with the older teen, who felt safe with Michelle, but frightened around grown men. In the process, Joshua and Michelle had developed a deep trust.

Michelle wore short, dark brown hair that reminded Joshua of feathers. She stood about five feet, four inches tall, with a square physique and an athletic grace. Like Denny, the other member of the team, Michelle would do anything for Joshua. And she would do whatever she could to rescue someone from New Brunswick City, especially a woman.

"What do we know about this woman?" Michelle sat in Joshua's living room stroking the long-haired, white cat.

Theresa entered the room with a tray of coffee cups, sugar and cream.

Joshua answered Michelle. "We know her name is Alice, that she has had numerous male relationships, and that she drinks heavily and uses narcotics, particularly the drug known as love drops. She's about sixty years old and has seven children, all of them fully grown, except Richie."

"Any indication that she would want to leave?" Michelle thanked Theresa for the coffee and started to stir in cream and sugar.

Theresa answered this question. "We know she is discontent with her life in the city. She is estranged from all her other children. But we've seen nothing to assure us that she would be happy to leave." Theresa sat in her favorite chair and put up her feet. The cat abandoned Michelle in favor of Theresa, with a quick bound and a small purr.

"Any attachments now that might put up a direct resistance to us talking with her?"

Joshua knew that Michelle could imagine particulars about Alice's situation, from her other rescue attempts, as well as from her own life. But he had little to offer.

"Richie hasn't been home much for quite a while. And the immortals who first brought him out haven't kept a close eye on Alice." He decided to stretch Michelle's worldview a bit. "But I'm sensing a strong affirmation from the King that this mission is something he wants."

Like many people living under the Reign, Michelle tolerated some of the supernatural abilities of the immortals, but mortals such as Joshua, who could see beyond the physical realm, unsettled her. To Joshua, the assurance that the King wanted him to attempt this mission, was the leading reason to do it. But he knew that Michelle looked for more concrete, human assurances.

She didn't respond directly to Joshua's last statement, instead turning toward Theresa. "Your people will get us into her house, or at least her neighborhood?"

Theresa hesitated for a second. The contrast between the two women went well beyond the one being mortal and the other immortal. Where Michelle majored in manipulating the pieces, Theresa didn't rely on logistics for her confidence.

"Yes," Theresa said. "We will land you all near the house, at a time when we know she's at home."

A noise in the kitchen punctuated Theresa's response. Then a voice explained the noise. "It's only me, Denny. I'm pretty hungry, so I had John land me in your kitchen."

Joshua laughed. Michelle looked concerned. Theresa just stroked the cat from ears to tail. John was Denny's mentor, an immortal who had lived in southern Africa. He was even smaller than Theresa, with pigmy ancestors. He had been known for his miraculous power in his previous incarnation. Apparently, John had dropped Denny off and left. Joshua found only the lanky young man in the kitchen when he went to investigate. Denny was assembling a sandwich. Joshua was glad he had thought to buy bread the day before. His kitchen wasn't always stocked with edible food.

As if reading his thoughts, Denny explained himself. "I checked first before I landed. I knew you had fresh bread. I also knew that if I didn't help you eat it, you would have moldy bread in about a week." That last part was no surprise. Joshua ate at home too seldom, and neglected good food even when he had it.

Patting Denny on the back, Joshua joked. "Well, maybe you should check my kitchen more often, so you can let me know when I'm out of stuff."

Denny didn't avert his eyes from his sandwich project. "Pickles would be nice, dill slices. You're out of those." Then he looked up and grinned.

Leading Denny into the living room, Joshua introduced him to Michelle. "This is Denny. He's a friend of mine who escaped from New Brunswick City when he was a kid."

Michelle stood up to shake hands, and Denny obliged by handing his milk glass to Joshua, wiping the condensation on his jeans, and then clasping her offered hand. Joshua could see a slight electric vibration pass from Denny to Michelle, much like what happened when he touched one of the immortals.

For Joshua, that electricity was the main reason for including Denny in the mission, followed by his hunger for adventure, and his experience in finding his way out of the walled city.

Denny joked with Michelle. "Well, I can see that I'm not the eye candy on this team."

Michelle scowled at that remark. Joshua had anticipated tension between Denny and Michelle. But he expected they could work together, once the mission began. He planned to keep them apart most of the time before they flew north but had wanted them to at least meet once before.

Denny took his milk back from Joshua. "Anyone want half a sandwich? I make a grand sandwich."

Michelle looked at the neatly divided sandwich with some interest but shook her head. Joshua sensed the barrier she was keeping up and started to head for the kitchen to get a second plate. But Denny stopped that move by pulling a plate from beneath the one with the sandwich on it.

He persisted. "Come on, I know you want it. I won't take any romantic meaning from you sharing my sandwich. I was just teasing you before. I'm not gonna harass you. You're probably old enough to be my mother. Heck, you might *be* my mother. I never met her."

After another hesitation, Michelle accepted the tall half of a sandwich when Denny extended it toward her on that second plate. Joshua chuckled quietly to himself while he bent to prepare himself a cup of coffee. As he did so, he noticed something.

"Hey, where did I get this little pitcher and these cups?" He looked at Theresa.

"I wanted to serve coffee, and you didn't have anything suitable."

"So you went shopping?"

"I made them, as you well know."

Joshua smiled at her and then returned to stirring his coffee with cream.

Denny brought them all back to business. "How's the kid?"

"Richie's doing fine. I checked in at Mirabelle this morning. He was putting up a good fight against the nervous waiting part, before we finally head out."

"We go as soon as the immortals see an opening, right?" Michelle spoke around a mouthful of sandwich.

Joshua looked at Theresa and then Denny. In his mind, the show would begin when Michelle became comfortable with the plan and the people. Her question clarified her level of readiness.

He answered Michelle while monitoring Theresa's internal responses. "Yes. I think we can go at any time. I know sooner is better than later for Richie. If we're all comfortable with our roles, then we're ready."

"We're ready." Michelle swallowed visibly.

Denny only nodded, clearly too intent on chewing to interrupt with words.

They all agreed to go to Mirabelle to await the mission's launch, in deference to Richie. He would certainly find some comfort waiting in a familiar place, even a place from which he had escaped more than anyone else. Denny had brought a small bag with him in preparation for a few days of waiting. Joshua packed for three of four days on short notice, and Michelle decided to take her chances on finding what she needed in Lincoln. Joshua noted her more Spartan outlook. Michelle's commando approach simply came with the package.

Joshua had never seen Theresa transport three passengers at once. But she seemed to ignore his attention to this accomplishment. The means for moving real objects instantly over long distances bypassed categories such as numbers and mass. Theresa had assured him, for example, that walking on water had nothing to do with whether one stepped lightly or danced a clog.

All she needed for this transport was three willing passengers.

CHAPTER TWENTY

They landed in the back yard of Mirabelle, where Theresa must have known they would be seen by the minimum number of people when they popped in. By chance, Shari was looking out the window at the end of a long workday. Theresa apparently sensed their audience and looked up. Joshua followed her gaze and waved at Shari and her young assistant. Shari was smiling.

Inside the house, Joshua introduced Shari to Denny and Michelle, both of whom had travelled through the rescue system without a stint at Mirabelle. But the most important person to introduce to his team waited in his room upstairs.

"Can we see Richie?" Joshua asked Shari.

"Of course. I'm glad you arrived so soon. He's going crazy waiting here. Go on up. He'll be glad to see you."

Joshua led the others up to the third floor of the house, to the east side, overlooking the back yard. With a gentle knock on the door, which stood open several inches, Joshua announced his presence.

"Richie, I brought some people for you to meet." He pushed the door open and stepped through.

Like a boy waiting for his name to be called, Richie spun in his seat and jumped up.

"Is this it? Are we ready to go?"

Joshua gave half a smile but shook his head. "Not just yet. We have to wait for word that your mom is at home, where we hope to meet her without any interference from anyone else."

Richie nodded and then turned back to his desk. "I've been drawing a map of her yard and her house from the last time I escaped back there."

Joshua followed Richie to the desk. Theresa, Denny and Michelle entered the room, the latter two somewhat awkwardly. On the desk lay a dozen pieces of white paper, smudged, erased and redrawn over and over. Joshua turned to introductions.

"Richie, I want you to meet my friends." He turned to Theresa first. "You met Theresa before, right?"

Richie nodded from where he stood by his desk, looking over the adults.

Joshua introduced Michelle and then Denny. Richie shook their hands solemnly, with something less than suspicion but also less than trust.

"They're both from New Brunswick City. Michelle escaped on her own, and we rescued Denny like we did you."

This information changed Richie's demeanor. "So, you think you can get my mom out?" He focused on Michelle.

Michelle spread a rare smile. "If she wants to come out, we'll get her out."

"But can you make her *want* to come out?"

Michelle flinched slightly. She glanced at Joshua, for some sign of how much to say.

Joshua came to her aid. "She can do a lot to persuade your mom. But it's too much to say anyone can make her want to come out."

Richie looked from Joshua to Michelle, to Denny and back. "I just wanted to see what she'd say."

Joshua caught a flash of annoyance from Michelle. But that settled quickly. She had risked a lot to escape from her own mother. But her sympathy for this boy who wanted to risk everything to reunite with his mother afforded Richie some extra mercy. Having just visited his own mom for the first time in too long, Joshua sympathized with the turmoil Michelle now fought. He marveled at the way she lashed herself to Richie's emotional determination, as if she hoped for some vicarious satisfaction regarding her longing for her mother.

After that initial meeting, Shari offered each of the adults temporary sleeping arrangements, in case their wait stretched from hours to days. But before Joshua and Denny had decided which one would sleep on the couch and which on the mattress on the floor, Theresa heard the news that Richie's mother was at home alone, and mostly sober. After delivering that news, Theresa headed to the front porch, leaving Joshua to inform Richie, and to gather his team for the ride north.

When the mortals arrived on the porch, they found Theresa with another immortal, a man nearly as tall as Joshua, with features that sent him to Mediterranean shores and ancient sculptures of Greek gods. Alexander greeted each of the mortals with a confident smile and what felt to Joshua like a breeze blowing directly from the throne.

"We go then, to do what we can," Joshua said.

With that, the immortals broke through physical space, and carried the four mortals with them to a quiet residential street on a sunny afternoon in New Brunswick City. The four stood in front of a house whose design would fit on a Caribbean island.

"That's my house." Richie's voice was reedy and trembling.

Joshua took a deep breath, still uncertain that it was worth risking the intense rise and fall of so much hope in Richie's heart.

CHAPTER TWENTY-ONE

Alice Harper, formerly Alice Phelan, formerly Alice Jenkins, formerly Alice Schuette, stood alone in her living room, looking out the picture window. Over the three-foot-high wall that bordered her front patio, she saw four people—three adults and a child—standing in the street. The child looked familiar, but she couldn't find the part of her mind that knew who he was exactly. Something had happened. A very sad thing had happened. A long time ago. Or maybe not so long.

As she stood there thinking about this, the doorbell buzzed, startling her. She began picking up cups and glasses from the coffee table and moving them to the pile of dishes in the kitchen sink, or along her kitchen counter.

The buzzer sounded again. "What? Who would that be?"

Someone called out. The windows were open. "Alice. Alice can we talk to you?"

"Who the hell is that?" She opened the inside door as she spoke.

There stood four people. One was a boy. Alice recognized the boy. It was Richie. Richie was home.

"Richie!" She shouted, a surge of energy. She swung open the screen door, with its missing screen.

Richie launched toward her, and they hugged on the welcome mat. Alice scrunched down to reach her little boy. But he was bigger now.

"How've you been? Oh, you look so grown up." It seemed like she should know *where* he had been. So she didn't ask. A mother should know where her children are. *Where are the others?*

Straightening to full height, Alice fixed a loose strand of her recently-dyed red hair behind her ear. There were two men and one attractive young woman on her doorstep. Had she seen them before? Did she know them?

"Hello, Alice." The tall man spoke with a charming smile.

"Hello." Alice let the "O" last a couple extra beats. This new man was very interesting.

The man nodded toward the living room, shaking something loose in her mind.

"Oh. Won't you come in?" She pulled that boy out of the way, so the tall man and his friends could enter. One of them pulled the boy into the living room with them.

Alice swallowed a gasp when she saw the room now. She had guests. She jogged to get past them. With a sweep of one hand, she cleared the couch, and then motioned for her guests to sit down. Room for the three attractive guests.

But there was that boy, too. Who was that boy?

He was looking at her. She knew him.

He sat on the arm of the couch, while the other three squeezed together on the cushions.

"Can I get you anything? Anything?" *Such attractive guests.*

The tall man spoke. "Alice, we actually want to *give* you something."

"What's that?" *This could be good.*

"Alice, do you have a headache right now?"

Alice had lost track of what they were doing here. Why the question? Headache?

But, in fact, she *did* have a headache, come to think of it. The strangers had distracted her from that pain when they showed up outside. How long ago was that?

"Well, I *do* have a headache. You have something good to get rid of it?" She tried to see if one of them had a bottle of something.

"Sure." It was a younger guy now. He stood up.

Had he been here all along? There were too many faces to see at once. This one was skinny, young. He was kinda interesting. Maybe he was the one with the drugs.

"I've got something that you can absorb through physical contact, skin to skin."

"Skin to skin? Oh." That sounded good. Sure. She could go for that.

He was getting real close to her. He moved too fast. But close was good. Maybe. She wavered. She backed up a bit.

The skinny one reached a hand toward her head. She had a headache. He had something to help her. But there was nothing in his hand.

The boy spoke up. "It'll feel good, Mom. He won't hurt you."

It was Richie. He was back. He was sitting on the arm of the couch. She knew that. She knew he was there. How long had it been?

Alice looked at Richie now. "Where ...?" But she wasn't going to ask that.

The skinny guy was touching her forehead. *Whoa. There went that headache. Gone. Poof.*

"Wait. What did you say?"

Something was happening.

Four people were there in the house. Who were they?

"Richie." It was her boy. She knew him. He was back. These others were strangers.

Richie got off the arm of the couch and stepped gently toward her, his eyes wide, like when he was little. He was so much bigger now, though.

"Oh, Richie! You're home!" She lunged at him and grabbed a big hug. He started crying. Or maybe it was her that was crying.

When she stopped grabbing at him, turning to look for a tissue, Richie spoke up.

"Mom, these are my friends. They came with me to get you out of here, to heal you up and get you out of this place, out of the city."

The young woman on the couch seemed in pain. She winced. She was one of Richie's friends? But she was so much older than him. And the others too. That tall man was certainly much older. Though he didn't look as old as Alice did in the mirror.

"Wait. Did you say, get out of here? Why would I do that? Now that you're home, I don't need to go anywhere."

Richie looked like he hadn't realized this before. *Where had he been? When did he leave?*

Before Richie could answer, the front door swung open. Darien was home.

"What the hell is this?" His dreadlocks swung over his shoulders as he looked around at the strangers. Richie's friends.

Alice wondered where Darien had been that day. But then, she couldn't remember where *she* had been before Richie and his friends arrived. She couldn't even remember what Darien was doing now in her house.

The tall man faced Darien. He reached his hand to greet him. "Hello, Darien, I'm Joshua Stippleman, and these are Michelle and Denny. We brought Richie home."

"Brought him home?" Darien looked confused.

But Alice couldn't blame him. It didn't make sense to her either. And now this Joshua had said something different from what Richie had said.

"Yeah," Joshua said, "we just came through that door a few minutes ago. Alice and Richie are just meeting now."

Darien shook his head and then excused himself from the living room. He only glanced at Alice.

She realized her face was still covered with tears, and she started to wipe at them as Darien went down the hallway.

Joshua spoke now. "Alice, if you want to be with Richie, you'll have to come with us, to leave the city. He can't stay here. It's not safe for him." He glanced toward the bedroom.

Did he think Darien would hurt Richie? Would Darien do that?

"Where would we go?"

"I will personally guarantee a good, safe place for you to live with Richie, in a prosperous and free community, with everything you need to care for yourself and your son."

As she stood calculating the offer, she compared it with her life with Darien. She thought about just having Richie stay with her in this little house. She remembered life with Richie's father, and with boyfriends that came after him. She was seeing the meanness now. Then she took a good look at Richie. Maybe he could take care of himself better this time. It seemed like he had taken care of himself by running away before.

Now he was back.

"You came to get me out?" She looked from Joshua to Richie.

Richie nodded.

Joshua glanced toward the bedroom. "Let's go outside, so we can get some fresh air and talk about this."

Alice turned her head toward the bedroom now, too. Joshua must want to stay clear of Darien. That was generally a good idea ... for everyone, really.

She heard Darien's phone ring. He answered it.

Joshua gestured toward the front door. Alice decided to go out that door with him, and with Richie and the others.

On the patio, she paused to look around at the crystal-clear air. The fog was gone, that fuzzy air so hard to see through, closing her in, keeping her contained.

An emerald hummingbird sampled a magenta flower that she hadn't noticed growing along a trellis against the house. Suddenly, she understood that the younger guy, Denny, had done more than heal her headache when he placed his damp palm on her forehead. She looked at him now, as he came out of the house.

Two jet-powered motorcycles roared past on the narrow concrete road in front of the house. Alice covered her ears, as did the strangers, at the pumped-up volume of the bikes.

That sound was more intense than she was used to. Just like the clear air. Clearer sounds.

Had her drugs been keeping her from seeing, hearing and thinking clearly? Had that young guy wiped away the effect of the love drops? How much had she taken today?

Joshua interrupted Alice's wanderings. "Let's take a walk." He pointed the opposite direction from where those motorcycles had gone. Alice followed his gesture and reached for Richie as she did so.

Behind her it seemed that that woman and young man were constantly checking for signs of Darien.

Breathing the fresh spring air, like a healing vapor, Alice continued to look around her, amazed at her new clarity. She could hear the video streams in the houses they walked past. Neighbors. Names came to mind. She was recalling some of their names.

But this Joshua guy, and Richie too, were asking her something really important. She needed her clear head to latch onto that.

"What if I changed? What if I made Darien move out?" She thought for a few seconds. "What if I stayed off the drugs and booze?"

Joshua walked beside Alice, with Richie on her other side. Her boy had faded a step behind.

Joshua said, "It takes a lot of effort and assistance to change that much, Alice. It would be significantly easier in a new environment, with new people around you." He paused for a breath. "You need the presence and power of the King in your life to make that kind of a change."

Alice looked hard at Joshua. "Would you be there? Would you ... be around?"

He looked concerned. Serious. "I would visit Richie. I'm responsible for him for the long term. But I'm not offering you a relationship with me, or with anyone except Richie. This is your chance to be his mother, to be a mother in a way that you regret missing with all of your children since Lauren."

Alice startled at the mention of her oldest daughter. She glanced at Richie to check if he had told Joshua about Lauren. Richie shrugged his shoulders and shook his head.

Joshua explained. "When you devote yourself to the true King, the Son of God, he gets inside your heart and inside your head, and you can hear him speaking. He told me about Lauren. It wasn't Richie."

"He knows about Lauren and me?" Alice's voice clogged a bit in her throat. "Does he know where she is now?" She stopped and hitched a strand of her hair over her right ear.

Joshua breathed a long sigh. He nodded. "Yes, of course. He knows where everyone is." He waited for something before going on. "She's outside the walls. She's living a happy and free life out in the world. She loves the King."

For a second, Alice's heart lightened at the news of her lost daughter's peaceful life. "Could I go see her?"

"Yes, you can go see her. I can't guarantee that she will welcome you back into her life. That's up to her. But you would be free to go where you want, along with Richie, of course."

Alice looked at Richie, imagining her youngest child meeting her oldest for the first time. Lauren had been born thirty years before Richie and had disappeared years before his birth.

That tough looking woman spoke up before Alice could respond. "Here comes Darien, and he's on the phone. I'm guessing he's calling the cops."

Joshua looked back again and Alice did too. She saw Darien striding toward them, with his phone bud in his ear. Seeing Darien looking concerned tripped something in her. She could see a sort of battle lining up. Darien against Richie. With her in the middle. That would be hard on Richie.

Darien put away his mobile device and burst into the circle that included Alice and her son. He ignored all the others and spoke to Alice. "What are you doin' with these people, Alice? Is your boy come home, or are you thinking of leaving?" He didn't sound mad, really, just anxious. Intense as usual.

Richie tried one more time. "Mom, the cops are coming. You need to decide to come with us before they get here."

Darien did that little sideways grin at Richie. But he seemed afraid of the others. He probably thought they were aliens. That was a scary thought. But they weren't, *were they?*

Joshua spoke to Darien. "Don't worry, we're not leaving with anyone that doesn't want to leave."

The sound of copter cycles filled the air. Four loud vehicles, each carrying a defense officer, rose above the roof tops from the east, the direction that they had been walking.

Alice squinted at the cops. She didn't want to get in more trouble. That would make it hard to get drugs again.

As the copter cycles hovered toward the ground all around the little group, a larger flying vehicle appeared over the rooftops. The other woman shouted above the sound of the surrounding engines.

"Spread out!"

Joshua seized Richie's hand and pulled him away from her and Denny. Alice, and then Darien, followed Joshua and Richie.

Joshua spoke close to Alice's ear. "You can stay or come with us. It's up to you. We came to get you out, to unite you with Richie and get you to a better place. We don't need cops where we live." He glanced around at the officers and their vehicles.

Alice weighed the situation. She felt the urge to flee, but not a clear desire to vacate the only home she could remember.

Again Joshua spoke into her ear. "Give it some thought. This is not the way it should be if you decide to come out. We'll come back for you. You think about it."

He led Richie toward where that woman stood.

She shook her head, but Denny was also headed for her. She looked ready to panic and run, when a large, padded net dropped around them. The big extraction vehicle was right above them. They didn't bother with Alice and Darien.

Joshua held onto Richie, who tripped as the rim of the net fell against the back of one leg. Even as he fell, Richie kept his eyes on Alice.

She backed away and let Darien wrap an arm around her shoulder.

CHAPTER TWENTY-TWO

He couldn't see what was happening on the ground, but Isaac Wilson could tell that the cops were grabbing some more disturbers of the peace. So-called peace.

Tuning in to the spiritual signals sent by the folks on the ground, he recognized someone like himself. A mortal who was a fighter for freedom. Definitely a disturber of the peace. And maybe there was more than one.

The big net was on its way back up into the extraction vehicle. Isaac leaned against the far corner of the detention cage to allow for new arrivals. He didn't move as fast as he used to, and he sensed the new arrivals were younger folks.

Four captives, squashed into a group hug, rose into the belly of the hovercraft. One young man laughed childishly. Isaac laughed along with him, as did a taller man, more substantial in every way. Isaac liked him immediately.

The guards surrounded the net as it rose to the ceiling of the craft, barking their orders which included closing the bay door below the net. Someone released the horizontal pull and the four new captives staggered onto the deck of the ship. They kept each other upright.

Speaking of upright. There was a young woman with them. No, the word for her was actually *uptight*. She wasn't like the two men. And there was a boy.

"Woowee, you boys caught four at one swipe. You're gettin' good at this." He wanted the captives to hear a friendly voice amid the military chatter.

The tall, blond man squinted toward Isaac, even as he seemed to be reading the hearts of the cops. It wasn't the same as the way Isaac read spirits. But it was strong. A strong gift of seeing into people's hearts. He really liked this stranger.

"Okay, let's see some identification from you folks." That was a tall man with military posture and a short afro. Isaac thought his name was Carter or something like that.

"We don't have any identification," the tall captive said.

That was the clincher. These were rescuers. Disrupters, like him. Not from around here. Not from the rebel enclave.

The cops knew that too. "Okay, so you're outsiders just like the guy claimed when he reported you?"

"Yes, sir. And we all came in together."

Isaac expected the tall man said this to make it clear that the kid was with *him*. Isaac suspected the boy came from New Brunswick City, at least recently, if not today.

"All of you came in together?" The commander was looking directly at the boy.

"Yes, sir." The boy spoke quietly but clearly.

Looking at all four for a moment longer, the commander turned toward the cockpit of the craft. "Go ahead to the drop-off point." He was holding an earpiece with two fingers, probably getting his orders from some technocrat somewhere.

"In the holding cage," another officer said. And the four obeyed, moving slowly toward one corner of the bay.

"Come on in, friends," said Isaac. "Standing room only in here, I'm afraid. But this won't be a long trip."

The obvious leader of this group reached out his hand. "Joshua Stippleman."

"Isaac Wilson." He took Joshua's hand in a firm grip. He couldn't stop smiling.

"You've done this before."

"Yes, I have—quite a few times, in fact."

Joshua introduced each of the others and they all shook hands with Isaac.

"Where are they taking us?"

"Outside the walls. They always drop us outside the walls far from an entrance, as if that would make any difference." Isaac chuckled.

"So, who keeps dropping you *inside*?"

"Oh, I have friends in high places."

The woman, Michelle, was clearly impatient with the merry banter. "Why do you do it? Why do you keep going in?"

Isaac studied her, saying a silent prayer to the King. "For the same reason you do. To save as many as I can."

As usual, they landed outside the fifty-foot-high fortress known as New Brunswick City. Now there were five of them. It was good to not be alone this time.

Of course, Candice was there. She materialized next to them, as did another immortal, a woman in a simple black dress. The others all looked at Candice. Apparently, they knew the other woman.

"Joshua and company, let me introduce my friend in high places, Candice. She's my transport in. And she's also my aunt." He couldn't keep the silly grin off his face. He knew the fact that she appeared much younger than him would confound the uninitiated. He still wasn't above such a small joke.

Joshua looked inquisitively at Isaac, and then glanced at the other immortal. "I thought relatives didn't get to work together across the divide between mortals and immortals."

The small immortal woman answered. "It's not a rule, just a pattern. While the connections between families after someone passes are not guaranteed, neither are they forbidden."

Isaac filled in. "I barely knew Candice in her mortal life. She's my mother's sister and lived halfway across the country. The first time I saw her after the war, I was just surprised that the immortal they sent to transport me was Aunt Candice. Of course, the years have been better to her than to me." He laughed some more.

Joshua clapped him on the shoulder. "Maybe so, but she doesn't get to ride in an extraction vehicle as often as you do."

Everyone except Michelle laughed at that.

CHAPTER TWENTY-THREE

Joshua noticed Michelle's reaction to his joke with Isaac. He stepped close and put an arm around her. "You still with us? I still need you." He spoke gently into her ear.

Michelle nodded. "I'm mad at myself for being so uptight. I know I'm looking at this all wrong."

Joshua edited. "Not *all* wrong. You're with us to keep tactics and strategy in mind, just the way you naturally do. You may just need to expand the boundaries of what tactics can be included in our plans."

"Plans?" Michelle smirked. "Do we have a plan?"

Joshua looked at Richie, conscious of the lighthearted talk around a critical event in the boy's life.

"What do you think, Richie? Did your mom seem like she was seriously considering coming out with us?"

Richie looked at the scraggly weeds at his feet for a second. "I think she is *trying* to decide. She seemed different after Denny healed her, and she kinda had to get used to that change."

Joshua nodded at the wisdom of Richie's assessment. "I think you're right." Then, he looked around at the little group. "How long do we give her before we try again?"

"Twenty-four hours seems like a reasonable time." Theresa was standing next to Candice. "That allows her to cycle through a whole day in her new condition, thinking about Richie, and about the prospect of getting out. I think we will get some help from her friends, who will unintentionally remind her of why people escape the walls."

"Is that agreed?" Joshua looked around at all gathered there.

All nodded, except Isaac and Candice. But Joshua had an idea about including them in his team.

"So what do *you* do next?" He asked Isaac.

Isaac cocked his head at Candice. "I think we might be able to pool our resources a bit, to work together some. What do you think?"

Joshua breathed a little laugh. "I think you already know what I have in mind."

Isaac smiled. He was a kindred spirit to Joshua, a rare find among mortals. Joshua looked again at Candice. She seemed to shimmer with some kind of visual vibration on a minute scale. After staring for a few seconds, he glanced at Denny, and then Michelle, to see if they noticed. Then he checked with Theresa. She smiled knowingly.

"What's happening to you?" Joshua asked Candice.

She grinned in a way that warned of uninhibited laughter soon to follow. But she held back long enough to explain. "I can only be in one place at a time. But time is relative. I am passing back and forth between where you are, and the throne in Jerusalem, in short bursts of time."

Joshua furrowed his brow. "You're bouncing back and forth between us and Jerusalem?"

Still smiling, almost mischievously, Candice nodded, and the fluctuation slowed a bit so that it was more obvious.

Richie stepped closer and reached toward her.

"Don't touch her." Theresa warned him briskly, yet still with a smile.

Richie looked from Candice to Theresa. He managed to resist the draw toward the electric air around Candice.

Joshua consulted Theresa. "Can *you* do that?"

"Yes."

"Then why haven't I noticed you doing it?"

"Just because I *can* do it, doesn't mean I *have* to." Theresa's playful dimples showed on both cheeks. Then she answered a bit more seriously. "I don't do it often. And I've never done it when you were around."

Isaac said, "Candice does it a lot. I'm used to it." He chuckled. "But I'm fully convinced that fifty percent of her attention is worth far more than one hundred percent of mine."

As Isaac looked at his shimmering aunt, Joshua could sense the deep longing in the old man, as if he contemplated his own future immortality. Seeing this, Joshua admired the old evangelist even more for his attempts to infiltrate the walled city.

Candice settled back into place, becoming more solid. She and Theresa exchanged a silent something, both appearing to suppress giggles.

Then Candice spoke to Joshua. "I'm sorry for the distraction. But it demonstrates a point, anyway. While you mortals couldn't tolerate the rapid movement I was just using, we *can* move you very quickly, if you're willing to endure the disorientation."

"The catch is, that it may scare Alice away if you appear to be as alien as they claim *we* are," Theresa said.

"But she doesn't have to see everything," Isaac said. "I can go into a crowd and start preaching, the way I do sometimes. That will surely cause a distraction. We just need Alice to be somewhere that there are a lot of people."

Alexander spoke up. "With the three of us," he motioned to Candice and Theresa, "one could be invisibly watching the timing, and the other two transporting people in and out of the situation."

"I could help Isaac," Denny said, "by healing someone, to increase the distraction."

Isaac smiled. "I like that idea." He looked at Denny admiringly, as if just discovering a secret weapon.

"Good," Joshua said. "That leaves Richie, Michelle and me to persuade Alice." He looked at Michelle, knowing she would be happiest with a role that depended mostly on human effort. She seemed satisfied. At least they had the outline of a plan.

"In the meantime, we need a better place to wait." Alexander stepped toward a struggling clump of shrubs fifty yards farther from the city walls. "How about some shade?"

The notion of shade in relation to the low scrub brush seemed absurd, until Alexander stretched out his hands. As they all watched, the tangled little clump of weeds, and dwarfed bushes, grew and changed. Whether he simply increased the size of plants already there, or transformed small weeds into species of trees, Joshua couldn't tell. Either way, the brush become a copse of trees, casting welcome shade in the midday sun.

Joshua laughed, and Richie clapped his hands once in surprise.

Denny ran to join Alexander. "Oh man! You gotta show me how t' do *that*."

CHAPTER TWENTY-FOUR

The team waited for an opportunity that fit their plan. They sat on outdoor chairs the immortals had conjured by some means that Joshua didn't notice. The conversation circled back to Isaac's offer of a diversion.

"How can you be sure that the authorities will show up when you preach? Or is that not necessary for the diversion?"

Isaac smiled knowingly. "DNA tracers."

"What?"

"They have my DNA. They monitor the air for microscopic traces of DNA that match that of known troublemakers."

As Joshua digested this fact, Theresa popped in, as if to listen to this explanation.

"They can get that out of the air?" Joshua glanced at Theresa.

Isaac explained. "It's not perfect, but they have sensors built into public buildings and streets all over the city. It's a very sophisticated system, with a central monitoring office. They've figured out how to recognize the smallest particle by its DNA origins. And they have me on their top ten most annoying list." He grinned a moment before suddenly frowning. "They have all of you now, as well."

"Huh? Us? They have our DNA?"

"The net." Isaac reminded him. "The cushions on the net aren't just to protect you from injuries that would certainly bring on the immortals' intervention. The surface of it also collects hairs from your head and your arms. The authorities would have monitored you on cameras and noted where you were in the net. Then they put your DNA in the database. I'm sure they'll have you in there soon, if they don't already."

"I had no idea."

"They're working hard on things like that in the rebel cities. Technology is their god, as if the walled cities weren't enough."

Joshua reviewed the new information and considered its implications for Isaac. "Have you found places where you won't be detected?"

Isaac nodded. "There are some places, mostly private homes and such. But I have to be invited there, of course."

After a few heartbeats, Joshua realized something else. "Do they have their own citizens in that database?"

"Of course. I think they completed that project a few years ago. That's part of their control system, knowing who is where, and what they're doing. Most of the video screens you see around the city have video cameras hidden in them, along with other hiding places, I'm sure. Matched with DNA sensors, the cameras can keep track of their people pretty accurately."

"How long would it take them to link Richie with Alice?" Joshua lowered his voice. Richie was sleeping on a folding chaise lounge a few feet away.

Isaac looked at the boy. "Not long."

Theresa interjected. "What can they do about it, though? It's still up to Richie, and to Alice."

Joshua nodded slightly for several seconds, thinking about what lay ahead. His main reason for concern was Richie's age and his history of emotional trauma. Even if the immortals could rescue him, it might not be before some struggle, especially a struggle inside Richie's heart.

The next day, while Joshua lay asleep on his own reclining lawn chair, Alexander received confirmation that Alice had left the house with Darien. They were headed for a local commercial district, where shoppers and diners gathered in numbers. Michelle woke Joshua with a gentle nudge. He blinked appreciatively at her, noting the tenderness beneath her shell.

Having decided to stay near the city, they had watched the day carry the sun across the face of the wall. Through the course of the day the concrete shone white-gray and then more golden, to pale orange. As if to keep himself occupied, Alexander had been growing lush, green grass around them. Candice lay contentedly in a deep field at the point where they were all roused to their task.

They had decided to stay there at Theresa's advice, instead of retreating to a more civil location. Such distance might weaken the focus and resolve of the team. Remaining in sight of the walls insinuated a siege of the city. Rest, food and water, provided by their immortal protectors, had eased the wait and softened the siege enough for Joshua to approve of leaving Richie in that place. Richie had never camped out for recreation, only occasionally sleeping in an unguarded barn, when on the run from his rescuers. He seemed to enjoy their brief stay under the miraculous stand of trees.

Settling on their plan, the points at which decisions would have to turn, and their timing, they divided their force. Isaac and Denny were to be transported by Candice, to Denny's great pleasure. And Theresa would carry Joshua, Richie and Michelle. They headed for an intersection half a block from the restaurant where Alice and Darien had gone for supper. The two immortal women would remain in place inside the city, but invisible. Alexander would provide the link between them, relaying and coordinating from a position unknown to the mortals.

Joshua noted Denny's boyish smile when he put his arm around Candice's waist, in preparation for his transport. And they all launched into the city.

The street had already succumbed to nightfall, artificial lights dimming the sky which had appeared twilit outside the wall.

Once they emerged from the sheltered alley into which they had been transported, Michelle nodded to a nook between buildings, where she, Joshua and Richie could pretend to be looking at an animated display in a store window. In fact, the display fascinated Richie, who had spent little time exploring the city in recent years. Technological advance had moved so rapidly that Richie seemed as awed by the city sites as Joshua and the others.

The small creatures in the window, fantastical inventions resembling conglomerations of actual animals or people, leapt and played in a pastoral scene. It was lit by very convincing artificial sunlight. Richie examined it closely, probably trying to discover the mechanism moving the little figures. Michelle and Joshua joined him. Joshua could hear a portion of Alexander's and Theresa's telepathic communication, and Michelle monitored the physical situation with furtive glances and reflected views in dark sections of the store window.

When a store employee appeared behind the display, checking the interest level of the apparent family outside, Joshua and Michelle engaged with Richie's curiosity about the moving figures. Joshua thought he could detect a combination of cleverly manipulated magnetics, with robotic automation on a very small scale. Michelle smiled at the store clerk but shook her head at the unspoken question about their intention to enter the store.

Joshua was impressed at Michelle's ability to look like a deferential window shopper, and not a commando on a mission ... if only for a moment.

CHAPTER TWENTY-FIVE

Next to the restaurant, where Denny could just see the back of Alice's head, Isaac scanned for idling people that they might engage in conversation. With the authorities on the alert for them, they had to act quickly, to deliver any meaningful message.

Denny spotted a woman with a brace on her wrist, the sort people used for repetitive stress injuries before the Reign. The healthcare situation inside the rebel cities resembled the pre-Reign medicine of chemical and mechanical solutions to physical ailments. Only from old movies did Denny know the type of injury treated with such a brace. Pointing her out, Denny drew Isaac's attention to the small woman with a chemically-induced olive complexion and artificially auburn hair. She appeared to be much older than Denny, but not so old as Isaac.

Isaac stepped off the curb and strolled to where the woman with the brace stood talking to a man, who seemed to be receiving directions. Isaac waited for the directions to be completed. Denny, at his elbow, prayed silently. When the man receiving directions finished and walked away, Isaac caught the woman's attention.

"Excuse me, my dear, but I couldn't help noticing your wrist brace. Do you mind if I ask what's wrong with it?"

The woman looked at Isaac and then Denny, and then at her wrist, which she raised to improve its position as the focus of the conversation. "Well, I don't mind, I suppose. There's no hiding it. I just get sore when I work at the checkout at work. We're so busy, and I'm ringing things up, ya know." She demonstrated sliding an item across a scanner. "It generally hurts all the time, but especially when I'm moving it like this."

Isaac nodded sympathetically. He explained himself. "Well, the reason I ask is that my young friend here has this amazing ability to heal things like that with this technique he discovered. And I wonder if you would be willing to let us make it better?"

The woman stared, clearly unsure what they were asking of her.

Isaac filled the gap. "I'm sorry, I should have introduced myself. I'm Isaac, and this is Denny."

"Rosalind." She offered her braced hand.

Isaac gently shook that hand. Denny did likewise but held on an extra second, until he knew that healing power had gone into her wrist.

Rosalind froze, her eyes on her wrist. Then she lifted her head to examine the two men in front of her more carefully. Perhaps she was checking for signs of mortality, signs of aging and imperfection. What she found apparently satisfied her. She didn't panic.

Isaac interrupted her confusion. "What do you think it would be worth for someone to take the pain away and heal your wrist?"

Rosalind flexed her wrist as much as the brace would allow and then wiggled her fingers. She began pulling at the straps holding the brace and removed it, now working her wrist vigorously, and clearly still finding no pain.

"I guess it would be worth a lot." Her brow furrowed and eyes squinted as she continued to study the men.

Isaac asked another question. "How do you think it's possible that ordinary people could heal just by touching someone?"

"You're not aliens."

"No, both born here on this old Earth, and getting older, as you can see. But, what if someone with the power to heal sent us to come and touch you and take away your pain?"

A short, middle-aged man with a long, straight nose inserted himself into the conversation.

"I know who you are. You're that preacher. I seen you here before. You're that preacher that the cops took away last week. Yeah, I know who you are."

Isaac nodded slowly. "Yes, the authorities will grab me in a little bit. But don't you wonder why they arrest people for healing, or even for speaking their mind?"

Rosalind just shook her head, which left room for that other man to hold forth. As that stranger began to answer Isaac, Denny gently rested his hand on the man's shoulder. This stopped his vocal cords. His mouth moved, but no sound came out.

"The God that created you, who loves you and healed you, wants you to know that you are not alone, and that you are welcome in God's family any time," Isaac said.

Another man, younger than the first, and a good deal less sober, began to shout. "Oh, oh, you're gonna get in trouble." He howled in a childish voice which degenerated into ridiculous laughter.

By now, two dozen people had gathered around Isaac and Denny. Denny scanned the crowd boldly. “Anyone here sick or in pain?” As he studied the strangers, he suddenly knew that a man standing to his right had a disease that was slowly killing him. Denny turned to the man, named the disease and then put his hand on the man’s chest. The heavyset man just stood there gawking at Denny’s hand on his chest.

At this moment, a squad of police officers ran around the corner in tight formation. They carried no weapons, the rebels having surrendered those decades ago. Nevertheless, they plowed through the crowd by virtue of their size, strength and precise training.

Denny’s little mission with Isaac was ending in a scuffle. And just as it was getting fun.

CHAPTER TWENTY-SIX

Joshua had received the signal to move to the restaurant. He, Michelle and Richie arrived at the side of the open-air establishment just as the police surged into the nearby crowd. He could hear the extraction vehicle approaching, when he made eye contact with Alice.

Alice started when she saw Joshua, but then smiled when she saw Richie. "You *did* come back." Her voice choked slightly.

The syrupy slur to her words warned Joshua that Alice was under the influence of something, probably the love drops like the last time they saw her. Richie could apparently see it too. Joshua tracked the collapse of Richie's hope. Still, he persisted with the mission.

Michelle stood where she could monitor the police, shielding Alice, Joshua and Richie as much as possible. Darien seemed less hostile than Joshua had expected. He was perhaps also flying on some drug. He regarded Joshua and Richie the way he might if they were street mimes performing for coins next to the restaurant.

"Alice, this is your chance to come with us, and to live with Richie out in the free world. We can get you both out of here in a matter of seconds, if you choose." Joshua noted a couple at the next table tuning into what he was saying. But he kept his eyes latched on Alice.

"Mom, this is our chance. Come out of here and we can start a new life."

Alice smiled at Richie. But her blank smile lacked the depth she had tapped when Denny had helped to sober her. Her son, and of the decision before her, apparently remained outside the sunny little orb formed by her drugs.

Alice eventually reached a hand toward her boy. "Oh, it's good to see you, dear."

Richie hesitated to take that hand, as if he knew that the offer was counterfeit.

Joshua prayed, even as he strained to feel something from Alice that resembled real emotion. Then he took a chance.

Reaching to take Alice's offered hand, Joshua increased his bid for the mission's success. "Alice, remember when my friend Denny touched you yesterday, and you saw the sky and the flowers so much more clearly? I can do that for you now, if you want."

Tipping her head, as if to align it with a tilted universe, Alice tightened her sedated face into a close imitation of a thoughtful look. She looked briefly at her hand, which Joshua held. He sent a simple blessing her way. Because he believed he could heal Alice more effectively if she received willingly, Joshua waited for her verbal agreement.

Richie spoke again. "Mom, let him clear your mind up, so you can decide whether you want to come with me." Richie seemed to believe that keeping his mother focused on her connection with him was their best hope.

When Joshua sensed that Alice had linked into what Richie was saying, he sent the first wave of healing to her brain. Though she hesitated, she did accept the initial blink of clarity. As he felt her opening, Joshua increased his effort, and waited to see what God would do in the tossing circumstances.

As Joshua started to gain some hope, Darien leaned through the envelope of his own inebriation. "Hey, you get your hand off o' my wife." Still, he didn't move, as if he were contained two glass layers away from what Joshua was doing.

The couple who had been listening from the next table were much more sober than Darien. The man, perhaps older than Joshua—his tanned face like leather and his hair unnaturally swirled over the top of his head—spoke up. "What is this? Who are you?"

Alice seemed to rally slightly, like awakening from a sleepwalk. She stood up, still holding Joshua's hand. She made a motion to Darien, as if to say, "Wait, I'll handle this," and she stepped away from the table, toward the entrance to the restaurant patio. She released Joshua's hand, in order to maneuver past other diners, and then reached out for Richie's hand, when he met her at the opening in the restaurant railing.

Richie looked hopefully into his mother's face. Joshua knew that Alice had decided something. Michelle remained focused on the police, who were scrambling to capture Denny and Isaac among the crowd they had gathered. She also kept an eye on Darien and the man at the table next to him.

Taking a deep breath, Alice held Richie's attention as well as his hand.

"You have a good life, where you live?"

Richie answered at half volume. "I keep running away, instead of letting 'em put me in a good home. I keep hoping you and me can be together."

Alice nodded. She was clearly struggling against remnant effects of the drugs, and perhaps years of brain damage. "I'm too stuck in all this stuff, in this life. I don't know what I'd do on the outside—probably escape back here." She inhaled deeply. "And I couldn't be a good mother to you here, either. I'm too messed up." She paused and almost grinned. "I'm so messed up that I like it the way it is, the way I am. This is what I know."

Alice stared into Richie's eyes, yet she seemed to feel none of the pain that Joshua read from the boy's soul. She looked at Joshua. "You take good care of him. I know you will." And she let go of Richie.

Darien had followed them, after an indecisive pause. He stood now waiting behind Alice. She turned to him and took his hand, not looking back.

Joshua gathered those bits of her cast-off responsibilities, to carry home with him, along with Richie and his crumpled heart.

But, as he put his hand on Richie's shoulder, Joshua sensed a resolute hope in the boy. Briefly, he feared that Richie had decided, against reason, to stay with his mother. Then Joshua understood that this irrational idea wasn't what was stoking hope in Richie.

As they walked away from the restaurant, Richie glanced back at his mother. Then he spoke to Joshua. "I'm gonna grow up and come back here. And I'm gonna be like you. And my mom's gonna come with me, 'cause it'll be okay for me to take care of *her* then."

Joshua gripped Richie's shoulder more tightly, holding back his own tears. He looked at Michelle, who was shadowing their slow escape. He drew strength from her steady calm. She benefited from distance between herself and the emotions of an eleven-year-old boy, who had already begun a lifelong mission to become his mother's caretaker.

The three rounded a corner into an alley and the immortals intervened. They snatched Michelle, Richie and Joshua away from the walled city.

Back at their oasis outside the walls, Denny and Isaac were laughing quietly with Candice when Joshua and the others arrived. Joshua appreciated their enjoyment of the way healing had challenged some citizens of New Brunswick City. But he welcomed their restraint when they saw him, Richie and Michelle.

John, Denny's mentor, appeared next to them, as if to temper the giddiness of his young student. Isaac nodded a greeting to John and spoke to Denny. "We should work together more in the future." His old eyes sparkled at Denny when he said this. Then they turned their attention to Richie and Joshua.

Michelle had taken a seat on one of the chairs unevenly resting on the ground beneath an impromptu palm tree. Joshua knew he would have some repairs to attend to later, with her.

The group debriefing took less than five minutes. The mission itself had lasted only a few minutes. And none of the crew seemed compelled to know every detail of what had transpired with the others. The essence of what had happened was clear enough. They would have days and weeks to live inside their own echoes of their brief foray into that colossal city.

Joshua regretted allowing Richie to stretch his childish hope beyond its breaking point, or at least the point at which a *healthy* boy would have found hope's limit. But Richie, for all the disappointment of this loss, demonstrated the resilience of a child raised on the border between two worlds. With Joshua's help, Richie had survived repeated crossings back and forth between the Reign and the walls of the rebellion.

More than the parental responsibility that had been transferred to him by Alice, and which he would soon transfer to a loving family, Joshua bore the responsibility of a teacher and mentor for the boy. And Joshua knew that he would do everything he could to help Richie fulfill his dream of leading his own team someday to try to rescue his mother.

CHAPTER TWENTY-SEVEN

For Theresa, every day included the hope and relief of that first triumphant day when the King rode into Jerusalem on his white horse. On that day, the light from the Lord of the universe reflected off a mighty steed, elevating that beast of burden to miraculous status. But then everything seemed alight and alive that day. No sports fans welcoming their championship team, no oppressed people welcoming the liberating army, no people on Earth ever celebrated a parade or procession so recklessly, so free from hesitations and doubts. She recalled his face as he rode past, looking right at her, deep into her. And she recalled knowing that he looked at everyone in that crowd with that same passionate recognition, and measureless love.

Every time Theresa visited Jerusalem, every day that she swung over the throne like a seagull lifted by warm sea breezes, or danced in the crowd, shoulder-to-shoulder, chest-to-back with throngs of unfettered lovers of the King, she relived that first day. She relived the fresh relief of the coming of the one for whom all of creation had been waiting. She never lost the newness, the discovery, the transcendent awe of that first procession into the city, no matter how many times she returned to the center of the human world.

When Joshua visited the royal city the first time, at the age of twenty, he had fought nausea and chest pains, excitement morphing into panic, and anticipation listing toward terror. He had looked into Theresa's eyes with questions and doubts. She knew he didn't feel ready to be so near that glowing throne, surrounded by a billion worshippers, even where he stood at the outer edge of that gigantic congregation.

Back then, eighty years ago, Theresa recognized his fears, and she knew that her prize student was fully embracing his place in God's universe. She celebrated quietly within herself the confirmation that her student knew the most important truth, that God alone was Lord, and that Joshua's own fragile human self-image, even one assembled in the safety of the Reign, couldn't stand up to the force which created all life and matter with mere words.

Once again, she watched as Joshua landed on the ground in Jerusalem. It was the first time in several months. This had been his longest time away from the city, just as he had recently broken his longest absence from his parents' farm in Iowa. Theresa knew that Joshua had become busy with his good work, fulfilling his destiny. He had slipped a little loose from his foundational attachments to family and creator.

She knew that she was supposed to allow her student to follow his human urge to work, and to accomplish more of those good and noble tasks he had been assigned. She allowed him to slip away just a bit, so that he could feel the draw back to his core, his lode star, the gravitational center. This natural human rhythm had to be revisited, to revive the inherent human experience of surrendering independence. Without the small steps away, he couldn't know the exhilarating return into the arms of the waiting father, who watched the road every day for when his son would come back from that far country.

Feet firmly planted on the gold-dusted ground, Joshua swayed as if he felt the Earth rock beneath him. This was no vertigo caused by his rapid transport from one side of the globe to another. This was his connection to the pulse of that globe, in the place closest to the heart of humanity's home. Tears began to run in streams down his face. Clearly, his mouth could form no words.

Theresa stayed with Joshua, at first, though they both knew she would move away and come back freely. He would be taken care of, even sustained, by the spirit of the King himself. On most of their previous visits, Joshua had simply lost track of Theresa, and had lacked the emotional margin to wonder what she was doing when she wasn't with him.

Before half an hour had passed this time, Theresa launched herself away from the royal city. She went to visit a friend of hers in New Zealand. A joyful trip that lasted some hours. She could monitor Joshua from that distance. She could feel him there, with his nose flattened against the pavement, his arms spread perpendicular to his body, his shoes off—lost somewhere already.

When Theresa greeted him next, he had returned to consciousness, responding to thirst and hunger beyond what the passage of time naturally demanded. Theresa laughed aloud when she saw his face, glad for the recharged light she saw again in his eyes. Joshua smiled self-consciously, never comfortable being the butt of her jokes. But that wouldn't stop her.

He slowly shifted to his knees and then to standing, stretched his back, arching and then hunching forward. Then he grabbed Theresa for a brief and vigorous hug. After recovering his decorum—to the degree possible for a grown man unused to being barefoot in public—Joshua drank juice and then water from glass bottles kept cold by her. He ate the bread and fruit she gave him and recovered visibly.

When he stood still for a moment, a bottle of water in one hand, Theresa introduced the next phase of Joshua's visit, gesturing to the man who now stood beside her.

"Joshua, this is David." Theresa nodded toward a tall, slender man who appeared a bit younger than Joshua.

And she excused herself.

CHAPTER TWENTY-EIGHT

David Adeyemi panted to recover his breath. He recognized in Joshua the tear-stained face and unsteady limbs of a mortal recovering from the blast of Jerusalem. With the songs of the multitude ever filling the spaces between thoughts, David smiled knowingly at a man that he could tell was reading his heart in the same way that David was reading his.

"You are Joshua Stippleman, from Chicago."

David had become accustomed to meeting immortals on his visits to the throne, and always hoped to communicate more directly with the King. But rarely had he come to the royal city to meet another mortal.

"David Adeyemi of Ibadan," Joshua said, apparently learning David's full name from the Spirit. He stepped up and gripped David's hand, returning his welcoming smile. Neither of them spoke aloud for a few minutes, but each continued to read the soul in front of him. Their handshake had become a conduit across which each of them listened. Without hesitation, they opened their hearts and minds to each other, and simply received the impressions they found there.

Unlike a verbal introduction, this empathic discovery process involved taking in a soul much the same way one takes in a landscape, like a view of the broad savannah in David's country. Instead of linear thoughts communicated through words, they each saw the other as an emotional and spiritual vista, each free to focus on minutiae, or to step back for a wide overview. David and Joshua saw in each other a sort of mirror image. That they lived on distant continents, that their skin, their hair and their faces looked nothing alike, didn't matter. They knew each other now, and each recognized himself in the other.

The King spoke to both David and Joshua in the middle of their encounter. As significant as David found meeting Joshua, the palpable presence of the King overwhelmed that significance. Into the mix of wordless communication between him and Joshua, arose the discovery of the image of God in the other man. He knew Joshua was seeing the same thing. And they slumped to the ground, their hands slipping free from each other.

As he rested on the smooth, golden pavement, a rushing crescendo of music and flying saints swirled around him. Like a thousand giant birds launching at once, worshipping saints responded to the influx of God's spirit onto these two men, coalescing and then whirling over, and around the fallen mortals.

Even in the epicenter of this surge, David knew perfect peace. He knew peace even as he knew that, in a heartbeat, the King could have him. He could extinguish David's mortal life. At the same time, he felt the King's delight in the prospect of two men such as him and Joshua continuing to represent the King in mortal bodies. He could feel the gravity of his own body against that of the Earth. David knew that God intended to walk and eat and sleep in mortal form, through him. The King had selected him and Joshua, and millions of others, to display divinity out of mere humanity.

When this revelation solidified, David lost his place in Jerusalem and landed in some peaceful, green place near an old hut, the grass and shrubs around it overgrown from neglect, no sign of occupants. When he lifted his face out of the long grass and pushed himself up to a sitting position, the King sat there with him.

The King looked eye-to-eye with him, as they stood together in the overgrown yard. "Your goal is not to become one of the immortals, nor to be more like them than any living mortal man. Your goal is to become like the mortal I once was."

David shivered as the profundity of those words seeped into his whole being. They were just words, of course. But they were words from the one that created the Earth and everything else with words.

"Now, I know it through and through," his spirit said, though he couldn't move his lips.

The King laughed heartily. "Yes, now you know!" He shouted. And he grabbed David in a powerful embrace.

The magnetic power of the King held David in a standing position. He felt as if his limbs no longer possessed the will, or the strength, to hold himself up. He had never been drunk, or high on drugs, but he knew that this is what it felt like.

David stirred himself from the ground, turning his head as he pressed up to all fours. He was in Jerusalem still.

Joshua was also beginning to rise. David could tell that his American counterpart had been with the King, as *he* had, and had also received some revelation that had altered his soul.

He stood, his mind spinning, his eyes blurry with the movement around him. Then one of the dancers veered from the flock and landed in front of David and Joshua. A boy of about eight years in human appearance, with golden twirls of hair all about his round little head, stood perfectly still in front of him—no panting, no sweating, no need to adjust from dashing to a sudden stop.

The boy enveloped them with his broad smile. "It's time for you to learn to fly on your own."

David laughed loudly. Though he could hardly hear himself. He spoke to the boy. "Lead on, my man. You are the teacher!"

Just as David discovered in his mental inbox that the boy's name was Randy, the boy took his hand and then Joshua's, and hoisted them into the air. He cut between passing worshippers, who missed them with the precision of an old Air Force flying squadron.

The weightless rebellion in which they now engaged pulled David away from Joshua. Their arms slipped from each other. But they caught hands again before David spun off and away from their little flight instructor. Firmly gripping his new friend, David turned to look at Randy, who was towing him by his other hand. Randy looked back with a smile that said, "You can trust me. You're going to love this."

The boy lifted them clear of the crowds, clear of the flying worshippers and into fresh, blue sky. From a thousand feet off the ground, David saw small white clouds in the west. The sun illuminated them up there, instead of the glow of the King and his throne.

Randy pulled his attention back. "How hard would it be for you to go back down?" He looked at the seething crowd below.

He had avoided using the word "fall," David noticed.

David laughed. "If you mean, do I know how to get down from here? Then the answer is, 'yes, of course.'"

"How hard would you have to *try*?"

This time Joshua laughed, a nervous laugh. "Not very hard at all."

"That's how it is to fly. You don't do it by trying hard. You do it by letting go and *allowing* yourself to do it."

David's first reaction was, "*That's easy for you.*" But he kept that one inside. Instead, he tried to let what Randy said fill his imagination. "*What if flying were really like that, just like cooperating with gravity?*"

"Which is stronger? Gravity, or the love of the King?" Randy seemed to converse with David's thoughts.

David replied by letting go of Joshua's hand. As far as he could tell, he and Joshua remained aloft by virtue of contact with Randy. This is how it had worked for him in the past, with his immortal pilots. As long as he hung onto Moses, his immortal tutor, then he could fly.

David let go of Randy now.

For a moment, he didn't fall. He didn't move. He could feel Joshua and Randy staring at him. Was he hovering there because Randy had extended his influence to sustaining him in the air? Certainly, the immortals could move objects, even mountains, without touching them.

But then he began to fall. This fall was not, however, a straight line toward the ground. Falling began to feel a bit like swooping. Maybe more falling than flying, but he felt more like a bird than a rock. He concentrated on surrendering and letting the King carry him. His angle toward the ground became even less severe. And then he caught a sort of updraft that kept him from crashing into the crowd.

At the same time, he heard a man shouting, as he would imagine someone would scream as they fell from a great height. He saw Joshua sailing past, toward the ground. But his descent slowed and Randy caught up to him, perhaps holding him in the air again.

Struggling to figure out how to steer, David veered left and then right before he found how to bank his turn back toward where Joshua had landed. David swooped to a stumbling landing just a few feet from Joshua.

David had flown. He had mostly flown downward, but that was part of his trick, part of how he convinced himself it would work. It was four parts gravity and one part flight. But it ended in a landing, and not a crash. Now he stood panting again in front of Joshua, they both laughed nervously. David's legs wobbled under him.

Joshua spoke through his gasps. "I always liked transporting better than flying, anyway. at least since I grew up."

David stood up straight and smiled. "Yes, transporting is definitely easier to do." As soon as he said it he could tell that he had surprised Joshua.

"Wait, you‘ve already transported yourself?"

David nodded. "It is true then, that you Americans have not mastered transporting?"

Joshua raised his eyebrows in a look of chagrin. "And you Africans *have* mastered it?"

David, still catching his breath, laughed again. "Haven't you heard the stories of preachers and missionaries transporting across miles, even before the Reign?"

"I never believed it, I guess." Joshua recoiled. "*Before* the Reign?"

But David could see a look of discovery settle onto Joshua's face. And then the tall American closed his eyes. His shoulders relaxed visibly. And he disappeared.

He reappeared twenty feet away.

Stamping his foot David exclaimed. "Yeah, man! You just transported yourself about as far as you could walk in two seconds." He bellowed wild laughter. But he knew his teasing couldn't break his new friend's triumph.

Randy duplicated Joshua's feat, popping from next to David to the space next to Joshua. Then he popped out of that circle in the crowd, and reappeared hovering over a knot of worshippers, who clung to each other, singing like New Year's revelers.

Joshua zapped himself into the space next to Randy. But, when he arrived there, suspended only briefly, he fell into the crowd below. They caught him, and he lay with arms and legs spread, playfully passed along the top of the crowd. Several others dove onto the uplifted arms of their neighbors and joined Joshua on the human conveyor that rolled him first one way and then another.

David laughed and laughed. And then he followed Randy's invitation to head for the sky. For another flying lesson.

CHAPTER TWENTY-NINE

After a winding and ticklish surf over the top of the crowd, Joshua returned to a place on the ground, exhausted. He sat down but then sensed a new presence. He looked up slowly. He wondered briefly whether Theresa had been waiting there for him, or whether she had only appeared when he returned to this spot.

Theresa smiled. She reached out to help Joshua to his feet, which proved to be more of a challenge than her simply offered hand implied. Joshua reeled and staggered, trying to keep an invisible surfboard under him, as he rode an equally invisible wave. Theresa laughed at his impaired state, though she had seen him like this on previous visits to the royal city.

Before Joshua could assemble enough of his wits to say anything in response to Theresa's laughter, a flock of children frolicked into view, running and leaping and singing like a herd of musical antelope. None of the children was as tall as five feet, but they followed a tall man in long robes who ran and jumped in a way that patterned the flight of all those behind him. As the man swept past, his robes trailing behind him, Joshua recognized the King, or at least he thought he did.

Seeing the King, he suddenly recalled what had happened before the flying lesson.

He had been alone with the King, near an abandoned house. Somehow, he knew the house was near his father's farm. The King had stood back, holding Joshua at arm's length, a serious look on his face.

"Now you begin to treat Theresa as your partner, your coworker, no longer your teacher. She knows less about your calling than you do now, though she knows me in ways that you haven't yet comprehended."

In his numbed state, Joshua had briefly thought, "I don't know if I'm comprehending *anything* right now."

"You are. Don't worry. This experience will stay with you for the rest of your life."

Now, here stood Theresa. She must know what the King had said to him. But Joshua didn't feel ready to discuss it with her.

Instead, he felt an urge to talk to his father. He checked with Theresa. She nodded. And Joshua knew that he was able to go directly to the farm in Iowa, on his own. Immediately following that epiphany of confidence, he was standing on the front porch of Rodney and Emma's house. No Theresa. He had transported on his own.

For the first second, Joshua gasped as if he had just emerged from a deep dive. Then he turned his head slowly, noting things his parents had changed about the front porch. Settling into concrete reality, he heard his father's voice. He recognized Rodney's playful tone as he said something to his wife. Momentarily, Joshua wondered if he might have popped in at an inopportune time, but that seemed unlikely, given the one who had ultimately decided that he should be there.

Lacking any better ideas, Joshua knocked on the front door. He could hear his dad's voice again, this time a questioning tone and volume rising, as he approached the door. Joshua breathed a brief prayer that he wouldn't give his father a heart attack from shock. And then the door opened and there stood Rodney, speechless.

"Hey, Dad. Just thought I'd drop in. Hope this isn't a bad time."

"A bad time? What? Of course, it's not a bad time. Why, son, it's a wonderful surprise." He swung the screen door and clasped his son with both arms.

"Rodney?" Emma's called from inside the house. "Joshua!" She sped her pace toward the front door.

After they had hugged and laughed a bit, wiping a few tears, Rodney looked around the yard. "So, did Theresa drop you off?"

Joshua started to laugh and worried briefly that he might not be able to stop. But he forced a dose of sobriety and tried to respond.

"Well, the thing is ... the thing is, Dad ..." and he started to laugh again.

Emma seemed to get it. "No, you didn't." She gasped, lifting her hand to her mouth.

"Didn't?" Rodney said. "Didn't what?" Then a light flicked on in his eyes. And he started to laugh along with Joshua.

When the laughter subsided, Rodney said, "So it's come down to this, has it? This is how I get to see my son more often? He has to become like one o' them darned aliens." And he started the laughter up again. Emma just shook her head at the two of them.

By the time they had caught their breath, Emma urged them to come inside for some strawberry lemonade.

Joshua joked. "I knew I could get more of Mom's strawberry lemonade if I would finally just let go and believe."

Emma waved dismissively and headed for the kitchen. Rodney turned serious. "So that's how it works? You just believe and you can pop from Chicago to Iowa like this?"

Joshua shook his head. "Not Chicago, Dad. I was in Jerusalem."

Threatening to fall back into unquenchable laughter again, Rodney just shook his head and leaned on the back of the couch. Joshua smiled at the sight of his father so full of joy.

Then he remembered another aspect of his conversation with the King that day. Was it really that day? The King had taken him to an abandoned farm near his parents' place. Apparently, he had taken Rodney there once, when Joshua was a teenager. And the King had spoken to Rodney as he did Joshua.

In his spirit, Joshua was back there briefly, staring into those loving eyes, returning the welcoming smile.

"Do you see?" the King had asked.

As obscure as that question may have seemed to an outside observer, Joshua knew the answer. He nodded. "I do see, more fully than I saw it before."

"Your sight improved when I showed you a man just like yourself."

"Yes." Joshua nodded, standing straighter. "I could see what is true of David and couldn't escape that it applied to me as well."

"Comparing yourself to the risen saints has left confusion in many areas of your heart. They are my purified servants. But they don't stand between you and me. I showed humanity how to live on this Earth while I was still a mortal man. You can follow *my* example."

Joshua shook himself back to the present, sitting on the couch next to his father.

"I saw the King today, over by that farm along the highway, the abandoned one just next to the sunflowers."

"Ah. I remember that spot. Went there with him myself, once."

"That's one of the things he showed me."

"And he showed you how to follow him and not wait for the immortals to do everything for you?"

Joshua chuckled. "Something like that."

Emma returned to the living room with two glasses of cold, pink refreshment. She folded her arms after handing off the lemonade. "Well, can you stay for supper?"

Joshua checked with his internal scheduler and received an okay. "Yes, Mom, I'd love to stay to supper." He smiled at his dear, old parents and at his new freedom to visit them.

CHAPTER THIRTY

After returning to Mirabelle for a week, Richie had flown with Shari in a jet. In Pittsburgh they rode a bus to a suburb up the Ohio River. First, they stayed at a halfway house in that old river town. Apparently, the town had been built up some since the capital moved to Pittsburgh. Shari, and then Richie and Shari, met with Mark and Karen Slater, to see if they could be the family for him.

For his second meeting with them, Richie joined the Slaters for supper, while Shari headed to a coffee shop, where she said she would catch up on some work.

Food had been the hardest part of Richie's transition away from the walled city. Mirabelle's staff knew that. They had been allowing him some sugar, salt and fat that folks under the Reign didn't normally eat.

The Slaters were typical. They served him salad, with really different nuts and spices in it, and then some rice dish and this spicy protein thing they called Lassah. But Richie knew he was there to impress them, so he ate all of that stuff without complaining. Days on the road, escaping without enough food in his bag, had taught him to not be too picky.

"Uh. Thanks. That was good." He suspected it really was good, even if he didn't enjoy all of it.

Mark grinned at him. "I think you earned a little treat, the way you put away that meal, which I know wasn't your favorite." He handed Richie a glistening, golden cake, factory-wrapped in plastic. Karen smiled supportively.

"You can get these down here?" Richie's voice squeaked. He touched the dessert as if it had come from a diamond mine on the other side of the world.

"There's no law against buying or selling them in this country. They're just not much in demand."

"They're not the healthiest food. So folks down here don't eat them much. But for a special treat we thought it would be okay." Karen was watching him as if she would get some fun out of seeing him eat it.

And, even though it was weird to have people watch him while he ate, that didn't stop him from chomping down the sweet and sticky cake in four bites. Maybe he should have taken his time. It disappeared faster than an immortal on the way to Jerusalem.

Mark had explained to Richie that he worked for the national government and commuted by electric train into the city. Apparently, his contacts at work helped him locate the sticky cake, from a food maket in New Brunswick City. In Pittsburgh, these things were rare. But Richie knew that, in the walled cities, they were more common than sliced bread.

Pittsburgh, a special treat and healthy food—this was all part of the picture. But it really came down to these two people. Mark and Karen. They seemed cool. He didn't think they were bribing him with the golden cake. They were just saying they knew things were different down here. That was good. They were good people.

After all, he was looking for new parents, somebody to basically take over for the job he had been doing himself. His mom was never much of a parent. And none of her men were anything like a father. So Richie had figured out how to get along on his own, once the last of his sisters moved out. And he couldn't blame them for moving out.

Richie was glad to get a visit from Joshua two weeks after the Slaters officially took responsibility for raising him. By then, he had gotten used to being a stranger in a strange land. His new parents were different, but mostly in good ways.

One weird thing was how they seemed to rely on no pharmaceuticals, at all, for anything. In a way, this made them seem sort of unhuman, or maybe superhuman. He expected Joshua to live that way, but not ordinary people in the suburbs.

Sitting in his back yard, trying to repair the wing of a radio-controlled airplane, Richie looked up when Joshua came out of the house. He figured that Joshua had already interviewed Mark and Karen about how it was going. He hoped that he would get Joshua to himself for the rest of the afternoon.

"Have a crash?" Joshua nodded to the plane.

"Yeah." Richie pressed the wing back into alignment. "That's pretty much what these things are for, though. You fly 'em until they crash. Landing doesn't seem to be part of the deal."

Joshua stuck his hands in the pockets of his tan pants. "I know what you mean. I used to fly one of those out on the farm in Iowa, and I crashed lots more than I made decent landings. But, as I remember it, I got pretty good at putting it down gently on our long driveway."

The backyard in Pennsylvania was pretty tight. That long driveway sounded good.

"I told Mark and Karen that we'd be going somewhere. You wanna try flying this thing back on the farm?"

"In Iowa?" Richie's voice cracked as he stood up, with the plane intact again.

"Sure, it's a great place to fly."

"Where's Theresa?"

"Spain." Joshua smiled like he had some joke bouncing around in his head.

Richie waited for the joke.

"You trust me?"

"Uh. Yeah."

"Enough to be my first transport passenger?"

"Oh." Richie tried to imagine what would happen if it didn't work.

Joshua was waiting with raised eyebrows. To tell the truth, he didn't look completely confident himself.

"Okay. I mean, what could go wrong?"

Joshua laughed. "Probably me looking silly is the worst-case scenario."

Richie snickered. "I could live with that."

Joshua kept laughing as he laid his hand on Richie's shoulder. Richie made sure he had a good grip on his plane and his remote.

In an instant, they stood on a long, smooth driveway in a flat land with wide horizons. Richie looked up at Joshua, who removed his hand from his shoulder, and wiped his palm on his pants. With the other hand Joshua pulled his communication device from his pocket and hit a button.

He spoke to whoever answered. "Well, I just wanted to warn you that there are two guys flying a remote-controlled airplane on your driveway."

Richie looked at the house when Joshua did. He saw an old man's face appear in one of the windows.

Joshua laughed and looked at Richie. Richie could hear an excited voice, but not the exact words from the other end of the call. The old guy seemed happy about it, at least.

"I just wanted to warn you, so you wouldn't call the cops, or run us down on your way to the grocery store."

After chuckling at the reply, Joshua said, "We'll come up to the house to see you, after we conquer this little machine."

When he hung up the phone, Joshua caught Richie watching. But he didn't say anything. He probably didn't mind being watched.

For almost an hour—as long as the battery and its solar charge lasted—Joshua watched and coached, as Richie tried to master flight and landing. Joshua told him that wind velocity and direction were important for calculating landing direction and speed. Part of the time, Richie had to cope with landing in a cross breeze. But mostly he was able to choose landing into the wind, like a real pilot.

On the very last flight, when the battery died and the little, top-wing plane had to glide to the ground, Richie managed to land it in the field next to the driveway—over bumps, and through flowers that shot petals all over. Joshua laughed and patted Richie on the back when he kept the plane's nose pointing up during that last landing.

"Thirsty?" Joshua walked with Richie to where the plane rested next to a clump of flowers.

"Oh, yeah."

Together they made the walk to the porch of the farmhouse. Richie imagined they were like workers coming in from the field.

The old man met them at the door, as if he had been watching.

"Well, did you master that thing, then?" He was grinning a lot like Joshua did.

"Definitely," Joshua said. "Dad, this is Richie. Richie, my dad."

Richie switched the plane to the same hand as the remote so he could shake hands. Joshua's dad was strong, even if he looked pretty old.

"I remember *this* guy when he was your size," his dad said, gesturing toward Joshua. "He spent hours and hours out there getting his landings just right. Funny that, though the point of an airplane is flight, he always seemed most interested in landing." Here, he looked at Joshua kind of curiously.

"I never knew you were watching that closely."

"Oh, I had to do it undercover, of course, not wanting to step on your independence. Besides, I didn't know half as much about flying as you did by then."

While the memories and new ideas kept the two men going for a bit, Richie watched closely. What he saw was more interesting even than Joshua's boyhood model airplane flying.

"*This is how a man talks to his dad,*" Richie told himself. "*This is what I want.*"

CHAPTER THIRTY-ONE

Joshua didn't use any superhuman means for his visit the next day to Ginny's new home. She lived in the suburbs of Chicago. He rode the train, fluid and silent, out of the more densely populated neighborhood in which he lived, through a luxuriant track of land formerly occupied by corporate headquarters. The concrete, glass and steel had disappeared, replaced by forests now fifty years old, part of the replanted woodlands that nearly stretched from coast to coast. Ginny didn't live far enough west of the city to bring Joshua into the revived prairies that now stretched for hundreds of miles.

For several weeks, Ginny had lived with Jonathan and Talia Berger, a relatively young couple, even by pre-Reign standards. Barely thirty years old, Jonathan worked remotely as a computer programmer, connecting to his office and to clients from the comfort of his home office overlooking the grand garden that he and Talia maintained.

Talia worked closer to Chicago, as the city manager for the town of Oak Park. Like most municipalities, Oak Park was the responsibility of a pair of immortals, who oversaw all aspects of the welfare of its citizens. Talia served as the top mortal employee of the town, cooperating with the immortals and operationalizing many aspects of their design for that town west of Chicago. At twenty-nine, Talia was the youngest city manager in the area. Her skill as an administrator and her willingness to cooperate with the immortals had won her that job.

With Jonathan and Talia lived Jonathan's mother Mary, who had divorced Talia's father nearly twenty years ago. Mary was a young and healthy seventy years old, an adult in her prime, under the Reign. Exactly how long those prime years would last, she and the generation before her were still discovering. Joshua, of course, knew from personal experience that those prime years lasted past a hundred.

As he rode, Joshua read a novel that was written within the past decade by a woman living in China, near where his sister Miranda worked. Miranda had recommended the book. As much as he loved his sister, her recommendations for literature seemed to miss the mark more often than not, so his mind wandered from the story, to the views from the train. A pair of giraffes, out of place but peacefully preoccupied with eating treetops, diverted him to recollections of his meeting with David Adeyemi, in Jerusalem. He recorded a reminder in his personal computer to arrange a meeting with David soon. Then he started thinking of Theresa and what she would be doing just then. She had promised to introduce him to someone.

Taking a deep breath and letting the tension of unfinished business slide off, Joshua looked outside again, allowing his little computer to fall asleep and the novel to fall off his radar completely. As if she had appeared in response to his thoughts about her, Theresa popped into the aisle next to his seat.

Joshua laughed. "You know you could just send me an email or something."

"Oh, you forget that I come from a community that rejected electricity. We licked envelopes and waited days for a message to arrive. But that wouldn't work for you. You're never in one place long enough."

Joshua patted the seat next to him. Theresa accepted the invitation, stretching her legs in front of her.

Her voice sank to a more serious tone. "I wanted to tell you how I admired your self-restraint the other day with Richie." She glanced at Joshua and then at the passing trees.

"How so?"

"The airplane." Theresa gave him her foxy smile, crinkling her perfect cheeks. "You didn't even seem *tempted* to take the controls away from the boy. Weren't you just itching to?"

Joshua nodded and thought back to his time with Richie. He had been so tuned into making a connection with Richie and listening for instructions from the King, that he had ignored the draw of that old fascination with model airplanes. Theresa was reminding him to pay attention to old feelings like that, and not get too caught up in the task at hand.

"I did enjoy the flying and the time with my parents. But I see what you mean. I could let loose a bit more."

Theresa grinned, apparently please with his easy acceptance of the lesson packed away in her comment.

Then Joshua remembered what the King had told him. "I thought you were supposed to stop being my teacher and start being my partner."

Theresa took a deep breath and maintained her tight-lipped smile. "Old habit." Then, more pointedly, she said, "Of course, partners can sharpen each other, from time to time."

"Really? Can you think of ways that I've sharpened you?"

"Oh, yes. Many ways. You've helped me to listen better to the thoughts and feelings of the people around me, and to do it sympathetically. Just because I *can* do it, doesn't mean I was always invested in engaging mortals in this way. It's more complicated, and less fulfilling, than listening to the thoughts and feelings of folks like me. You, my friend, are a living bridge between the mortal world and the immortal. But then, that's what we're all supposed to be."

Joshua looked hard at Theresa, and he recalled ways he had mediated between Theresa and the mortals with whom they both worked. Then he thought about Ginny.

"So, I expect you have something to tell me about Ginny."

"Well, we're right on topic, as far as that goes."

"Okay, you want me to introduce someone to Ginny and her family?"

"Yes. But first I need to introduce *you* to her."

With that scant prelude, a young woman appeared, dressed in all white, as if flying in from the heavenly choir. She came in the form of a teenager, dark caramel skin and shiny black hair, as if her ancestors came from the Philippines or Indonesia. Joshua noted a scar on her neck which ran as far as he could see. She had landed in the seat in front of Theresa and Joshua. She knelt on the red cushion and leaned over the seat back.

With no warning, the girl kissed Joshua on the forehead. Then she sat back and smiled at him for one second, before bursting into musical laughter.

Theresa introduced her, accompanied by that laughter. "Joshua, this is Mita. Mita, Joshua."

Before Joshua could reach up to shake her hand, Mita slipped through the seat, onto Theresa's lap. One thin arm wrapped Theresa's shoulder, and her thin legs crossed toward Joshua's. She stared expectantly at him.

When Joshua had learned, at the age of eighteen, that his new mentor would be a woman, he worried that this might distract him, given the perfect beauty of the immortals. It was someone like Mita that Joshua had in mind back then. Sitting there so close to him now, he could barely resist wrapping his arms around her and kissing that luscious face. When he calmed that urge, Joshua realized that Mita was blocking him from following such an inappropriate impulse, even as she inspired it.

"You have slightly elevated chemicals predisposing you to anxiety. Would you like me to fix that?"

The way Mita leaned in as she asked this implied that she wanted to extract something with invisible tweezers.

He nodded. "Yes, of course."

Instead of producing those tweezers, Mita leaned in closer. When she had nearly touched her nose to his, she lunged at him. It felt like she reached inside his head, as if her face had penetrated his.

She pulled back and looked satisfied. "There, I replaced the tiny part of your brain that was overactive. You should feel less anxious from now on."

Joshua was glad he was sitting down. Even so, he reeled from the experience of part of this young beauty penetrating his skull.

Mita laughed at the dazed expression on Joshua's face, looked at Theresa, and patted her on the shoulder.

"He *is* a good sport, just as you said, dear."

Theresa nodded, quiet amusement behind her reserved exterior.

"So, let's talk about Ginny."

"Wait," Joshua said. "I'm wondering what you just did to me." He emerged from his daze.

Mita grinned like a puppy about to pounce on one of her siblings. "I pulled that part of your brain out with my teeth."

He paused to discern whether she was kidding. His intuitive powers didn't work well on the immortals. "Why did you have to use your teeth?"

"'Have to?' Of course, I didn't *have to* do it that way. I just wanted to. Besides, I knew you could handle it." She was more than a few steps ahead of him. "Don't worry, I will be more subdued with Ginny's new family ... at first." As if to reinforce this latter point, Mita twirled off Theresa's lap and back to the seat in front of Joshua. There she crouched, resting her arms on the shiny railing along the top of the seat.

Releasing a cluster of other questions like a handful of captured fireflies, Joshua shifted to thinking about Ginny and her new family. "So, how is it going between them?"

Mita grew more serious. "Do you want to tell him or should I?"

"You go ahead." Theresa bowed slightly.

"All right. Well, the first thing you should know is that her new mother and father are both devoted to the King. They've been to Jerusalem once each, not together. They are young and busy professionals, but their real passion is for the King."

Joshua nodded. "I knew they were worshippers. It's good to hear your assessment. How is Ginny taking that part of their life together?"

"She's fascinated with the King, as you know. But she's dealing with the complication of the grandmother. Mary is not so devoted as are her son and daughter-in-law."

"But that works to Ginny's advantage, allowing her at least two options to choose from." It was like thinking aloud, for Joshua.

Mita smiled at Theresa. "You're right. He *is* sharp."

Though she appeared to be a teenager, Mita spoke about Joshua as if she were much older. Joshua was familiar with this disconnect. And he willingly ignored the patronizing tone in Mita's comment.

The train pulled into the station just then, and the three stood to exit when the final brake eased the lightweight train to a stop. Just like ordinary people, Joshua and the two immortals walked the three quarters of a mile to Ginny's new house.

CHAPTER THIRTY-TWO

Ginny ran up the stairs to her room again. She decided that it was better not to wear any shoes or slippers. She wasn't dressing up for this visit with Joshua and the holy people. She was just meeting them at her new home. No need to show off. She kicked her sparkly pink sneakers into her closet.

Then she heard the clacking of the brass knocker on the front door. She turned and ran down the stairs right up to the door. The door was open already. She jumped right into Joshua's arms. From up there, where he held her in his strong arms, she noticed the pretty, young woman with him. She studied the dark-skinned teenager from her place leaning on Joshua's shoulder. That new girl was beautiful. She must be one of *them*.

Ginny laughed, but she could hear the grownups all sniffling around her. That was okay. They could cry. But she didn't feel like doing it.

"It's so good to see you, little one," Joshua said. "It's especially good to see you so happy in your new home. This is all I ever want for any of you children." He ended with a little sniffle, as he lowered her to the ground.

Then the grownups got busy with introductions. The new girl was named Mita. She was so interesting. So beautiful. Was she here for Ginny? Really?

Talia, her new mom, reached out to shake Mita's hand. But instead Mita wrapped her arms around Talia and hugged and kissed her a bunch of times. Ginny could see Jonathan sort of stand up straighter like he was ready to get some of those hugs and kisses. But Mita just shook his hand. The look on his face made Ginny laugh. She couldn't help it.

"Where's Theresa?" Ginny was looking forward to seeing her.

As Joshua entered the hallway, he answered. "She flew off to someplace far away, no doubt. Just me and Mita for now."

"Shall we go into the living room?" Talia put a friendly hand on Joshua's arm, as she pointed toward the living room. Joshua and Mita nodded, following her directions.

Having guests here made Ginny think about the house. It wasn't new, but it wasn't very old either. She had seen some of the really old houses around town. Some of them were famous. But she liked this place. She was walking next to Joshua, trying to guess how he might be seeing her new home.

A tray with glasses, an ice bucket, tea and water, waited on the coffee table in the living room.

Ginny ran ahead of the grownups. "Can I serve everyone?"

Talia and Jonathan both smiled and agreed.

When Joshua sat down, he asked Jonathan something. "Mary isn't around?" The way he said it seemed as if that was a bad thing.

Jonathan shook his head. "We thought it would be better to ease my mother into things slowly." He was talking quietly, as if he didn't want Ginny to hear.

But she heard, and she knew what he was talking about. Mary wasn't happy like the other two. She seemed sad and angry a lot of the time, though she didn't say bad things to Ginny. Mostly, Ginny could tell that Mary didn't like the Jerusalem people. Though she couldn't really tell why.

"I wish you would call her to have her come as soon as she can." Joshua had a straight, little smile on his face. A sort of serious smile, maybe.

Getting his phone from his pocket, Jonathan stood up and went out of the room. Talia looked a bit worried, but she was good at keeping quiet even when something upset her.

When Ginny finished pouring water and tea for everyone, she sat in the big rocking chair by the bay windows. Mita sat on the end of the couch opposite Talia and just an arm's length from Ginny.

"How are you liking your new school?" Mita looked only a little bit too old to be in school herself.

Ginny rocked and nodded her head. "It's pretty good. My teacher is really friendly. She's not one of the holy people, but she's just as nice." Ginny looked into Mita's eyes and found a sort of link there that reminded her of the time that Joshua showed her the sound of worship around the throne. It was as if there was music in Mita's eyes.

Even though she was pretty magical, Mita kept asking Ginny really normal questions about school. They were the kind of questions that Ginny could answer without trying very hard. So she had some time to really look at Mita. That was the best part of the questions. They gave her an excuse to look at those eyes and that beautiful face.

Ginny noticed that Joshua moved a bit closer to her new mom then.

"What are you thinking?" Joshua asked Talia, just as Jonathan returned to the living room. Joshua's voice was low, as if he were trying not to interrupt Mita and Ginny.

Talia sort of gulped and looked from Mita and Ginny to Joshua. "I have all my life envied mortals who have close contact with the immortals." She looked at Ginny and Mita again. "I get to work with them to some extent, but that's more task-oriented and less personal." Here she lowered her tone a bit more. "I guess I'm just feeling a little jealous."

Ginny got distracted back to Mita again, but heard Joshua say something a minute later.

"Have you ever thought to ask for a closer relationship with one of the 'holy people?'" Joshua smiled when he called them the same thing that Ginny called them.

She lost track of what the grownups were talking about after that. That happy grab that she felt from inside Mita to inside herself was getting deeper and warmer, somehow. Maybe the ordinary questions Mita was asking weren't that important. Maybe it was just words to cover up what was really happening. And all Ginny could think of was how much she hoped that Mita would get to be her teacher, like Theresa was Joshua's teacher.

Jonathan must have called his mother before. Because she came into the house a few minutes later. Ginny could hear her close the front door a lot more quietly than normal. Probably, Mary was afraid of what she was gonna find there that day. She didn't like "aliens." Even if she didn't really think that's what the Jerusalem people were.

Mary's face was pretty dark when she looked at Ginny talking with Mita. Ginny waved at her, hoping that would help her feel welcome. It was *her* house too, after all. Now Ginny tried to see Mary the way strangers would. She was small for a grownup. Her yellowish hair was colored that way. Ginny didn't even know what color it was supposed to be. Mary was as full of energy as the other grownups, even if she was older. She must have been older, of course, since she was Jonathan's mom.

Clearing her throat, once she stood in the living room, Mary seemed worried she was interrupting something. She kind of was. But Ginny didn't mind. Mary needed help. She was sure of that. Maybe Joshua and Mita could give her that help.

***

"Joshua, this is my mother. Mother, this is Joshua and Mita."

Joshua arose from his seat and shook Mary's hand, noting Jonathan's elevated anxiety level in the presence of his mother. Joshua sent a pulse of peace that he expected Jonathan would receive gratefully.

Smiling bravely at the two strangers, Mary nodded her greeting. Mita diverted her attention from Ginny, even as she reached out and touched Ginny on the arm. Then Mita stood and swept across the room to greet Mary. But she didn't greet her with a polite handshake. Instead, Mita grasped her shoulders and stared into Mary's face with the intensity of a mother's love. Mary stood in shock at the string plucked in her heart by that small smile. Joshua could tell that her defenses had fallen. Could it be that simple? Did she simply need to meet one of the immortals face-to-face? Or had Mita given her more than a warm greeting, opening some gateway into her wounded soul.

Joshua sampled Mary's emotional tumult for a few seconds. He found something like abandonment, alone with hopelessness inspired by that abandonment. Mita seemed to have slipped right into that place of need in a way that Mary was ready to receive.

Turning his attention to Ginny, Joshua stood up and slipped into the place on the other side of her, opposite where Mita had been sitting. He could tell that the stubborn opposition in Mary's heart had introduced a sort of harmony with Ginny's character. Ginny had formed her emotional defenses against the bankrupt rebel culture in which she was raised. Mary seemed soured against the Reign in a similar way.

"What are you feeling now?" Joshua spoke low so only Ginny could hear.

She turned to study him. Then she seemed to discover what he was asking. "She's really sad, and that makes her angry. And she knows about all that. But she can't find a way to get out of it."

Joshua tempered his smile at the profound insight of this little girl. "So how would she find a way out?"

Ginny shrugged with one shoulder. "I don't think I'm supposed to worry about that, but just be kind to her."

Joshua nodded for a few seconds. "You don't have to solve her problems or take care of her. You're right about that. But you will feel things that come from Mary, and from other people too. And you will need to talk to Mita about these. It wouldn't be good to store other people's feelings inside yourself."

"Is that what she's here for?" Ginny nodded toward Mita, who was just now releasing Mary.

"That, and many other things. Some of them will be really fun, like flying, for example."

Ginny swung her head around like she was looking for a joke in Joshua's eyes. When she found his eyes locked on her, she pressed her lips together and looked at Mita again. Joshua almost burst with the excitement he could feel building up inside the little girl. The most thrilling part was anticipating how much better her life was going to be, even better than in Ginny's excited imagination.

CHAPTER THIRTY-THREE

Back in his apartment in Chicago, Joshua woke earlier than he had planned. No meetings scheduled for the day, he had hoped to sleep in a while. The bright spring sun tugged at his eyelids until he lay awake and disappointed. He rummaged around for the leftovers of a dream that had charmed his sleep.

In that dream, he met a woman that he wished existed in the waking world, not just his own subconscious. He savored the feeling of connectedness—intimacy offered, accepted and returned—in the dream. He had been visiting an old friend from school, a friend who had two sisters that Joshua could remember. But here his friend seemed to have another sister, a tall, slim woman with blonde hair, a fine face. She was sharp and ready to smile, especially at Joshua. He relished sitting shoulder-to-shoulder with this woman at a crowded family dinner, their souls squeezed as close as that warm, physical contact.

Who was she? A teacher? A preacher? Educated at the best university, bright and engaging and knowing Joshua instantly. Who was she?

As much as Joshua maintained his celibate intimacy with mortal women, he longed for more symmetry, a giving to match the taking, freedom from the dissatisfied tension often openly aired by his female friends, such as Franny. That symmetry would require a woman determined to genuinely know Joshua on his terms, genuinely confident in her own identity and purpose.

To extract himself from the spiral of regret into which he now spun, Joshua adjusted his breathing to a more relaxed pace. He listened for the voice of the King. More than just as a ruler or instructor, the King offered himself as a friend—the closest, most thoroughly engaged, friend. Here Joshua found ultimate intimacy with the ultimate lover, the infinite lover—always open and always seeking connection with him. Joshua's internal links all latched onto the spirit of the King and he rested there, satisfied again, for as long as he could maintain that spirit-to-spirit conversation.

Though this rescued him from building on the sense of loss from falling out of his dream about that woman, it didn't erase her from his memory. It didn't extract her from where she had become embedded in his soul.

CHAPTER THIRTY-FOUR

In Portland, Oregon, Natalie Warren turned beneath her sheets and drew her spare pillow closer to her face. She was trying to stay asleep. What was that dream? Who was that man?

Her brother had brought a friend home with him, a home she hardly recognized, a family assembled from paradigmatic parts—a father not really her own, a mother only slightly like her mother. And, since she knew her brother's friends, how could this be his best friend that she only now met for the first time?

And yet she felt sure that she knew him. There was no consternation in there that she struggled to remember meeting him. There was just the certainty of recognition, forgetting inconvenient lapses in memory, or unaddressed holes in logic.

There, seated around a crowded table and comfortably leaning on this nameless man, she felt at home, as if any place she had called home before was only a waiting room, a transit station, to this true place of belonging. Yes, this was a true connection, a true kinship, more than a brother, more than a friend—more, but without leaving out what *those* relationships included.

And then she had awakened from it. It was a dream, after all.

Staring over the horizon of her spare pillow at the half-open window and the shade drawn to block the light that would have ended her sleep within an hour or so, she took a string of deep breaths. She let go of the feeling from her dream. She abandoned the stalled vehicle left where the dream stopped when she woke.

She had planned to sleep later that morning, but she knew from experience that attempting to go back to sleep wouldn't serve her well. The urgent hope of returning to that dream would inevitably prevent the sleep that would make it possible. She threw back the pale sheets in the predawn room and swung her legs over the side of the bed. She pulled her shoulder-length blonde hair back from her face with both hands and released it for a stretch with arms lifted toward the ceiling. And she laughed.

Rising from her bed and stepping lightly across the floor, Natalie wove past Solomon, her black, long-haired cat. She hummed softly as she performed the mundane morning ablutions of a mortal woman. A smile tightened the corners of her eyes and the corners of her mouth.

By the time she was washed and dressed and fed, Natalie's song expanded from the comforting hum to a few words sung aloud, words in a language she didn't fully understand, a language she had heard around the throne in Jerusalem. These morning songs served to tune her soul, the way a guitarist adjusts her strings to harmonize in the ears of her audience. The worship songs from the throne resonated with that part of her that heard the voice of the King, even while she spoke to her neighbors, to town councils and to the Congress in the Capitol. These songs soothed any hatchling anxiety she might have, any furrowing concern. In their place, she received a glimmering peace that she had seen infect others around her on many occasions.

But Natalie knew that her need to nurture that soothing feeling testified to a missing piece in her life. As much as she contented herself with a life of celibacy, she longed for an intimacy fitting more symmetrically with her soul. In all her relationships she had experienced the mismatched intentions and conflicting connections between what she offered and what she needed.

This morning, the one disturbed by the promising dream that she hummed to forget, she was meeting with three of the immortals. She was hoping to receive a fuller explanation from them of their expectations regarding harvesting fallen trees in the recovering rainforest that now filled every uninhabited valley and hillside from the city to the coast, and north into Washington State. Part of Natalie's mission would be to convince the congressman from Washington to relax his campaign for greater logging rights on behalf of mortal lumber companies.

The leader of the little committee of immortals with which Natalie would meet, Jeremy, had made a habit of meeting at the top of Mount Hood, a short flight from Portland. No longer the snow-capped peak of centuries past, that volcanic mountain had finally become overgrown with pine trees nearly to its peak. At that peak stood two large stones on which Jeremy liked to sit and look out over the suburbs and the city of Portland. Natalie loved the flight up to the top of the mountain but envied the immortals their superior eyesight, which allowed them to include the entire Portland area in their survey.

When Natalie arrived atop the mountain, the sun had climbed above the tallest trees, even from the perspective of the lower elevations around the city. In his usual roost, she found Jeremy seated with one knee pulled up to his chin and his powerful arms wrapped around it, his gray-bearded chin resting on that knee. A mortal man of Jeremy's girth and apparent age wouldn't have the flexibility required for this pose, a posture which clearly strained the ageless man not at all.

As she arrived, Natalie witnessed the instant appearance of two others, both women, but very different from each other in appearance. Joanna stood smiling down at the valley, including the other people on that peak in the sweep of her welcoming eyes. Though she had lived to a very old age a hundred years ago, she now appeared as a young woman whom one might expect to be a bride or a young mother. She wore a simple cotton dress, the color of the sky, and light sandals. Her golden-brown hair hung free to follow the breezes.

Opposite Joanna stood Natalie's favorite among the immortals, if she slipped and admitted that she really *had* a favorite. Anne wore her hair in impossibly tight braids, beaded artistically and dangling just short of her round shoulders. In her mortal days, in the twenty-first century, she had been a social worker in Detroit. She resembled more the shape of the boulders on that mountain than the swaying trees. Like Jeremy, Anne moved with far more flexibility and grace than a mortal of her years and dimensions. And she loved to laugh, even in the face of tough conversations and world-changing tasks. Natalie loved that laugh.

"Like the gods arriving on Mount Olympus," Jeremy said. "What misery shall we impose on those unwitting mortals today?" He guffawed. In his mortal life, he had been a machinist with calloused hands and rough speech.

Natalie grinned, as the sole representative of those unwitting mortals. However, she had flown from her house to this lofty perch on her own power, so she could feel some of the power of the gods even as she identified with those powerless humans.

"Our golden girl has some ideas, I'll bet," said Anne. "Revenge on those greedy loggers, do you think? Maybe a plague of termites in their lumber yard? The whole locust thing has been overdone."

"Locust get such bad PR," Joanna said wistfully. "I think they're quite handsome, really, and so good at what they do. Really, I think the

King owes them some rehabilitation, at least for the rest of mortal human history. Don't you?" And she stepped like a mountain goat over to where Jeremy sat, folding her girlish frame and leaning back against him, as if he were part of the rock formation.

Natalie wondered whether the thin, pine-scented air was making the immortals giddy, but sensed some method in their teasing introductions.

"I see we've abandoned all pretense of solemnity this morning."

Anne managed to look somewhat sober, as she leapt effortlessly from one boulder to another and stood looking over the animated sculpture formed by her two immortal companions. "After enough time in the presence of perfect power and ultimate meaning, you completely forget how to take yourself seriously."

Natalie nodded. "I suppose so." She was still searching for the hidden agenda behind the levity and the little lesson.

Anne read her thoughts. "'Agenda' is a politician's word. Looking for our agenda is gonna lead you in the wrong direction, because there are desires and passions that blow all agendas to smithereens." Anne looked at Natalie, as if diagnosing some skin disease on her face. But she looked deeper, of course.

Jeremy chimed in, his voice low and jolly. "You better keep an eye on that, Natalie, that assumption that it's all about agendas and tasks. Don't let the machine of government suck you into their slots-and-boxes way of dividing up the world. And don't lose your passion and your romance."

Natalie raised her eyebrows at that last word. "Romance? Why romance?" She had come to this lofty meeting place to discuss land usage and forestry, to prepare for tough negotiations between private business owners and the government. How could romance have any place even in the preliminaries to this meeting? She began to feel as if she had been ambushed, invited there under false pretenses.

Joanna answered this latter thought. "It's only false, if you believe that the world is static all the time. The world rolls on. The whole planet is on the move. Our meeting 'agendas' have to keep up with the new realities."

Anne lowered her eyes sympathetically. "The new situation is that the head of the lumber association has had a visitation from a higher power. And that visit changed his attitude considerably. You're not gonna have to contend with him, just arrange an amicable deal for everyone involved. And we *know* you're overqualified for that task."

Smiling at the good news and the compliments, Natalie joked. "Then, maybe I can send my assistant to handle the deal." She knew this would breech protocol and she didn't *actually* intend to flaunt her freedom from the system so blatantly.

Joanna joked along. "Sure, a child could lead them. You could send Maggie." She referred to Natalie's youngest niece, a nine-year-old.

Natalie smiled again. But only half of her question had been answered.

Jeremy addressed what remained, rising to his feet and putting an arm around Natalie's waist. "You, my dear, need to follow your dreams more often, and more recklessly."

Looking into his frosty blue eyes, she searched for the connections that Jeremy's words skipped over. Instantly she caught a whiff of her dream from that morning, and she knew where that word 'romance' came in. She shivered suddenly.

"You mean he's real?" She was sure that everyone present recognized who "he" was. They certainly felt the electric buzz that ran up her spine.

"Very real." Anne smiled slyly.

"Though we haven't actually met him," Joanne said.

Jeremy chuckled. "But you have."

She allowed the meaning of these playful words to land on her like a thousand raindrops. "What does *he* know about this?"

"His name is Joshua," said Anne, "and he knows a bit less than you do. You see, he had the same dream this morning, only he hasn't gotten the Mount Olympus briefing on it yet."

Someone less familiar with the ways of the immortals might have wondered if they were challenging her commitment to remain celibate. That commitment arose from Natalie's quest to be like the King, and like the immortals, who abstained from sexual connections without shying from emotional intimacies. Raised in the atmosphere of the Reign, free from the machinations of the master tempter, and trained by the loving and free immortals, Natalie knew that she could maintain her commitment and still pursue relationships. She had, however, bumped into that asymmetry of many of those relationships, especially with members of the opposite sex. And then there was the scar left from her marriage.

She sighed heavily.

Jeremy added to Joshua's introduction. "He's cut from the same cloth as you, my girl. But he's all man, just as much as you're all woman. The matchmakers among the immortals have been salivating over the prospects of getting you two together for some time."

Natalie furrowed her brow, doubtful that there were legitimate matchmakers among the immortals, but also feeling a bit uncomfortable at being the subject of such personal consideration by strangers, even heavenly strangers.

"Nothing's changed. You're still free to do what you want, to be with whom you want. The King hasn't sent us to order you two to get together." Anne spread a motherly smile. "This is a gift to you and to Joshua. You're free to do what you want with it."

CHAPTER THIRTY-FIVE

Joshua stood in his kitchen, listening to music from his living room, the deep drums reverberating in his chest. His neighbors were all at work, or otherwise absent from the surrounding apartments, so he had raised the volume considerably. Slicing some homemade bread with a knife, he stopped and listened more closely. The volume of the music had definitely increased, just as the recording approached his favorite section of the song. After briefly considering the possibility of a malfunction in his music player, Joshua turned to guessing which one of his friends would be in the living room cranking up his music. That he couldn't read their feelings implied an immortal had done it.

Theresa stepped into the kitchen and grinned at him. She waited for that favorite passage of frolicking percussion and rocketing melody to rise to its climax, before raising her finger and lowering the volume from where she stood.

"Yes?" Joshua said to her, as one would to a friend calling on the phone. He knew Theresa came with an important message. She had allowed that much of her thoughts to lie open as she entered the room.

"You busy?" This was, of course, facetious. She knew his schedule.

"Never too busy to see you. Bread?" He lifted a fresh cut piece of honey whole wheat.

She took the bread in one hand and bit a curve out of one corner. She put her other hand on Joshua's shoulder and looked at him while she chewed.

"Ummm. That's the best yet. And that wonderful fragrance might just attract a couple hundred of my friends."

"Yes, and all coming with an important message for me, of course." Joshua bit into his own piece of the warm bread. He nodded his agreement. It *was* his best.

Theresa paused before her next bite. "Remember that I promised to introduce you to that mortal woman who could fly?"

Joshua nodded. "I remember something about that. But I don't really remember if you said it was a man or a woman." They both knew that the prospect of a woman so free that she could fly had captured Joshua's attention.

Theresa laughed as she chewed. "Today's a good day to introduce you."

Joshua looked down at his old, white t-shirt and sweatpants sagging onto his bare feet. "You think I should change?"

"Of course. And I'll just watch over this bread while you run along and do that."

Joshua laughed as he went to his bedroom to change clothes. He selected his usual dark slacks and light button up shirt, untucked and square cut, in the style of the day. Instead of nervous anticipation, Joshua rode a levitated hope at the prospect of a new friend, one that was a match for him. He thought of Franny. Their friendship modulated between a dance and a contest of strength. And there had been other women as well, always the same let down.

Theresa sat on the couch petting Gwendolyn when Joshua appeared in the living room, briefly straightening his short-cropped hair with one hand.

"Did you wrap up the bread?"

"Bread? What bread?" She chuckled. "Yes, dear, I wrapped it up and put away the butter."

"Thank you."

"Save that winning charm for Natalie." Theresa stood and waved the cat hair away with no great effort.

"Her name is Natalie? How much more do you want to tell me about her?"

"Oh, nothing more than that." Theresa waved his curiosity away with the same hand that vanished the white cat hair from her black dress. "I am staying out of the middle of you two, just doing my part to give the invite, and leaving it to you to figure out the rest."

This called to mind a time when Joshua was thirty-five years old, a young adult by Reign standards, when Theresa had introduced him to Vera. The dark-skinned, dark-eyed young woman who had first broken Joshua's resolve to celibacy, had been Theresa's idea for him. Misinterpreting the meaning of that introduction, led to more than he or Theresa intended. He had allowed the pull of passion to loosen his grasp on his destiny and his emotional security.

For just one moment, Joshua allowed himself to relive the visceral intensity of those hours with Vera, listening to her speak in her Venezuelan accent, watching moods wax and wane on her face, even as he sensed her heart turning this way or that. He knew that his physical bond with her would last his lifetime.

"Have you met her?" Joshua sensed that Theresa didn't know this mysterious woman personally.

She shook her head slightly. "I got to see the dream, of course. Though I didn't get to feel it like you did, I feel like I've met her."

"The dream?"

Then it all clicked together. "That dream was real? I mean, the woman in the dream is real? She's the one? I mean, I'm going ... She can fly?"

Theresa snorted her amusement and grinned shamelessly at him. She held out her hand.

Joshua took her offered hand, but then remembered something. "You know I can do this on my own now?" He might prefer to show up without a chaperone.

"I know you can. But you don't know where we're going." Theresa smiled mysteriously.

Joshua grinned and nodded a concession. His powers hadn't yet advanced to that stage.

CHAPTER THIRTY-SIX

Joshua stood alone on the sidewalk along a steep street, the shade of a cottonwood tree sheltering him from the morning sun. Theresa had not appeared in this place, even though she had directed his transport. Across the street a small café invited him for a morning coffee. He accepted that invitation, confident that Natalie had done the same.

How do you greet someone that you've met already in a dream? How do you meet someone for whom feelings of serendipity have been launched by messengers from Heaven? For Joshua, the counselor, the only answer was directness and honesty.

Natalie stood up from a small table in the back corner, where she seemed to have just settled her coffee and herself. She appeared to hesitate a fraction of a second during her rise to her feet.

Joshua was shaken by anticipation and fulfillment all at once. And it wasn't only his. He was reading this in Natalie. There was a sort of mirror in her. He hadn't intended to read her heart and mind when he saw her. Instinct stepped forward and decided for him. Her receptive heart and the echo in his own heart literally shook him.

Joshua didn't hesitate or wait for permission. He walked directly to Natalie and took her in his arms, hugging her gently and then pulling away just enough to look full in her face. She exuded pleased surprise at that greeting. Her face seemed to shift toward laughter and then tears before she settled into equilibrium.

To play fair, and start their alliance honestly, Joshua knew he should explain his intuition to her immediately. "Natalie. It's wonderful to finally meet you."

"Finally? I only learned about you in my dream this morning."

Joshua nodded. The memory of the dream was still with him like an aftertaste of fine wine. But here she was. More than a faint taste.

"Yes, that *was* just this morning. But my mentor teased me months ago with the prospect of introducing me to the mortal woman who could fly."

Natalie laughed. "My claim to fame." She tipped her head slightly. "Certainly, I'm not the only one."

"It's a very rare gift. From what I can gather, there are only a couple of dozen who've succeeded. And I don't count myself among them. My flying attempts resemble falling more than they should."

Natalie smiled at him, leaning back just a little. "Well, maybe I can teach you."

In that instant, Joshua sensed that Natalie also possessed a sympathetic perception beyond the body language and voice tone that humans normally read.

"You have another gift that I'm more familiar with," Joshua said.

"You can feel what I'm feeling, can't you?"

They smiled at each other as chills ran through them both. Then they laughed.

"This is crazy." Joshua snorted. "I was planning on letting you know that as soon as we met."

"We better sit down."

He drew his hands away from her waist and let her ease into her chair. Then he remembered that they were meeting for coffee. She had a cup already.

"I'll just order something." He pointed toward the counter.

That was when he noticed the two young women staring at him and Natalie. He had completely lost track of the fact that they were in a public place. He snickered uncomfortably as he approached the little staff of the café. They busied themselves when he stepped toward them.

When he returned to the table, Joshua bypassed preliminaries again. "You know this reminds me of great therapy sessions I've had in the past." He sat down and looked squarely into Natalie's eyes. "It's a lot like meeting a part of myself that I had known was there but had struggled to see."

Natalie shook her head and sucked in a quick breath. "Wow." Again they laughed together.

During these debutant moments, as they introduced some of the specifics of their lives and work, Joshua struggled with a feeling that he had seen her somewhere beside his dream. He searched his memory for news images of her once she mentioned she was a congresswoman. But that image eluded him. Perhaps the adrenalin of that first meeting overpowered his ability to access those video images.

Joshua and Natalie didn't come to this place to drink coffee. They came to look at each other, to try to say cogent things, and to hear the way the other responded. Joshua focused on the warm entanglement of their hearts. And the coffee mugs went untouched.

The stir they were causing with their intense mutual interview came to Joshua's attention. The patrons and staff of the coffee shop were straining to hide their fascination with the strange couple. He felt like he owed it to those folks to find another venue. Natalie glanced at the two young women behind the counter whispering and watching them. With only a nod, she agreed to take their first meeting outside.

Joshua stood, feeling a twinge of guilt at neglecting his coffee entirely, but forgot it as soon as he turned with Natalie toward the door. He rested his left hand lightly on the small of her back, as they slipped toward the open door of the café. He noted the bounce of her hair and registered the satisfied grin on her face as they left together. These he collected like delicate shells from a sandy shore. Of course, he would see her face again, would see her animated eyes and mouth many times in the future—just as there were more of those shiny shells still waiting on the beach. Still, he collected.

That they were meeting in her home city, put Natalie in the role of guide. When they reached the sidewalk under the massive oak tree in front of the café, she took Joshua's hand. "I want to show you something."

Joshua signaled his acceptance with a smile and a gesture with his free hand.

"We'll have to fly."

Joshua tilted his head slightly. "I can transport us."

As far as impressing a woman, this had to be his most successful moment. Natalie raised her eyebrows as high as he had seen them. Then she nodded toward the mountains. "Mount Hood, please."

Joshua snapped them from the street in Portland to the top of Mount Hood. He landed them on the side of the peak that faced away from the city, overlooking the forests and valleys to the south and west. Her smile implied satisfaction at his delivery.

CHAPTER THIRTY-SEVEN

Natalie saw Joshua gaping at the eagles soaring overhead, and she turned her attention to them as well. Then she did a trick that she expected would impress him. She screeched like an eagle, with both hands cupped over her mouth like a small megaphone. The pair of eagles banked simultaneously toward the summit.

Joshua laughed at this trick, and then seemed to hold his breath as the huge birds swooped in closer and closer.

She had first met this pair of eagles on that peak with Anne and Joanna, a few years previous. Joanna had taught her how to call them, and Natalie had often drawn them in to visit her, after watching them riding the thermals off the face of the mountain. As they swept nearer to Joshua and Natalie, the pair of eagles parted, one landing on each side of the two humans, the female by Joshua and the male next to Natalie. The male settled on the strongest branch of a small, twisted pine and bowed his head toward Natalie. She responded by petting the feathers on the back of his head and down to the shoulders of his half-furled wings. He made low clucking sounds of pleasure at her touch.

"Is this your roost, or theirs?" Joshua was making an obvious effort to get comfortable with the big raptors.

Natalie chuckled. She pointed to the female, who had edged up next to him. She certainly wanted some of that affection her mate was receiving. Joshua followed Natalie's example and petted the glossy, brown feathers of the mature eagle.

"Now I know why I felt I'd seen you somewhere before my dream, ah ... I mean, *our* dream." Joshua looked from the eagle to Natalie.

Still attending to the male eagle, she bent a little grin. "Lunatic congresswoman who communes with eagles?"

"Well, I don't remember the lunatic part, just the beautiful woman who defends God's forests and animals."

Natalie felt herself blush. "I see you haven't remained single because you don't know how to charm the ladies."

Joshua turned his eyes toward some movement among the trees to their right. Out from the dense cover of pines, into a flowered, green meadow burst six wolves, romping and playing with a man dressed in jeans and a red flannel shirt.

"Friend of yours?"

Natalie laughed. "No. I've seen him before, but I've never really met him."

Joshua tipped his head toward the exotic stranger. "So let's go meet him." As he stood, both eagles took flight.

Nodding agreement, mixed with surprise, Natalie followed Joshua's lead. She had forgotten his description of his flying capabilities until they were airborne. Joshua did seem to calculate the right downward trajectory in his bold leap, but Natalie soared after him with an eye to preventing a crash.

She could see that the man with the wolves had slowed down and turned to watch them. He clapped as they landed. Perhaps he was reacting to Joshua's obvious fledgling effort. He landed with a small stumble, but not a grand crash.

The stranger shouted. "Okay, you've outdone me for bizarreness. Two flying mortals beats one guy dancing with wolves."

Joshua took Natalie's hand when they both stood firmly on the ground. They ignored the natural intimidation of approaching the six furry predators. And the man in the lumberjack outfit reached out his hand.

"My name's Jesse. And, of course, I know who you are." He stood a bit under six feet tall, with wiry limbs and gray hair flying in all directions. His beard looked like a wheat field after a strong windstorm.

Natalie, and then Joshua, shook his hand. Joshua grinned at the wolves with some trepidation, perhaps. Natalie squatted, and a smallish female approached her with a sniff and a brief tail wag.

"They're still wild, just not dangerous, and getting somewhat used to *some* humans. That is if you can count one of us as a human." Jesse stroked a large male that rubbed against his leg.

"Can they tell the difference between mortals and immortals?" Joshua stepped a little closer to the animals.

Jesse nodded. "They can tell the difference, though I can't explain to you entirely how much it matters to them. I think it's the spirit of the person that really matters most."

As Jesse said this, the female wolf next to Natalie laid down at her feet, rolling over to get a scratching on her stomach. Natalie obliged, allowing a little "huh" to escape her throat.

"Like I said, it's the spirit of the person that matters to them most."

As the young female lay at Natalie's feet, two others settled down a couple of steps away from her. The other three, two males and a large female, wandered toward where Jesse and Joshua stood together. The female sniffed at Joshua and the largest male slowly circled around him sniffing at the air, as if getting closer wasn't his style.

"I wonder if they mind the smell of my cat." Joshua held one hand out for the female to sniff more thoroughly. She began to lick his hand.

Jesse smiled. "I supposed, but they sure do like the sort of mortal that comes flying down off the top of the mountain."

Joshua knelt and began to scratch around the thick fur of the big female's neck. The second male sidled up to Jesse again to get his share. Jesse squatted and granted his friend's quiet request.

"How often do you come up here?" Natalie looked at Jesse. "I know I've seen you a few times."

"Lately I come here every day. This is my main assignment these days."

"Very nice." Joshua beamed at Jesse.

"You may not envy my former job so much," Jesse said. "I used to work with food reallocation." He grinned at them and waited.

Natalie laughed. "I heard about this. Some of my constituents still complain about the reallocation."

Joshua shook his head, apparently unfamiliar with the issue.

Jesse responded to his unspoken question. "Back at the beginning, when the economy of the Reign first offered food staples to everyone, some of the mortals began to hoard. Given the plague, famine and war they had survived, this was naturally tempting. Instead of stopping them at the front end, we simply removed excess supplies from whatever hidden cellar or vault they used. And we put the goods back on the free store shelves."

He glanced at the alpha wolf still standing aloof, as if protecting the lounging pack. "I remember the first guy that figured out what was happening, where I was in New York. He started secretly marking the boxes of rice and beans, and such, that he had stockpiled under his barn. Finding three quarters of his stores missing again, he went to the store in town and found his marked boxes there. We didn't bother to erase his markings. We weren't afraid of getting caught." He laughed.

Natalie added her experience. "Some folks still feel the urge to save up for a day in the future when food isn't so abundant. I assume they learned it from parents born before the Reign. I had to figure out what was happening when some of these people started finding canned goods missing." She sat down in the grass to relieve her knees. "This one couple just could *not* get over the idea of the immortals stealing from them, as if some form of amnesia had wiped out the memory of where the food came from in the first place." She laughed but then sobered a bit. "I think that couple is living in one of the walled cities up north now."

Jesse and Joshua both stood silent for a second, as if in mourning for the loss of two souls whom they had never met. Natalie cleared the air by ruffling the fur of the wolf at her feet and standing up. She brushed grass from her tailored tan slacks and flipped her hair off her face with the back of her hand. She blushed again when she realized Joshua was studying her movements.

Jesse stood up straight and began to howl up toward the peak. All five of the lounging wolves rose and took their place in the chorus. The alpha turned toward Jesse for a moment and then cast a glance at Natalie and Joshua. Then the tall, dark gray male added his voice to the report issued up the mountain. Joshua grinned at Natalie and then faced the top of the mountain and howled along. Natalie did the same.

Jesse stopped his call and the alpha ended with several deep barks. Joshua and Natalie followed their leaders and fell silent. The alpha looked at them as if he approved, at least Natalie thought so. Then she stepped up next to Joshua and hooked her right arm around his left, while he stood smiling at the pack.

"So you spend your days running around with the wolves now?" Joshua grinned at Jesse.

Jesse smiled. "Oh, not all day every day. But often enough. I pop off to Jerusalem throughout the day, And I visit other creatures around the mountain. There's also a woman who has responsibilities in this area. We get together most days."

"What's her name?" Natalie asked.

"Oh, you know her. I was speaking of Joanna. She gets to be mother to these creatures, just as I get to be father. It's a great big furry and feathered family."

Joshua studied Jesse for a second. "So, what is it you *do* for the animals?"

Jesse looked around at the wolves, who had remained close after the chorus, rubbing against each other. "I think of it like salt. The King has spread us throughout the entire Earth to salt the whole big salad, to add his flavor to every big and little thing. He's not just a King sitting on a throne away off there. He's the creator come back to take his rightful possession, and to get it all ship-shape for the Father. We get to be part of that."

"So you communicate the thoughts and feelings of the King to the creatures?" Natalie didn't know everything about this part of Joanna's work.

Nodding, Jesse scratched each of the wolves as they pressed against him. "I communicate in the largest sense of the word, I'd say. The wolves and bears and cougars don't need to hear a report or get instructions. They just need to know that they're being taken care of. They seem glad to know they're part of a peaceful and prosperous world. They know all that by sensing my moods, by the tone of my voice, the attitude of my face. They know they're loved. Since they seem to sense my connection with the source of all life, my attitude gives them confidence."

After answering a few more questions along this line, Jesse looked from Natalie to Joshua and back. "I think it's time for the wolves and me to get going. You two need some time to talk."

Natalie exchanged a smile with Joshua who might have been as surprised as her at getting relationship advice from this rustic man who lived with wolves and bears. She and Joshua left the pack with some final scratching and words of thanks and farewell.

Joshua followed her down the grassy slope. "So when is your meeting?"

Natalie pulled a lock of hair off her face. "How did you know about that?"

"Well, it could have just been a lucky guess. You must have meetings pretty much every day." Then he shrugged. "But I could sense your thoughts wandering toward some sort of appointment that's been concerning you, but that you've decided recently not to worry about."

Natalie chuckled. "I'm glad to hear that I really *have* decided not to worry about it. I wasn't completely sure that was settled." They smiled at each other again. "So, you can't read my mind so much as you can sense my feelings?"

Joshua raised his face toward the midday sun. "Yeah, that's right. But you could mostly block me out if you wanted."

"Why would I want to?"

Joshua's grin grew. "Well, Theresa, my immortal friend, blocks me for my own protection sometimes. She says it would be too much for me to mix in with all that she's feeling."

"But otherwise you can read her feelings as well?"

Again Joshua nodded, allowing the wind to speak next. Maybe he was pausing to read her feelings about her own intuitions. Could she learn from Joshua? Was she supposed to?

She broke the silence. "I do have that meeting." A small hitch tripped her voice.

"Let's say goodbye here."

Natalie tilted her head at him, knowing words wouldn't scale to the height of her feelings.

They hugged for a few seconds and looked at each other again, the smile muscles in her face beginning to weaken under the constant strain.

"Happy negotiations," Joshua said, though she hadn't told him the nature of the meeting.

"Thank you." She kissed him on the cheek.

Then he disappeared from that sunny mountainside. And Natalie launched herself toward her congressional office in Portland.

CHAPTER THIRTY-EIGHT

Theresa transported to the coast of Spain to meet with her young student. She found Osana in the small yard behind her house, tying tomato plants to stakes, to straighten their posture against the strain of abundant fruit. Instead of being startled at the arrival of her immortal mentor, Osana kept her eyes on her work and greeted Theresa with only a glance from the corner of her eye.

Speaking in Spanish, Osana jumped right into a pressing need. "Knowing that you would arrive soon was a great relief to me, my teacher. I have had a very disturbing vision that I need to talk to you about."

Theresa noted the mature tone of Osana's words and blew a reassuring breeze into the angular young woman. Osana acknowledged the refreshment and smiled, as she finished with her last knot in the strip of white cotton cloth.

"I wish I could send such calming feelings into the hearts of my family." Osana's voice and face both bowed under the burden she bore.

Theresa nodded, receiving all the information she needed from the voice of the King inside her and from the tone of her student's voice.

"It's about your grandmother."

Osana nodded slowly. "I know that I just needed the courage to face it. Just seeing you clarifies all of it for me."

"All of it?"

"Yes." Osana stood, staring introspectively at the ground. "In my vision, this big, old mother hen finally stopped her running around and sat down, but not in the nest as she should. Rather she sat on the floor, in the middle of the chicken coop. As she settled to sleep there, I realized that she would die if she slept. And I tried to intervene. But that was impossible, of course." She took a deep breath. "Then, just as the hen began to sink lower and lower—more than just into sleep—a great flash transformed her into a seagull, and she launched out of the door and flew away."

Osana sighed. "This is not the sort of vision I can tell my parents about, or my grandmother. This is just what they all fear about grandmother's approaching death."

Theresa stepped close and placed a hand on Osana's shoulder. "They survived your visit to Madrid, didn't they?"

Osana nodded. "But that was only a short time."

"Any loss is easier to bear if you know that it is only a temporary loss." Theresa allowed a silence to hang. "Let me show you."

Still resting her hand on Osana's shoulder, Theresa reached with her other hand to gently touch the smooth, golden forehead of her pupil. At that touch Theresa closed her physical eyes, so that her spiritual eyes could travel with the impulse that she sent through Osana's mind and heart.

In a moment of ecstatic elevation beyond the physical world, Osana saw her family—mother, father, brother, herself, and her grandmother—hugging each other as if meeting after a long trip. It was her grandmother who had been traveling. Now she looked young and strong, stronger than Osana had ever seen her in the natural world. This new grandmother lacked the bitter edge of regret tightening her lips, the tired air of longing in the tilt of her head, and the hard eyes that had seen more loss than she could recount.

"She will fly away, but she will be back, many times," Theresa said. "And they will be *happy* times."

Osana opened her eyes. She waited for her soul to absorb the glimpse of the future that Theresa had provided. For one so young, Osana had easily grown accustomed to stepping back into the present from a future that ran far beyond her sight and dropped off into the gulf of the unknowable. Seeing those things that are not yet, strained her soul. But Theresa served as a sort of knotted tie, anchoring her to the one that propped her, and straightened her posture.

Now Theresa did something she rarely did, she wrapped her arms around the young woman. "Most of your revelations come purely as information, with little of the feeling that goes into God's plans. I want you to step in closer to what the King is saying about the future, so you can *feel* what he feels, and participate in his plans more fully." Theresa pulled back to look into Osana's eyes, inches away. "I will show you what I mean." She hugged Osana again, gently, in silence.

For Theresa, the experience was like turning on a faucet and being the faucet at the same time. For Osana, that embrace united soul and spirit, linking her spiritual line of communication to her heart, her deepest feelings, even her identity. She began to cry quietly and profoundly. But the tears carried neither sadness nor pain. It was an opening where she had been closed, a flow where she had been stopped up.

After a few minutes, Theresa unwound herself from that embrace and paused to wipe tears from Osana's cheeks. Osana spoke first.

"His heart for us is so sweet, so pure, so true. I had missed that many times."

"Have you ever wondered why the Lord hasn't yet sent you to speak to other mortals on his behalf, even though you hear from him so often and so precisely?"

"I thought I was still being trained. Not ready to speak to them, yet, I guess."

"You're right. But it is a different sort of training, it is really growing that he awaits. He is not looking for someone who is merely older, or even more experienced at hearing. He is waiting for you to feel his heart, so the messages you deliver carry all of what he wants to communicate. He has feelings for his children, not only information."

Osana pursed her lips soberly. Then Theresa watched her student reenter that vision of the old hen dying and rising again as a seagull. She watched her take in the revelation in a new way. The colors and sounds sharpened. And Osana knew that what was happening to the hen was not happening outside the realm of the King. The passage from one life to another occurred within the sight, and even within the heart, of the one who created and cared for all things. The hen didn't die alone, she didn't suffer pain, didn't regret loss. All of this reflected the intentions and desires of the King. And he drew the old hen, Osana's grandmother, into his Kingdom more deeply than during her—sometimes painful—mortal life.

When the image of the seagull flying away, with a departing squawk, had passed from Osana's spiritual sight, she laughed. Theresa shared in her joy, inside and out. And she joined in the laughter.

CHAPTER THIRTY-NINE

Joshua arrived outside the little safe house next to Humanity City, where he had met several survivors just weeks ago. This visit was only as supervisor. The immortals had sent Denny to meet five survivors in the little, gray house this time, his first such assignment. The agents of the King had determined that Denny's healing gifts would serve these particular children well, and that he would be able to sense enough of their emotional state to begin the healing and integrating process for all five. They sent Joshua in only to check on Denny's work with the children, and to address a particular issue for one of the girls.

Denny stood facing away from the dark front door of the house, tossing a small, red ball to a boy with almond eyes and skin the color of varnished pine. The boy's straight, black hair clung to his forehead in little spikes, damp with sweat.

Joshua approached the house from the south, having landed himself a hundred yards away, to avoid startling any of the children. He worried that the children might mistake him for one of the "aliens," which some of them still feared at this point in their transition.

Looking away for a moment and smiling at Joshua, Denny turned back just in time to catch the bright, red ball before it hit him in the head. The little boy laughed at the quick recovery of his older playmate. The boy stopped laughing and cringed at the sight of Joshua. Joshua could see firsthand why the immortals had chosen the boyish Denny to meet Peeno. The boy had been traumatized by abuse from an adoptive father.

"It's good to see you, my friend," Joshua said.

Denny smiled at him, and patted Joshua on the back as they pulled out of an embrace. He handed the ball to Joshua who was facing Peeno. "Who's this bright young man with you?" Then he gently lobbed the ball toward Peeno, who arose from his fear to capture the ball with two hands.

"This is my new friend, Peeno."

"How are you, Peeno?" Joshua held up his hand to invite a return throw.

Peeno tossed the ball a bit short but Joshua stepped forward and caught it before it hit the uneven ground. Joshua smiled at Peeno, sending a message of unconditional acceptance—something unfamiliar to the little boy, for whom cringing was a familiar state.

Knowing that his task lay inside, with a girl named Kiely, Joshua tossed the ball to Denny. "I'll let you get back to it."

Turning toward Peeno, as he reached the porch, Joshua said, "Good to meet you, Peeno."

The sun outside left Joshua adjusting to the dim interior of the house. To help him, a spry, little woman with long, black hair brightened the living room briefly with a wave of her hands. The homemade light faded gradually and Joshua's eyes adjusted with it.

Seeing more clearly now the other occupant of the bare living room, Joshua bowed to her. He had met Aerin once before in the company of Theresa. The slight woman smiled at Joshua and bowed in return.

"Good to see you again, Joshua. And I know that Kiely will be very glad for what you bring her." Aerin's face seemed to strain against the inadequacy of a mere smile.

Joshua furrowed his brow a bit. He didn't know what Aerin was referring to. But he often entered therapy sessions, or healing opportunities, with no clear expectation of exactly what would happen. He trusted the details to the King and enjoyed the discoveries in each moment of his work.

Noting that the house had been carpeted since his last visit, Joshua paused to allow Aerin to fill in more detail if she felt it necessary. She just kept smiling. Joshua laughed softly, as he entered the playroom.

He spotted Kiely immediately, sensing a much greater openness in the round-faced girl with slightly rumpled hair and a plain, pink dress. The other three children in the room eyed him with suspicion but said nothing and returned to drawing or playing at the low table that dominated half the room.

In return for his unabashed observation of her, Kiely looked hard at Joshua, as if silently asking whether he was the one for whom she had been waiting. Joshua responded with an answer, of sorts.

"Hello, Kiely. My name is Joshua. Would you like to go for a walk?"

Kiely stood up and allowed deep concern to bend her face. "Are you going to show me the King?" She carefully wound around table and chairs to follow him out of the room.

In that instant, Joshua received a revelation about the little girl. Since Kiely had escaped the walled city, she had been asking if she could see the King. One of the immortals had assured her that a man would come to take her to see the King. Discovering all of this sent an excited charge up Joshua's spine. Now he knew what Aerin had been smiling so intensely about.

Kiely caught up with him by the door.

"Why do you want to see the King?" He asked this, not in a challenging voice, but curious and friendly.

"I just need to know that he's real, and that he's good."

Joshua gestured out the door and Kiely pushed her way outside without taking her eyes off him.

"How will you know?" Joshua pointed to the east, away from Denny and his game of catch.

Kiely squinted at him, speeding to keep up with his long strides. "I can know by seeing him."

Joshua nodded. "You will know that he is real, a real person and a real king. But how will you know that he's good?"

"He won't hurt me." Then, after a moment, she added, "But I think I'll know by his face. I could tell when I saw *you*."

Joshua nodded, but he didn't say anything for several steps, picking his way over clumps of wild grass, and between thistles brandishing bold, pink flowers before the brightening sun. Kiely reached out and took his hand in the silence. At her touch Joshua knew more clearly what was happening to this lost little girl. He saw her long days of quiet, imposed by her fear of being seen—seen by her own parents. They hadn't greeted her birth with joy. As she had grown, she had learned that she could escape their disgusted looks and resentful tones by being invisible.

In her efforts at invisibility, she attracted the attention of one of the immortals, a woman that lived in China before the Reign, a woman who introduced herself to Kiely, without appearing visibly. As if this invisible stranger confirmed her own desire for invisibility, the girl accepted the friendship of the disembodied voice.

"What was the lady's name, the invisible one that was your friend?"

Kiely slowed and looked up at him. "Her name was Bai Ming. She stopped being invisible when I asked her to take me out of the city."

Joshua slowed to a stop. He had been monitoring input from the King, even as he talked with Kiely. Now he knew that taking her to the throne was what the King wanted. He gave Kiely a crooked smile, as her hair riffled in a rising breeze. He noted that the expectant question in her eyes remained unmoved. He gladly relieved her suspense.

"I can take you to the throne. But that's many hours from here in a plane." He let go of her hand and lowered himself to one knee, approximating eye level. "I can take you there in an instant, by the power that comes from the throne, if you don't mind."

Clenching her sparse eyebrows slightly, Kiely looked deep into his eyes. "You mean like the magic ones? But I thought you weren't one of them."

"I can do it by the same power that Bai Ming uses. We work for the same king."

The look on Kiely's face bypassed the need for supernatural revelation of her thoughts. As bold as she seemed, she couldn't easily leap from the iron and concrete world of the walled city into a world of supernatural human transportation across the planet.

Joshua could see that a lesson was in order. Checking the ground behind him, he sank from his knee to a seat on the ground, the thin cushion of grass and ragweed sufficient for momentary comfort. Kiely followed his example, crossing her legs in front of her in the same pretzel style as Joshua.

"You see, Kiely, the King has been on the Earth before. In fact, he created it all. And because he created it all, he doesn't have to obey all the rules that he put in place. When I say rules, I mean what scientists call laws, like the laws of physics. You've heard of that, right?"

Kiely nodded. A bright student in a school system dedicated to technology, she would know what Joshua was referring to, even if she couldn't imagine anyone being above those laws.

"The rules that you learned in school, about chemistry and biology and physics, were put in place to govern humans during the days before the King came to Earth the first time, as a teacher and healer. Now that he has come as ruler of the entire planet, his followers are discovering that we, too, are free from the rules that used to make people feel safe."

Measuring whether he was talking over her head, Joshua paused to sense Kiely's internal response. Instead of finding her confused, he found her childish soul already reaching out for the freedom of which he was speaking.

"It's available to all of us who want to serve him." Joshua's words seemed weak in the face of the readiness of Kiely's heart. "I'll show you."

Joshua craned his neck at a small collection of bushes behind him. "Let's go over there." Then, without further explanation, he blinked them fifty yards away, still sitting in the same position, still facing each other.

For a second, Kiely froze, her head high, her neck stiff. The look on her face said, "*Did that just happen*?"

"You okay with that?"

Kiely began to nod, her affirmation growing moment by moment. "Can we go to see the King now?"

"Let's go see him."

He stood, and Kiely extended her hand again. As she rose to her feet, Joshua felt the fear mixed in with her boldness. He squeezed her hand once and smiled, to reassure her. Simultaneously he prayed, trusting his mission to more worthy hands. A surge of anticipation came in response to his prayer, and Joshua laughed briskly, just before transporting Kiely and himself to the congregation in front of the throne.

As he had seen happen every time he had been transported, Joshua arrived in a small clearing among the worshippers. Immediately the crowd around them seemed to sift so that most of the worshippers near them were approximately Kiely's height. Included among these supernatural worshippers was Bai Ming, whom Joshua recognized, though he hadn't physically met her before.

Kiely looked around her and then up at Joshua. Joshua was still laughing. The girl's blue eyes had sprung wide, but she smiled for the first time Joshua had seen. Bai Ming stepped in and whispered into Kiely's ear. Joshua didn't try to guess or discern what she said. He was being swept up into the worship.

Just as Joshua had fallen in with the beat of the worship, he heard a sort of disturbance next to him, tugging him out of the ecstatic flow. He had never heard such a break in the worship in all his visits to the throne. His spirit rose in protest against the sacrilege of interrupting the worship of even one person before the throne. Then he realized that the disturbance was a small shrill voice calling out over and over.

"Hey, I want to see you, King. I want to see you. Hey..."

That voice was affecting the worshippers around him. First the children near them, then worshippers in an ever-widening circle, fell dead silent. Within half a minute, the silence had circled out to the congregation as far as Joshua could see and hear. Total stillness, utter silence surrounded him. All heads turned toward Kiely.

She shouted one last time. "King, I want to see your face. I want to see you." Her voice faded and cracked under the pressure of the stillness crowding around her.

For a moment, Joshua wondered how the King would respond to this cry. Challenges from unbelievers hadn't always received the desired response in the past, as far as he knew. But he felt that Kiely wasn't challenging the King, nor feeding her own skepticism. She seemed to want the King to be real. She genuinely wanted to see him, and to *know* that he was real.

Five seconds of silence, where one has never heard silence before, is a long time. Kiely's silence lasted only a little longer than that.

Like a wind stirring leaves, like water gently rolling over submerged stones, a whisper rolled from the direction of the throne.

"Kiely."

The King whispered from where he sat. He was calling Kiely by name.

She stood up straighter and looked hard into the great light, as if the whisper might have opened a tunnel to the one who spoke her name. As soon as the whisper ceased, the worshippers began a roar that swept from all sides, colliding around Joshua and Kiely. A moment later, a half dozen children surrounded Kiely and lifted her into the air, pausing a moment and then sweeping her forward toward the throne.

Joshua stood in place, clear that he would have to wait there, not invited to be part of Kiely's face-to-face encounter with the King. He looked at Bai Ming, who nodded sympathetically. She, too, would have to wait at a distance.

To his left, Joshua felt a new presence, and turned to find Theresa, accompanied by a lovely young girl with long, dark hair and ethereal eyes. He knew instantly that this was Osana. The look of ecstasy in those eyes clearly accompanied some new revelation that she must have sealed in her heart there in front of the throne. As he watched, Osana was also lifted by the hands of several immortals, who appeared no older than she. Like Kiely before her, Osana flew forward toward the throne and away from her teacher's sight. Theresa spread a satisfied smile as she watched her go.

Joshua wondered at the confluence of Kiely's call to the throne and Osana's. Were they meeting together with the King? Would they even recognize the presence of the other in the blinding glory of the throne? His human curiosity danced in and out of his spiritual rest, subsiding as he sensed the King's voice emerging from that rest, alerting him to his next mission.

The first word that formed in his mind was "Siberia," and he laughed at the thought of a call to the other side of the world. Next he realized that the convergence in front of the throne was not between Kiely and Osana, but between himself and Osana. *He* was to take *her* with him to receive several children from the walled city known as Glasnost.

He wondered how this would work for a boy from Iowa and a girl from Spain, in a Russian-speaking territory. Those complexities made him laugh some more.

CHAPTER FORTY

After her return from the throne, Osana couldn't speak for several days. But those weren't silent days. She heard many voices, including that little girl saying she wanted to see the King. And, of course, she heard the King. She heard him more clearly than ever before.

This was very fortunate, because Osana was being given her first real assignment, to go with Joshua to help rescued children. They would be children like that little girl shouting at the King. But perhaps they wouldn't be so unruly as she was.

Joshua met with both Theresa and Osana by the Mediterranean Sea. She struggled past shyness with Joshua, like pushing against a strong current. She focused on his briefing to distract her from her timidity.

"We will be meeting one of the immortals outside the city. He is bringing others to assist with transport and security." Joshua glanced at Osana and then turned back to the sparkling waves in front of them.

Theresa and Osana had met Joshua on a bench next to the sea, not far from Osana's home. She knew those warm, blue waters like a family member. Joshua seemed distracted by the sights and sounds.

But Osana was focused on their mission. "Why security? We cannot be harmed."

Joshua nodded as he turned from the sea, a little delay as he heard the translation from Theresa. "We will be safe. And the children will be safe. But they are unpredictable, as are the authorities in Glasnost City."

That was where they were going. The city was named from the Russian word for "openness," a word that had a political meaning in that region, before the Reign. That region was once an Arctic wasteland. But the warmer climate had turned the north shore of Asia into a temperate zone, the sort of zone to which resisters had fled to escape the influence of the King.

Joshua continued to assure her. "The King always sends more than enough people to deal with whatever obstacles we might run into. So far, for me, the excitement has been just enough to get an adrenalin boost or two." He smiled as if he was making a little joke, perhaps.

Osana had to confirm with Theresa that phrase "adrenalin boost." She smiled at the translation, trying not to let Joshua know how little she wanted such a boost. But he could probably tell.

The next afternoon, Joshua and Osana stood in the street in front of her bright and tidy house in Valencia. They had done the family good-byes inside the walls of the home, taking their disappearing act outside. She had watched as Joshua tried to reassure her family, passing a pulse of confidence through his handshakes, she suspected. Her family needed a lot of reassuring.

Out of sight of her family and any of the neighbors, Osana launched into space with Joshua and Theresa, feeling the dreamlike transport once again. Their landing in tall grass south of a dark gray wall, fifty feet high, was not so dreamlike.

For a moment, the swaying, wild grass was their only greeting. She thought instantly of the dancers around the throne, swaying with the breath of the King. That connection spread peace through her heart, like warm steam from homemade soup, full of childhood recollections. Those recollections gave way to alertness and tension, however, when she saw three people approaching from behind an old barn, a structure with fewer timbers upright than those fallen to the ground in tangled heaps. People hiding behind that barn, or inside it, seemed a bad sign.

Theresa nodded at the approaching trio, an older man with a rough beard, a bouncy twelve-year-old boy and a small woman with jet black hair and small, quick steps. Theresa's familiar gesture comforted Osana. Joshua offered his hand to the strangers.

"You are Joshua?" The old man spoke with a thick Russian accent.

"You must be Sergei."

Joshua shook the Russian's hand. "Your English is very good."

Sergei laughed hard. "And so is your Russian." He laughed harder, his head tipping toward the ground as his amusement clenched his whole body.

"Russian?" Osana was as confused as Joshua appeared.

Sergei sobered, even as Osana noticed Theresa covering her mouth to conceal a smile. The boy with Sergei grinned broadly.

"It is the holy ones." Sergei swept one hand toward Theresa and that boy. "They are translating what we say right inside our heads."

Joshua just glanced at Theresa, his lips pursed. Osana had spoken with him through her teacher's simultaneous translation. But what she was hearing now was past that, a sort of automatic translation in the voice of the speaker. This is surely what surprised Joshua.

Sergei and Joshua took turns giving introductions. The twelve-year-old was Misha, a gangly boy who seemed to weigh nothing. His smile was warm and deep. He was one of the immortal translators. The third person in that party was Zhongli, barely over five feet tall. She was perhaps as old as Joshua, but that was very difficult to tell from her perceptive eyes and hint of a smile, set in a child-like face.

Theresa completed the introductions. "Zhongli does what you do but wants to learn more from seeing you at work." She spoke to Joshua without looking squarely at him. "Osana and Zhongli have complementary gifts, which will allow them a range of insights into emotions and needs regarding the children."

A whirring, clipping sound from behind them drew Osana's attention away from Theresa's explanation. Turning around, she saw a stout figure flying toward them, his feet just grazing the tops of the tall grass. Ripe grass seed swarmed around the approaching person in a shiny, golden-green cloud. Osana could hear a chuckle from Sergei, behind her.

"Da Jin," he said. "He keeps me young and is driving me to my grave." Sergei's earthy belly laugh did an encore.

Jin landed next to the gathered group with a bow and a giggle. "I specialize in entrances." He flourished one hand and exchanged glowing smiles with Theresa. Misha shook his head and chuckled like an old man.

"Welcome to my fields." Jin reached out and seemed to zap Joshua. Osana had felt the spiritual charge that jumped from the immortals into her body. But Jin apparently used it more like a defibrillator. Joshua shook with a jolt and then vibrated where he stood.

Seeing Joshua vibrating like a man in the back of an off-road pickup truck, Osana refused the hand offered her. Jin smiled and released an invisible wave of blessing that landed on her like a silk scarf. A whole gallery of anxieties fell away from her in just one moment.

Theresa filled in answers where Joshua might have asked questions, were he not still shaking with that electric shock.

"This is Jin's territory, the land outside the wall, and some of what is inside."

Joshua's voice wobbled as he spoke. "Inside the wall?"

"Yes, there are many of us who have responsibilities inside the rebel cities." Jin giggled again, as a great crowd of hovering saints suddenly appeared around the earthbound people. As quickly as that crowd appeared, they returned to invisibility, or to their place by the throne, or wherever they wanted to be when not summoned like that by Jin.

"You must be special," Sergei said to Joshua. "He never showed me that before." Sergei was still staring after that suspended choir of immortals that had disappeared.

Joshua seemed to recover from Jin's touch. "It's good to know that we have your protection." He spoke to Jin with respect, but not gushing awe.

Awe seemed in order, for Osana. She sensed that Jin was one of the most powerful immortals she had ever met. He seemed to have wide authority. How else could he summon all those other immortals for his little show?

"The way is open for you," said Jin. "There will be no interference. The children are ready." He gestured toward that old barn, where a house appeared out of bright, sunny air.

Osana gasped at the appearance of the hidden building.

Joshua began to step toward that house but paused. "Do you keep it invisible from the rebels all the time?"

Jin nodded. He had begun to levitate again, floating around the rest of the group until he was between them and the house. He gestured for them to follow, then he zipped the hundred yards to the front door of the house and waited there. None of the others, even the immortals, followed his example. They merely walked on the ground, the grass shushing against their knees, grasshoppers launching with each step.

Misha seemed fascinated with the flying grasshoppers, watching each as it leapt into the air and buzzed away from the humans. The immortal appeared to be studying them, until Osana understood that Misha was actually communicating with each of the insects.

When they reached the door, half a dozen sets of feet drummed up the steps and onto the wooden porch. Sergei stepped aside to stand next to Jin. Theresa and Misha took up a position on the other side of the door. Only Osana, Joshua and Zhongli would be entering the house.

The front door swung open and a young woman with chocolate brown skin and ebony eyes smiled at the guests. "So glad you could make it." She wore her hair in a puffy afro which sagged slightly around her face as she leaned forward to hold open the screen door. The sound of children quietly talking and playing eased over her shoulder.

"Angela?" Osana hadn't met her before, but often received a revelation of the name and character of someone as she met them.

"Hello, Osana." Angela took her hand, and then nodded to the others. "Joshua, Zhongli. Please come in. The children are looking forward to meeting you."

Zhongli led the other two through the front door. Angela held up a finger from which emanated a candle-like glow, making it easier for Osana's eyes to adjust to the dark interior of the house. A bluish light led the way to the playroom deeper in the house, where the children's voices could be heard rising and falling.

Angela seemed to be from North America, based on her English and her manner of dress, but Osana knew not to trust appearances. It seemed an odd choice, nonetheless, given that they were in old Russia. The children, as Osana stepped into their playroom, all appeared to be from that area. Just like Sergei, they seemed to be speaking Spanish with rich Russian accents. But Osana now knew that this was an effect of the automatic translation process. The weight of their accent was such that she couldn't forget that Spanish wasn't their native tongue, but their intonation was still easy for her to understand.

Entering the playroom with them, Angela made the introductions. "Children, this is Joshua. The man I told you about. And these are his friends, Osana and Zhongli. They have all traveled a long way to meet with you and help you with any questions you have about what comes next."

Clearly, it wouldn't do to explain that these specially gifted people were here to bring healing and hope to the children's wounded souls. Answering questions was merely a child's explanation for what would happen there that day.

What wasn't clear to Osana was how her ability to see into the future, or to other places and times, would be used in this mission. Joshua's emotional sensitivity was of obvious value here. She could only hope that he would lead her into her part of the healing process.

CHAPTER FORTY-ONE

Joshua sampled the landscape inside the heart of an obese girl, her weight rare both among the rebels and under the Reign. Behind the protective walls of cities like Glasnost, the culture of cosmetic beauty had pressed technology forward for managing weight, even in the youngest children. That this little girl had increased her weight by more than fifty percent of what was healthy for her, testified to her rebellion against her culture. Her name was Berta.

During those first moments, Joshua sensed a question from Zhongli. She said nothing but followed him with her eyes as if waiting for him to receive her silent query. Without even knowing the nature of that question, Joshua released Zhongli to do the thing that had come to her mind. He glanced at her with a slight bow.

Here, Zhongli seized an advantage over Joshua. Over a foot shorter than him, she folded herself comfortably into one of the child-sized chairs around the big oval table. Joshua chuckled at her ease at fitting in.

Zhongli was like Joshua, sensitive to the feelings of the children in a way that was informative and empowering. It's one thing to sense the emotions of others. But something more was required to identify an emotion's source and a possible cure, where a cure was needed.

This group of children carried a range of needs, as usual, but Joshua could sense none who were in critical emotional condition. Zhongli certainly sensed the same and had determined that she could place herself among the children as a sort of infiltrator. Joshua focused again on Berta. He stepped into her field of vision, though he said nothing and only offered a modicum of eye contact. This provoked the girl's defiant need for control, as he expected. An adult watching her wordlessly annoyed her, disturbing her far more than the small woman seated at the table coloring now with the children.

"Are you here to *evaluate* us?" Berta stared defiantly at Joshua. Though she was older than she looked, due to her excessive weight, Berta was also much more assertive than most ten-year-old girls.

Joshua smiled softly, knowing Berta wouldn't expect that response to her challenging tone. "Evaluate? Are you used to being evaluated?"

"My parents had me evaluated a bunch of times."

From his internal briefing, Joshua knew what prompted this parade of experts. Her parents, who were accomplished professionals, were at a loss how to change their defiant daughter. He could imagine their frustration in that control-oriented culture. He also knew that Berta had perceived that treatment as confirmation that she was no more than a piece of property to her parents, assessed and valued like a plot of real estate.

Joshua was glad he could do more than put on a sincere smile, to reassure the children. He sent warmth, acceptance and love to the defiant girl, from his spirit to hers. Berta could refuse the offer, of course. But that offer hung there in front of her.

Letting up on his press toward Berta's wounded soul, he switched his attention to the boy sitting next to her. The thirteen-year-old seated next to Berta wore his hair in a cloud of spikes, a *silver* cloud at present.

Raising his glittering head, Leo returned Joshua's interest, just as Joshua learned his name. At the same time, Joshua detected Zhongli trying to link into his thoughts. He opened that door and let her into what he was thinking. He then checked with Osana, who had different gifts and wouldn't be able to hear his thoughts in the same way as Zhongli.

The intensity of Osana's wrinkled brow was limited only by her young skin and inexperienced facial muscles. Joshua slid closer to her and put a hand on her back to release some of the tension she was stockpiling. The human reminder to relax, as much as the spiritual communication of peace, loosened her brow and induced a couple of calming breaths.

Back in contact with Leo, Joshua sensed the young man's frustration. He was too old for the arts and crafts, let alone the toys, in that little room. Somewhat small for his age, nevertheless he resented the children's table he had been placed at. Joshua offered an escape.

"Wanna go for a walk?"

Leo nodded gently, his eyes squeezed to thin slits and he turned his head a few degrees, as if weighing other offers. As Leo began to stand, Joshua motioned to Osana.

"Okay if she comes with us?"

Though he knew he should keep Osana near him, Joshua had also read some interest from Leo directed toward the lovely teenager.

"Yeah, sure. That's okay." Leo was attempting nonchalance as his cover.

Joshua had found that having a boy Leo's age a bit distracted—with a pretty girl nearby, for example—helped to break down his defenses. Leo was a voluntary refugee, so he didn't need much convincing. But he still needed help at opening his soul to begin his healing.

Zhongli started a conversation with a slender, dark-haired boy seated across from her, to help distract the other children while Joshua and Osana led Leo out of the room. Joshua smiled at her when she glanced his way, communicating approval of her tactic.

Once outside the little house, Joshua stopped to breathe the fresh breeze coming from the south. Leo, on the other hand, cowered slightly at the sight of the city wall over Joshua's left shoulder. He kept his face turned away, like a boy trying not to see a scary scene in a movie.

"Osana can tell you things about yourself that no one else knows, including your future." Joshua tipped his head toward the girl who was just stepping off the porch a pace behind them. More than an additional distraction, this boast was intended to build some trust for Leo, assurance that he was in competent hands.

Osana looked a question at Joshua. He returned an encouraging smile, and no further instructions. He had a sense that she knew what to do here.

"You like to dance," she said. "It's a frenetic dancing, a hard and vigorous dancing. I don't know what you call it. But I see you going with some older boys to a club where they show you how to slam your body around without getting hurt. It reminds me of what I saw when I went to Jerusalem."

These words flowed freely from Osana in Spanish and landed in Joshua's and Leo's ears in perfect English and Russian, respectively. Leo perked up at the mention of Jerusalem, having already straightened his back and brightened his eyes as he listened to Osana speak of his dancing.

CHAPTER FORTY-TWO

Leo Rachofsky was a city boy. A survivor in Glasnost City. Just surviving. He hated his hometown as much as he loved it.

He pulled himself away from staring out the window at the new tower rising two blocks away, a monstrous crane lifting some prebuilt structure toward the top level. To Leo it felt like the world was closing in around him. The only way he knew to escape any of it was in the clubs. It was still early, but he couldn't wait.

The dance club that allowed young teens like Leo opened at seven and closed at eleven. Rules. Of course. Rules. This city was all about rules. Even pleasure had its rules. Even dancing.

"Hey, you, Leo." The landlord called to him as he put his first foot on the pavement in front of his apartment building.

Leo sped his steps, not wanting another go-around with the landlord.

"Where is your mother? When am I gonna see the rent in my account?"

Leo didn't have answers. He shouldn't have to answer for his mother. He shouldn't have to talk to the fat landlord.

"Hey, where you going? Wait. I want to talk to you." The burly man's voice faded as Leo skipped away, mixing in with the foot traffic of people leaving work or going out to dinner.

"Idiot." He said it under his breath. But he said it aloud.

"What? Who ..." A middle-aged man next to him growled a challenge.

"Uh. Sorry. Not you." And Leo picked up his pace again.

The doors weren't opened yet. Five more minutes if they were gonna open on time. But Leo saw Kevin and Piotr in line, huddled together as if it were cold out. It hardly ever got cold this early. It was just the way those two stood together on the street. Maybe it was from some old movie they had seen from before the alien invasion. The good old days.

"Leo."

"Hey, Leo." Piotr pulled his shelter of orange hair away from his eyes.

That was a new color for Piotr. Leo could just see a spike of his own purple hair out of the corner of his right eye. He wasn't interested in Piotr's shade of orange.

The color of his friend's hair wasn't attractive, but his own obsession about such things was wearing him out, like a strap on a backpack rubbing in the same spot for too long, the skin starting to get sensitive and then sore. Irritated. Leo felt irritated most of the time.

He strung together his favorite obscenities. "When are they gonna open those doors?" He looked his friends toward the club entrance. He was anxious to get away, to escape the landlords, towers, rules, and obsessions about hair and clothes.

"Yeah. Any minute now." Kevin nodded sympathetically. His Russian was childish. He had been born in North America, only coming to the Siberian city when he was ten. His dad had a job here.

Leo had no idea where *his* dad was.

Glancing past Kevin, Leo noticed a spidery girl with jet black hair over half her face. She was watching him. The one eye that he could see seemed to understand him. Of course, the kids that came to this club were all looking for the same thing, a way to kick against the world without getting detention and reprogramming.

The doors opened a minute later, and the mass of teens began to push inside like commuters packing a levitron train at rush hour. That girl bumped against Leo, shoulder-to-shoulder.

"You're Leo, right?" She was being pressed close against his right side.

"Yeah." He glanced at her. Did he know her from somewhere?

"Arya. We were in school together a long time ago. When we were little."

"Arya? Oh, yeah. Arya. You went away. You moved."

"We got an apartment on the one hundredth floor of some downtown fright fest and I had to lose all my friends when I was seven."

He swore sympathetically. "Grownups."

"Exactly."

"Have I seen you here before?" He suspected that he had.

"You didn't recognize me. I had white hair before, in twirls." She tossed her head toward a girl with bright yellow twirls that reached nearly half a meter above her head.

"Ah. Yeah."

They were at the door now, passing between the guards. New guys, as far as Leo could tell. Piotr sneered at the big adult male to his left. The guy might have been propping the door frame with his bulging shoulder muscles. He could probably play attack ball, with shoulders like that. Maybe he had. Bad knees maybe. But Leo didn't plan on finding out if that guard could run tonight. Piotr seemed in a mood to test him.

Curious what Piotr would do next, Leo followed his red and black spikes bobbing above the heads around him. Piotr was three years older and fully grown. Leo would probably never be as tall as Piotr.

Arya stayed at his shoulder as they flowed with the mob into the main dance arena, after passing the billing kiosks and getting their chips clicked. This was where Leo had to hold his breath these days. He never knew if his mom had filled up the chip with credits.

But he made it past that checkpoint this time and into the flashing lights of the arena. Some older guy was shouting obscenities and shouldering other big guys to get them riled up. Leo wanted to be one of them, but he wanted to stay close to Arya too. She was even smaller than him, so he doubted she would want to bang with the big guys.

Piotr ran right at that loud dude with the bald head. They chest banged and the music seemed to crank up just in time to turn that into a dance move. Shouts on all sides rose toward the ceiling and its complex of screens and beams of colored light. The dance was on.

Gripping one arm tightly, Arya started to swing her weight against Leo's. She was stronger than he would have thought, and he let himself swing with her and bang into the bigger boys and girls around them. After a minute she let him swing her against the bangers on all sides. He hair flew around her head, a black fountain, revealing her other eye when the light flashed on them.

Pulsing, pounding, jumping, swinging, rubbing, grabbing, bumping and banging. Time disappeared. Space became free and three dimensional. They slammed each other over the gravity lifters, two feet off the floor for seconds at a time. But it was too crowded there, everyone wanting to fly like aliens.

Landing back on the floor, Leo got his first look at Piotr in what must have been an hour. He could only guess the time by how soaked with sweat he was, spikes of hair hanging onto his forehead now.

Piotr was banging against a bigger guy who seemed on the prowl for someone to hurt. That was so typical of Leo's angry friend—ramming toward the nastiest dude in the crowd. And the fight was on. Six or seven teens, both boys and girls, all collided next to the gravity lifter in that one corner of the arena. The drumbeat had taken over the song and those pounding percussions seemed to drive the fists of the fighters.

One of those massive guards rushed past Leo. He felt instant relief when the guy surged past without crushing him. But that turned to horror when he saw Arya tossed right into the middle of the fight. Leo let out a shout and followed his own voice toward that mosh of human hands and heads and feet.

He squeezed past two large girls who were part of the wall of spectators to the fight. They cursed him as he pressed his head and then his body between them. Arya was on hands and knees crawling to get clear of the stomping shoes and flashing fists. This was why combat boots had been banned for teens here. She would have been smashed to bits if those guys had been wearing hard shoes.

Just as Leo reached out for Arya, a big guy flew past and landed squarely on top of her, back to back where Arya still crawled on the floor. She disappeared from Leo's view. Squashed under that guy's bulk. A guard had thrown that guy and now he piled on.

"Arya!" Leo screamed her name as he got dumped into the pile.

Then absolute silence stopped the melee.

Everyone seemed frozen in place for several seconds. Leo felt the weight of the two guys piled on him suddenly lessen. It was like sound and gravity were being sucked out of the room.

Instantly, Leo was in the lobby. From total stillness, to instant transport, to lying on the tiles in the lobby, in less than a second. And Arya was there too, lying on the floor next to him.

A beautiful woman with golden brown skin and magical hands was touching him. All his pain, which he recognized only as she placed her warm hands on him, vanished. He turned his head toward Arya, and she looked at him with both eyes. That same woman had apparently touched her as well. She was smiling like a kid who falls from a jungle gym only to land on a soft mat, unharmed.

"Aliens." Arya grinned at him and looked at the woman who was now standing over them.

The woman laughed at Arya's commentary.

Leo laughed, too.

CHAPTER FORTY-THREE

"You've been there? You've danced in that huge crowd?" Leo was addressing Osana, but also checking with Joshua, as if for confirmation of the young woman's story.

Joshua nodded at Leo, his lips pressed together. He wouldn't one-up Osana's story with his own more extensive experience in front of the throne.

Osana answered the question. "I've been there. It took me over a week to recover from meeting the King last time." She spouted this as if venting her wonder at her own experience. She was flowing, not calculating.

"Did you dance? I mean, do they let regular people dance there? Or are there other places where you can just let loose like that?"

While Osana explained her experience, and the numerous options for Jerusalem worship around the world, Joshua checked the time. He was thinking of an old friend.

Lonnie Taggert, his best friend from high school, was as enthusiastic about Jerusalem worship as Leo. Joshua paused to remember the language gap, which was so easy to forget under his present circumstances. But he received a go-ahead from his link to the throne.

Joshua checked with Theresa. "Is Lon Taggert available right now?"

Theresa, who was in Jerusalem, beamed an answer back to him. "You will shock him when you zap in, but he should be available to talk. He's in Westchester right now, training a group."

She was referring to Westchester, Illinois, not far from Joshua's home. The irony of popping in to see Lon in Illinois, from the northern coast of Russia, was worth a chuckle, before Joshua introduced the idea to Leo.

"Let's go see my friend, Lonnie. He leads tours to Jerusalem, and is always attending Jerusalem worship closer to home, when he can't be in front of the throne." Joshua checked for interest from Leo, the way humans have always checked, watching the expression on his face. But he also took the boy's emotional temperature in the way that had become common only in the last hundred years.

"Where is this guy?"

"Illinois."

"Illinois, America?"

"Yes. I can take you there in an instant."

"An instant? I thought you were one of us ... I mean ... normal, y'know ... human."

Joshua *did* know what he meant but smiled at Leo's clumsy politeness. "Welcome to the land of freedom."

Leo stared at Joshua, as the shifting breeze pointed his puff of hair to the east.

"I'll show you," Joshua said. He turned to Osana. "You can go join Zhongli inside. I'll be back in half an hour or so."

Osana accepted this assignment with a grateful nod. She didn't seem eager to experiment with a mortal transporting her just yet.

When Joshua and Leo landed on the street in front of the retreat center, under giant elm trees that had been growing prodigiously for nearly a hundred years now, they stood still for a moment, recalibrating for their new location. Leo looked as if he suspected that the street beneath his feet wasn't entirely solid, bending his knees and holding his hands out to his side in preparation for a big plunge into ... what, Joshua didn't know.

Gaining his equilibrium first, Joshua touched Leo on the back gently. The fragile rookie transporter started and nearly fell on his face. Joshua caught him. "Sorry, I know it's a shock until you get used to that."

Leo straightened up and finished Joshua's thought for him. "But you get *do* used to it?"

"Yep. Mostly." Joshua let out a chuckle.

Up the long mauve sidewalk and into the open door of the retreat center, Leo followed Joshua, swiveling his head and craning his neck at the sculptures and landscaping that ushered him into this place of celebration, this place of beauty. They stood in the lobby for a moment, waiting for their eyes to adjust, and waiting for Joshua to sense what direction they should go. Theresa was invisible but present, translating and facilitating. But another voice turned Joshua's head and answered that question.

"Joshua!" Lon skipped forward and grabbed his old friend in a bear hug.

Joshua clapped Lon on the back as they broke their embrace. "Sorry to pop in on you unannounced." Gesturing to Leo next to him, still rubber-necking at the sights, Joshua made introductions.

Lon shook Leo's hand vigorously and studied his face. "You look familiar. Like someone I'm gonna get to know real well."

This greeting left Leo with his mouth open and a drifting focus to his eyes. He adjusted his gape slightly as a thin man with a glow to his young face paced peacefully down the marble hallway out of which Lon had arrived. The stranger approached Leo and locked in on his face and hair.

"Hey! I like your hair." He stared unapologetically. Then his own hair began to grow and stand on end and then soften and turn that same silver hue. The immortal had adopted Leo's hairdo in a matter of seconds.

Leo uttered an unchecked curse, still holding the handshake that the stranger had initiated. Joshua was glad not to have that curse automatically translated for him.

Leading with a big laugh, Lon turned to more introductions. "This is Kenny. He helps us with the Jerusalem worship. He leads worship in the royal city, but flies in to lead us here as well."

This explanation intrigued Joshua, who had given little thought to the need for worship leaders around the throne, having seen no evidence of anyone orchestrating. He had assumed that the King orchestrated invisibly.

"Not entirely." Kenny replied to Joshua's thoughts. "He likes to watch what we can do with more than just our individual bodies. Think of it as kingdom choreography."

More inviting still was the idea of immortals leading worship among the mortals away from Jerusalem. This, Joshua had heard of, but hadn't yet seen in action.

Again, Kenny replied to Joshua's thoughts. "Come and join us." He waved an invitation as he turned back toward the hallway from which he had emerged.

At the end of that hallway, they followed Kenny into a brightly lit room, illuminated by sunlight from huge skylights and open windows. Birds flew around the room just below the high ceiling, and then out to the sunny air, and back again. Dozens of mortals stood around drinking from bottles, some still huffing and puffing in recovery.

Within a few seconds, a band materialized outside the windows, an orchestra with two dozen instruments. And, with no introduction or instructions, the music began. Joshua and Leo were merging into a worship training session already underway. Lon smiled at their surprised faces.

Leo shook visibly, like a newborn fawn just corralling his spindly legs.

Music filled the air with the viscosity of honey. Joshua felt the gravity being filtered out of the room. His feet began to lift clear of the polished wood floor. Only with focused effort could he recover contact with that solid surface. But, as soon as he touched down, he bounced toward the fourteen-foot ceiling.

A glance at Leo told Joshua that his-low gravity experience wasn't universal. The thirteen-year-old was still firmly planted on the ground. Joshua associated the floating feeling with his attempts to fly, which had been few and somewhat shaky. But perhaps his flight experience set him apart from the average mortal in that room.

Others in the room seemed immediately oblivious to their surroundings. Whether flailing, leaping, stomping or pirouetting, many of the dancers closed their eyes, checking out of observing anyone around them. There were no mirrors on the walls of *this* dance studio. No one was watching ... except Leo.

Leo stared. But his gawking wasn't the shock of someone offended at the odd behavior of mortals trying to imitate the immortals, of clumsy dancers stumbling about without inhibition. His was the dumbfounded look of the gold miner, who comes home to find his old shack filled with nuggets that he didn't have to dig from the ground. Though his whole body shook with the shock of the discovery, Leo looked like a boy who had finally found a home.

CHAPTER FORTY-FOUR

As soon as he returned to his living room, even before feeding the cat and changing clothes, Joshua sent a message to Natalie's mobile device:

"Just popped back home from Russia. Portland seems pretty close. You busy?"

After feeding Gwendolyn and tidying up the kitchen a bit, he received this reply:

"Will have time later. 8:00 p.m. my time. Too late for you?"

Even walking next door to talk to Franny would take more time than transporting himself to some spot in Natalie's area. A slim available timeslot seemed no inconvenience at all. When he agreed, Natalie gave him the address of a restaurant in old downtown Portland, between the rivers, not far from the old rail yards. In the meantime, he made himself a light snack.

A rare evening rainstorm, complete with high lightning, changed Joshua's plans to read in his living room. It so rarely stormed during waking hours, that people often altered their evenings for a walk in the rain, or just to sit on a porch and feel the cool, moist air. Joshua sat out on his back porch, overlooking a small wooded lot, and read an electronic book while listening to the patter of drops counting leaves with playful fingers.

The peace of that evening calmed the rough edges of anxiety about seeing Natalie again. The rain soothed a restlessness in Joshua that he hadn't known for decades. Feeling that urgency drip away with the gentle shower, reminded him of one reason he had chosen a single life—a life without romantic entanglements of any kind. He had plenty in his life to stir up his adrenalin. He didn't need added excitement. But he did feel the need for a compatible companion. Variety is good and spicy, of course, but finding someone with whom you fit comfortably well, is a need as deep as there is in a mortal soul.

At fifteen minutes before his date, Joshua began to clean up a bit, giving brief consideration to not appearing overly self-conscious with his grooming, while still sparing Natalie the discomfort of a disheveled dinner companion. That calculation didn't last long. This relationship wasn't for validation, as much as for multiplication. Just as a musician can enjoy playing his instrument on his own only so long before finding an opportunity to join in with others, Joshua had a life to share. He enjoyed his life more when harmonizing with another, especially with this particular musician.

A minute before eight, Pacific time, Joshua landed on the street in front of the restaurant, relying on divine air traffic control to protect him from popping in on top of an unsuspecting pedestrian. He was just a bit too old to enjoy the fun of such misadventures.

Eight o'clock in Portland, in the spring, was twilight and cool breezes. No rain fell, despite the old reputation of the Pacific Northwest. Joshua could still feel the fresh ozone from the rain in Chicago in his nostrils, even as he inhaled his first breath of Oregon after sunset. He wore slacks, a button-up shirt and a light jacket, typical of the day—neither the suitcoat of pre-Reign generations, nor a windbreaker from those days. Clothes styles generally blurred for Joshua, under the influence of immortals who seemed to dress in the manner of any era they chose. Their freedom from fashion had infected Joshua, but he was on a date this night with a popular politician. She may have different standards from his usual oddball associates.

Just before he reached the door of the restaurant, Joshua heard a dainty throat clearing. "Ahem."

Turning to see Natalie smiling at him with bright and playful eyes, Joshua wrapped her up in an athletic hug. He assumed she had flown in behind him to catch him by surprise. He was grateful for the gentle alert, as opposed to an eagle swoop. Did she swoop like an eagle when dressed for a date?

CHAPTER FORTY-FIVE

"I really didn't mean to startle you." She sensed that her approach had done just that. "But I did calculate that your transport would get you here a minute or two early and timed my flight to arrive after you."

"All of that calculating is supposed to be a secret, you know."

Natalie laughed. "Just wanted to come clean from the start."

He smiled. "Okay. Then I'll tell you that I was debating whether to contact you and offer to pick you up, to transport you here. It occurred to me that flying might be a bit rigorous for someone dressed for a date. But then I wasn't sure you were going to dress up." He stopped there as if he might have said too much.

"You're welcome to pick me up anytime you want to. Tonight I was thinking first dates. And meeting at the destination has been the protocol for decades, right?"

"Protocol?"

Natalie shrugged, it was a political word, she knew. She was more familiar with politics than dating.

He held her with one arm, from the side, as they entered the restaurant. She welcomed the comfort in that close contact. And she shifted to holding his arm with one of hers as she spoke to the hostess at the station just inside the dim restaurant.

Joshua surveyed the place as Natalie negotiated with the gatekeeper at the reservations desk.

She kept her voice low, hoping Joshua wouldn't hear her pushing for a certain table that she liked. More calculations, probably. She was also self-conscious that this restaurant wasn't run by immortals. This place lacked the feeling of Jerusalem, and she knew the owners simply lived and worked right there in Oregon, instead of commuting from the throne. Would Joshua notice? Probably. Would he mind?

A brief duet of laughter between Natalie and the hostess pulled Joshua back from his inspection. He smiled like a man who missed a joke. She was glad he missed it. Brandy, the hostess, was teasing her about being on a date. The dark-skinned woman with curly blonde hair handed the menus to a stocky young woman with short hair bleached in streaks. The pasta blonde highlights caught the glow from the yellow lights along the walls and in the ceiling, leaving the feeling that those locks of hair floated along on their own through the dark restaurant, past the little islands of light at each table.

As they neared their table, Joshua joked. "Have you brought me to this dark restaurant so you can escape me, if necessary?"

"Will that be necessary?"

They had arrived at the table she wanted and were seated by the nervous, young waitress. Natalie regretted the young woman's mood. The server probably believed she was serving celebrities and would be scrutinized for her performance.

Before the young woman turned to walk away, Joshua touched her on the forearm, and made eye contact. "No worries, Andi. No worries."

Natalie didn't see him look at the girl's nametag.

"Oh." Andi perked up, as if he had surprised her. It must have been more than his words. Maybe there was something in that touch.

"Thanks." The waitress turned toward the kitchen with a smirk on her face.

Natalie was watching Joshua, waiting for an explanation.

"Habit. She was stressed about serving us. I think she should look forward to it, not dread it."

Natalie raised her eyebrows and allowed a chuckle. "Of course, she should. We're not the least bit scary."

"As far as *she* knows." Joshua grinned provocatively.

For the first time, Natalie actually giggled, but cut that short. *Act your age, Natalie.*

When they had settled in and ordered drinks, Joshua asked her about her parents.

Natalie took a deep breath and cast her eyes toward one of the dark corners of the room. "They're both gone. They were pretty old when they had me. Mom passed just two years ago. She was a hundred and sixty."

"Wow. So she had you when she was about seventy."

"She was a pioneer. No one knew what was possible." She shrugged. "I'm not sure we know everything, yet."

Joshua nodded slightly. He looked a bit distracted.

"You thinking about *your* parents?"

Snickering, Joshua confirmed her guess. He told her briefly about his parents and his own birth. Then he turned it back to Natalie.

"So, what did your parents do to inspire you to believe so deeply in the King and his Reign?"

She paused under the weight of that question. "I don't know. I don't think they hindered me at all. It was really my mentor, and the other immortals, who turned my heart so thoroughly toward the throne." She took a sip of water. "Joanna was my mentor when I was young. She was like a mother, or maybe a shepherdess, caring for me and leading me to good places, by little and by little."

Considering the man across the table from her, Natalie opted for diving deeper. "She was the one that convinced me that letting go of my life was the way to wake up and come alive. And she was the one who taught me to fly, about twenty-five years ago. Her ability to connect my heart with the deep love she had for me, and the love from the King, freed me from the laws of gravity. She used to say, 'The so-called laws of physics aren't really laws, just precedents.'" Natalie laughed. "I had studied law, of course."

Joshua laughed aloud. "That's a great analogy." He slowed his laugh. "That thought might just improve my flying."

Natalie grinned. "Gee, I was hoping we could go for an old-fashioned *walk* after dinner."

For the rest of the evening, their joking alternated with piercing revelations of their deepest feelings and thoughts. When they had finished small desserts, Andi brought them the electronic check. Joshua seized the little tablet, signing his name with his finger before Natalie could object. Given the guaranteed provision of the Reign, and the abundance of resources available to them, this was merely a token gesture. But Natalie sensed that Joshua had done it to catch *Andi's* attention, rather than to impress his date.

The young waitress hesitated when Joshua grabbed the tablet, and she waited for Joshua's signature rather than leave and return for it.

"So, Andi, how long have you been outside the walled city?"

The young woman glanced down at her clothing, as if looking for what had given her away. After that, she stared at him open-mouthed for a second. And then Natalie saw a tear form in her near eye. Andi wasn't the only one surprised by Joshua's insight, but she seemed more deeply moved by it than Natalie would have expected.

When Joshua motioned for Natalie to join in, she did what came naturally. She stood up and rested a sympathetic hand on Andi's shoulder. Joshua remained seated but slid his hand from Andi's forearm down to her shaking hand.

"Time to put together some of those broken pieces, I think."

Andi began to breathe hard, then to gasp and sob, until her whole body was heaving. Natalie tightened her grip around Andi's shoulders, shoring her up, as if the girl were a bridge under repair. Joshua began to address specific emotional wounds—accusations, loss and fear that had taken root from years and years of neglect and emotional abuse.

After five minutes, under the cover of the dark restaurant, Joshua gently pulled Andi into the empty chair next to him, and Natalie lowered herself back into her seat, leaning now toward the shorter woman who wept quiet tears. Andi spurted small exclamations, as childhood memories received some repair or adjustment.

Natalie expected that Joshua hadn't solved all of Andi's issues there that night. And she knew he didn't do this to impress her, though it was quite impressive. She could tell that he saw a need, as obvious to him as a broken-down vehicle parked on the side of the road. Joshua wasn't the sort of person who would merely offer best wishes and drive away from the stranded or suffering.

That small portion of the evening taught Natalie more about her dinner companion than the hours of conversation had. Though her view of it was incomplete, she was picking up some of the emotional communication passing between Joshua and Andi. The tone of that spiritual interaction showed her the purity and intensity of his ministrations. It also offered Natalie a good chance to calibrate her own intuitive abilities. She wasn't comparing herself to Joshua. But his advanced gift helped her understand more of what she often felt about people around her and couldn't articulate.

The hostess came in search of Andi, it seemed. She stopped her stealthy pursuit when she came upon the scene at Natalie and Joshua's table. Brandy's eyes relaxed when she saw that the waitress was receiving care from the famous healer. Natalie saw her turn back toward her post, pausing with instructions for another waiter along the way.

After some check-in and explanations, while Andi dirtied all the untouched napkins at the table, Joshua and Natalie finally rose from their seats. They wound their way back out into the cooling evening.

A slight chill invigorated Natalie's body and shook her from the soothing conversation and dreamlike encounter with the waitress. And Joshua seemed to lead the way in lightening the evening. The pair stepped up and down the hills of the restored city of Portland, joking and sharing stories from childhood.

Joshua told her about the time that he was nearly trampled to death by a stampede of wildebeest in the African central plains, discovering that the lion-and-lamb effect of the Reign wasn't as automatic as it sounded. Theresa, along with another immortal, rescued the twenty-two-year-old Joshua from learning that lesson the hard way. He confessed that it was one of the times he felt like he was just there for the entertainment of the saints.

"They teased me that the herd just wanted to lie down with me. But it wasn't clear to me just where we were gonna do that."

"You mean you don't speak wildebeest?"

"Well, I was young then. I'm sure I could tame them *now*."

"We'll just have to give that a try, some time."

Even as Joshua's reminiscence reminded her that they could transport to any part of the planet—to watch the sunset in the mountains of Alaska, to stand behind a great waterfall in the Amazon basin, to sit in the tall grass among herds of elephant and giraffe—Natalie was glad to be walking with him on cobblestone streets hand-in-hand in her hometown.

CHAPTER FORTY-SIX

Brice Katonah was getting a new assignment. Instead of supervising one children's home, he would take over the entire network of North American homes for rescued kids. He was getting a promotion in the fight against the dysfunctional system of hodgepodge rebel governments.

He had been hired to replace Ray Martinez. Ray was taking a job in India, where he would directly work with children from the walled city in the Himalayan Mountains. Ray said he was excited to get back to face-to-face interactions with the children. To Brice it seemed like a demotion. But that was no shame in the free world. They weren't competing for accolades or money.

Today, the transition between supervisors was being facilitated by a virtual face-to-face across the Internet. The holographic images were clear and almost convincing. One of the images joining him in his office was that of Joshua Stippleman. He was the star of the rescue program. Brice's intention in this call was to introduce himself. But he kept slipping into fan mode.

"I just hope I can do justice to what you do—I mean, not get in your way, or anything." He paused, hearing himself do that crawl below humility, into groveling. "But I guess I can do it, because they appointed me to this position." He tried to sound more than half-convinced.

Ray replied, certainly hearing Brice's fake confidence. "So, Joshua, do you have a suggestion for how to start Brice out in his new position?" He and Joshua exchanged a smile over the virtual link.

This was one of those times when Brice was on the outside looking in. He often felt that around the immortals. Working with Joshua would probably be like that.

"You should come out with me, to see some of the kids at Mirabelle." Joshua spoke directly to Brice.

Brice nodded. That sounded like a good idea, though he knew there were logistical limits to how close he could get with the kids when they met with a therapist or healer. He was thinking about how that would work when someone suddenly appeared in his office.

Brice squeaked his surprise. Instant regret at that loss of dignity jumped away as he tried to grasp what had just happened. Joshua was now in his office. His arrival had created a brief breeze, the first hint that Brice wasn't just seeing a glitch in the hologram. He was seeing a real person in place of the bluish image he was looking at up till now.

"Wait, you can do that? Why didn't anybody tell me that you could do that? How ...?" Brice had launched from his chair and slammed his legs against his desk, which scooted forward six inches on the smooth wood floor.

Joshua laughed. Even still, he tilted his head in a sympathetic way.

Brice took a deep breath and let himself laugh along.

Joshua bypassed Brice's blurted question. "I want to show you what I do, show you the kids, and how they first come into the free world. But there aren't any rescues on right now, so we should go to Mirabelle and see who's still there."

All of this came without formal introductions and not even a pause for a breath.

Brice was still catching *his* breath.

"You mean, just pop over there, just like that?" Brice fanned his raised hand at the spot on the floor on which Joshua had just materialize.

Joshua looked back at that spot. He did pause for a moment. "It's perfectly safe. Safer than bullet trains and bicycles."

Brice nodded without answering. It felt a lot like the time he climbed up to the high dive when he was ten.

As if reading this in Brice's mind, Joshua began to catalog all the times he had transported himself and others, with not a disaster in the whole history of those impossible feats. It was hard to argue the basic point, because the tall man making that point now stood in Brice's office in Denver. He had been in Chicago a few seconds before.

Laughter in the background reminded Brice that Ray was still linked to his office. His presence was still virtual, however.

"I'll let you two gentlemen get to it." Ray ended his part of the call, still chuckling.

Had Ray ever been transported? Was that why he was laughing?

Joshua held out a hand as if for a shake. And Brice reached for that hand, wondering if he had agreed to anything yet. He was still working on this when they landed in the back yard of a large house.

"Ah!" And he couldn't stop the hysterical giggles that came after that sharp expulsion of air.

"Holy ... I mean, wow."

Arching his back slightly as if to make room for his chuckles, Joshua just watched Brice adjusting to the new experience.

The most bizarre part of what was happening, in Brice's head, was a little debate about whether *he* could do something like that. It would actually be very practical at times like this.

The next stream of thought was much less hopeful. He realized that he was Joshua's prisoner now. How was he going to get back to Denver? And where in the world ...? *Nebraska. That was where in the world.*

CHAPTER FORTY-SEVEN

Theresa arrived a second after Joshua and Brice, appearing just behind them. She cleared her throat to warn them of her arrival. That feminine sound reminded Joshua of that night just four days ago when he had last met Natalie. He turned and smiled at Theresa.

"Why am I here?" She smiled at Brice now, asking the question he might ask when his head cleared. "I'm here to translate for you, so you can understand what Joshua is doing inside the hearts of the kids."

She was waiting for Brice to settle his nerves and get himself oriented to what was happening. He seemed to be undergoing a kind of rapid immersion therapy cooked up by Joshua and the King.

Joshua nodded toward the back door and led the way to the house. The back door was already being unlocked by electronic controls as Joshua reached for the bell. Theresa knew that Shari, the director of Mirabelle, had received advanced notice from Thomas, her mentor.

Inside the big old house, immaculately restored and maintained, the three visitors could hear someone coming down the stairs at a fair pace. Joshua smiled in anticipation of seeing an old friend. But Brice was holding his breath.

"Joshua." Shari smiled her greeting when she reached the bottom of the stairs. "Thomas told me you were coming." She looked at Brice. "And he said you were bringing a special guest."

"He knew ...?" Brice wasn't quite caught up yet.

Joshua introduced Brice. And Shari got right to business. "I don't feel like it's a coincidence that you're here now. We have a hard case that we need to make a decision on. She's driven everyone on the staff to tears at least once." She took a deep breath. "Well, nearly everyone."

"Okay. I would like Brice and Theresa to monitor on camera, so he can better understand our work."

Shari nodded. "I already sent Ken and Lydia to try to move her to one of the playrooms. Her name is Jezz, short for what you would expect. Come on up to my office for some more background."

In her office, seated behind her desk, Shari told Joshua and Brice about the girl they would be meeting today. Theresa listened to Shari at the same time she listened to the heart of the King.

"Jezebel Lacoste lived in the far Northwest, one of the smaller of the walled cities. The city, named Goldrush, had abandoned its walls before they were finished. Living with her parents, her father a security officer and her mother a travel agent, Jezz spent a lot of time with her maternal grandmother for the first few years. From the grandmother, she had inherited the family's legacy of hatred for the aliens. The grandmother lost two children to the King when he returned. She had seen those children later, but she hated the aliens even more for the way they had changed her kids.

"That hate had passed to her daughters and to her granddaughter by the time the grandmother died of cancer, refusing all help from the 'aliens.' Her eldest daughter, Jezz's mother, built a travel business that specialized in thrill destinations within the realm of the Reign. Her mother, Diane Lacoste, has led many of these tours herself, leaving Jezz at home with a nanny. It seems the nanny ignored the girl most of the time.

"Jezz's father worked long and unpredictable hours, or so he told his wife and daughter. While his security job, working for the administration of Goldrush, did require a rotating schedule of hours both daytime and night, much of the time he spent away from his family had nothing to do with work. While Jezz didn't know the details of his infidelities, she knew something was wrong.

"By age ten, Jezz had experimented with familiar forms of attention-getting misbehavior. When those failed, she turned desperate, attempting to set the house on fire, releasing the family car onto a busy street, and telling authority figures grandiose lies about the abuse she was suffering at home.

"The immortals began to consider her rescue when it became clear that the one core value she shared with her parents, and the one thing she held onto with all her might, was fear and hatred for the aliens and their king. The immortals intervened because her family fed her only with hate, which was poisoning her soul. Jerusalem decided that Jezz needed rescue before she harmed herself or someone else.

"Whether Jezz *could* be rescued is still debatable." Shari looked at Joshua at this point.

Theresa knew that Shari was feeling a bit desperate, not an unfamiliar state in her job. But she also knew that Shari trusted Joshua and his skills.

With Brice, Theresa settled into the viewing room next to one of the therapy/playrooms in the house. Three cameras would give them varying angles on what transpired in that room. The viewing room was used for the protection of both child and therapist, recording interactions to document what did, and what didn't, occur in the room. But the cameras also allowed others to observe the private interaction between therapist and child, where a visible observer would change the balance, muddying the mix of personalities.

Having Brice and Theresa in the room with Joshua and Jezz would have been unthinkable. As many myths as Jezz thought she knew about the aliens, she was quite good at detecting a real immortal when she sat in their presence. For Jezz and others, a sort of spiritual aroma entered the room when Theresa or one of her companions was present.

To get Jezz into that playroom, Frederique, an immortal who worked often at Mirabelle, had to transport Jezz against her will. Joshua would be in a locked cage with a frightened young girl. This was his specialty.

Jezz was a solid girl of average height and slightly above average weight. Her hair had been cut in what used to be called a pageboy style, and then dyed white, light blue and purple, in vertical stripes. This was popular among young people, especially in Goldrush. But Jezz was younger than most kids who wore their hair this way.

She fixed Joshua with her large brown eyes, a snarl forming on her lips. Jezz had seen very little of the aliens she had been so effectively taught to fear, but she believed that she was seeing one now. Something about this man was unusual—not normal, not human. On the other hand, Theresa knew that Joshua didn't fit neatly into what Jezz thought she knew about the aliens.

Her momentary confusion about what sort of man this was didn't stop her snarl. And she launched herself at Joshua, certainly expecting that he would avoid violence by any means available. But Joshua allowed Jezz to land her awkward two-handed punch in the middle of his chest. She weighed less than half as much as Joshua, but she had two steps to build momentum. Her blow landed with a "whump" and a slight moan from Joshua.

As Joshua winced in pain, Jezz recoiled. She stood back and stared dumfounded at him. She hadn't expected to actually land that punch. She had no idea how to deal with what had just happened. She couldn't apologize, because she had done it on purpose. Part of her regrouping was certainly to consider whether she had been wrong about this man being an alien.

Theresa explained Joshua's decision to Brice, who was sitting with his arms crossed over his chest and one hand over his mouth. "He knows that it was risky to let her hit him. Generally, we don't allow it, for their own good. Later they will most likely suffer guilt, and even shame, at having hurt someone. So we try to spare them that when possible. Joshua believes that it is worth risking that feeling of guilt, in order to convince Jezz that he is first, human, and second, not her enemy. He also calculated accurately that she would not hurt *herself* in the process. I believe he even refrained from tightening his muscles so as to soften her landing."

Brice gasped at that little detail.

Joshua began to breathe normally again, after a few seconds. He smiled slightly at Jezz—a soft smile, not taunting her. He would let her hit him again, if she chose to. But neither he nor Theresa believed Jezz would try another physical attack.

Jezz slowly turned away from Joshua. She squatted in the opposite corner, pretending interest in a carefully carved wooden truck.

"You'd rather be running and kicking a ball, than sitting in this tight little room with a truck and a strange man." Joshua spoke sympathetically.

Theresa described to Brice Jezz's internal agreement with that statement. Equally, she felt the girl's refusal to give in to the opening which that agreement invited.

Jezz remained with her round back toward Joshua, her bright pink shirt stretched tight as she hovered over the painted wooden truck.

"My name is Joshua."

"I'm Jezebel." She pronounced her name defiantly, as if she knew how rebellious that name sounded in this part of the world.

"I know." He spoke sedately, his tone coasting down a bit.

Joshua looked at one of the hidden cameras and communicate wordlessly to Theresa. She knew what he wanted and sent a silent message through her divine network.

"We're going to do a bit of traveling." Theresa alerted Brice.

"Traveling?" A weary sigh completed his mostly rhetorical question.

Back inside the playroom, Joshua tried again to get a response from Jezz. "You like soccer, I think."

"Or football." Jezz corrected Joshua. Her response implied that she was listening, at least.

"Yeah, football. That's what I meant."

Jezz didn't say anything.

"Wanna go and kick a ball around?"

Jezz continued to focus on the toy truck.

"I'll take us to a really beautiful football field high up in the mountains."

Jezz looked up at him, perhaps distracted from her resistance by the strangeness of his offer. "You're one of them, then?"

"An alien? No. I was born in Iowa a hundred years ago, and never left this planet. I'm as human as you are."

"So, yer gonna let one of them aliens take us to some far-off place to play soccer?"

"No, I can do it."

She just shook her head. Theresa could tell that Jezz was confused by Joshua's claims, but very curious. She shared this with Brice.

Joshua persisted. "The new mountain-top stadium near Santiago, Chile is wonderful. I'll take you. Someone will meet us there with a ball."

Theresa explained that Jezz was now calculating whether this bizarre playdate might be a way to escape, even if she wasn't sure where Chile was.

Joshua could tell that Jezz wanted to go, but he was waiting for some external sign of assent. He wouldn't transport her against her will if he didn't have to.

"Who's gonna be there?"

"A friend of mine, a woman who plays soccer all over the world. She's one of the greatest mortal players, and not a lot bigger than you. She's from Chile."

"I suppose that's better than this dumb old truck." Jezz stood and ventured a brief look at Joshua before studying the carpet at his feet.

"Hang on for a ride." Joshua and Jezz vanished from the room.

Theresa and Brice followed. They landed in the fourth row of seats in the magnificent stadium which hosted a variety of events but was most famous for its soccer teams. On the field below, they saw three very distinct figures—Joshua, over six feet tall, sandy-brown hair and broad shoulders; Jezz, a stout ten-year-old in bright pink tee shirt and purple shorts; and Rafi Sanchez. At only five-foot-one, Rafi was closer to Jezz's size. But her skin was the color of maple syrup, her hair black with golden highlights. She was dancing with a soccer ball, playing it with each part of her body in turn, juggling and dribbling. To Jezz and to Brice, it certainly looked like showing off. But Theresa knew that this was just a normal warm-up for Rafi.

Immaculate grass framed the three figures in green, as Theresa and Brice watched. Rafi did do a bit of showing off. For one, she turned away, kicked the ball high above her head and did a back flip, bicycle-kicking the ball to Jezz. Most amazing was the way that gymnastic pass landed gently at Jezz's feet.

The girl had clearly played enough soccer to instinctively receive the pass. Rafi seemed to note Jezz's ease with that pass and picked up the pace when Jezz kicked it back to her. The ball banked off Rafi's head before she stepped back and caught it on her chest, then onto her thighs and then back to Jezz.

Jezz surprised Joshua with the next pass. And the game was on—each one passing, receiving and showing off a little. Joshua had played soccer from when he was a child, but, lately, he only touched a ball in situations like this, with children for whom it was a medium of connection. For Jezz, this connection was more open than with any of the rescued ones Joshua had met recently.

When Theresa looked at Rafi, she recalled a pugnacious little girl who wouldn't talk, but who would play pass and dribble with Joshua all day, if he was willing. Theresa could see now that Rafi was observing her likeness in this little, freckle-faced girl from the North.

Theresa began to explain this history to Brice, speaking quietly enough not to call attention to the people in the stands. She explained that Jezz was captivated by the experience because the adults were demanding very little of her, and she had the attention of a very pleasant man and woman. With the ball at her feet and Rafi's skills stirring her imagination, Jezz had no time to worry or fear. It was a sort of brainwashing.

Theresa had often heard Joshua joke that brainwashing shouldn't be so despised. After all, who wants a dirty brain?

Brice laughed with his hand over his mouth at this comment.

Rafi said something in Spanish to Joshua. He translated for Jezz. "She says you play like a wild tiger."

Theresa knew the fierceness that Rafi was observing, the gritted teeth and furrowed brow, along with cat-like agility. But she wondered why Rafi, who spoke English herself, had said this in Spanish. Instead of pausing to figure this out, Theresa narrated what was being said, so Brice could keep up. She also provided some commentary on what Joshua was learning from watching Jezz and listening to her soul. But she wanted Brice to see more deeply.

"Do you want me to show you what Joshua is feeling, more than just hearing me describe it?"

"Ah, okay. Sure." Of course, he had no idea what he was agreeing to. But Theresa loved his childlike willingness.

For a few seconds, she connected to Brice's heart and then linked it to Jezz's. There he could sense her freedom and joy in the game they were playing on the field. But that light was surrounded by darkness. Theresa showed him how Jezz was numbing herself against the weight of a great pain about her parents, and against some confusion about the hate that was her family legacy. Theresa only allowed a brief sampling of this direct connection, knowing that Brice wasn't used to that sort of emotional link. She had worked long and hard with Joshua to teach him how to endure the intense anger and fear of others when their heart connected with his.

Joshua and Rafi finished their game when Jezz showed signs of getting too tired to enjoy it anymore. After Rafi proposed to meet with Jezz again, perhaps at Mirabelle, Joshua persuaded Jezz to go back to the house for a cool drink and snack.

She was a good athlete, but not in good condition. The twenty-some minutes of intense play was all she could take. This was part of Joshua's plan, in fact, wearing her out with some fun activity in order to take away some of her energy to fight. She would sleep well that night, and not be so much trouble in the hours before bed.

Rafi shook hands with Jezz and said goodbye in English. The transformation in the girl's mood was clear, if not complete. She actually smiled as Rafi turned to leave the field.

As Rafi dribbled and juggled her way into the stadium tunnel, Jezz turned to Joshua.

"So, is this how the reprogramming works? I mean, is it always this fun?"

Joshua let loose a grand laugh, smacking himself on the thigh. "Yes, it *is* usually this fun." His voice settled. "We don't want anything from you, Jezz. We're here to help you. And whatever helps is what we'll do, anywhere in the world, anything you need. That's the way the King takes care of people."

Still serious, Jezz squinted at Joshua, against the bright sun just visible over the top of the stadium. "I might be okay with this, then."

As hopeful as that sounded, Theresa knew that Jezz had no idea what she could take and what she needed. Neither could she anticipate the power of missing her parents, or the loneliness of living in a strange new world. But it was a start. Joshua, the staff of Mirabelle, and eventually Brice, would do all they could to provide her a joyful and resolved life.

All the travelers returned to the rooms at Mirabelle, where the adults debriefed with Shari, while Greta delivered a healthy snack to the exhausted girl. Then Joshua and Brice returned to Brice's office, where they sat down and talked about the experience, as well as the job ahead.

CHAPTER FORTY-EIGHT

After that day of five transports—from home to Brice's office, to Mirabelle, to Chile, to Mirabelle and back home—Joshua was ready for some geographical stability. That he had mastered the physics of transporting, didn't immunize him from the effects of hurtling from place to place without the normal human process of travel and movement. Though it was perhaps not physically tiring, nevertheless, Joshua had noticed a bit of transport-lag since he had begun doing more of it on his own.

In the morning, Joshua attended a video conference, of the 2D kind, and then spent time meditating, to clear his mind and focus on the mind of the King. He knew he needed to do this more often than he had lately and resolved to set a new habit.

Another habit he revisited was cycling with Peter Welch, the neighbor in the apartment below Franny. The three of them had biked together, but Joshua and Peter had a similar pace and compatible preferences for cycling. They had explored the expanding network of trails around Chicago several times.

Peter knew more about those trails than most people. He worked with the parks and recreation administration for the area and knew who to consult about new trails or improvements to existing trails. Infrastructure work was being done constantly, by mortals and immortals. So tracking new development was part of the fun.

A brick-and-mortar kind of guy, Peter understood less about Joshua's work than Joshua understood his. But they bypassed that with conversation that stayed close to the ground and the spin of their wheels.

At one o'clock in the afternoon, Peter was available for a ride, his work schedule as flexible as that of Joshua and so many others in the new economy. Though it wasn't directly part of his responsibility, Peter arranged to check some of the new work for his colleagues in charge of improvements. A few photos and a short video would fulfill that commitment.

Peter devoted much more time than Joshua to fitness and bodybuilding and showed it with a brawny physique suited to a professional athlete. Joshua was a natural athlete and outdoorsman, but weighed forty pounds less than Peter, though three inches taller.

Squashing his thick, black curls under his helmet, Peter teased Joshua, where they stood behind their building straddling their bikes. "Even if they can heal your brain, it still hurts until they do." He was referring to Joshua's decision to ride without a helmet.

Joshua didn't explain his new success, limited though it was, with flying. He just let Peter think of him as daring and carefree—which he was, sort of. This was a fun ride, and Joshua put little thought into any prospect of injury.

The day was perfect. Eighty degrees Fahrenheit, with a breeze and low humidity. They lived north of the greatly reduced downtown area. Their planned route that day would go north, out toward what used to be the suburbs of Chicago, before the earthquakes and wars that preceded the King's return.

The immortals had implemented a dispersed urban development that integrated green space and agricultural areas with residential neighborhoods and commercial property. They had also begun to alter the landscape to more closely resemble the natural geology of the area. The template they were using predated most humans who had ever lived in the land around the southwest shore of Lake Michigan. Where the former urban development had striven to eliminate hills, valleys, woodlands and wetlands, the new regime turned back the clock to a time long before a tight grid of streets and high-rise architecture.

Joshua and Peter sailed over smooth pavement, through lofty corridors of full-grown elm and oak and poplar trees. As usual, Peter took the lead, being more familiar with the pathways and a more powerful rider. Joshua teased him about breaking the wind for him, given his greater girth. But the wind ruffled Joshua's hair and he grinned into forty-mile-an-hour resistance when they hit top speed.

Joshua was enjoying the connection between effort and result, the physical sensation of propelling himself. Even more than a commuter of previous generations, conveyed by planes or automobiles, Joshua was accustomed to being carried by the efforts of others, either natural or supernatural. He owned no vehicle beside the bicycle and did most of his traveling by train or instant transport. He loved the feeling of his legs driving him into a headwind.

Peter, in contrast to Joshua, still felt the need to prove himself. He would have been quite uncomfortable if he had known how much of this emotional laundry was obvious for Joshua to see. But Joshua chose not to focus on the posturing and comparing—laughing it off and granting Peter the victory wherever he craved it.

They both enjoyed the woods and prairies along the pathway, and Peter often slowed down when there was something particularly beautiful to see. This is what he was doing near a series of bogs, interlaced with stands of maple and ash. Instead of the trees, however, Peter slowed suddenly at the sight of another kind of beauty.

A golden-haired woman sprinted through the trees, trailing a gossamer gown along with her flowing hair. Joshua saw Peter slow in time to avoid a collision, and then saw what had distracted his riding companion.

Something about the young woman, an immortal no doubt, struck Joshua as odd and unrealistic. Of course, the definition of realistic included a long list of amendments these days. Nevertheless, the young woman had an air of fantasy to her, or perhaps it was a sort of dramatic fiction.

Suddenly, the young woman vanished, as if she had run behind a tree and stayed hidden there. The problem with that interpretation was that the tree she had disappeared behind was a slender sumac tree, and her pace made stopping behind it seem very unlikely.

Peter swerved and stopped. Again, Joshua had to avoid a crash, stopping suddenly and getting his feet onto the path with little warning. Before they could say anything to each other, a man who looked a bit older than Joshua stepped out onto the path. He wore a cowboy hat, baggy gym shorts and a long tee shirt that nearly reached his knees. He was barefoot but walked like a man who had nothing to fear in the whole natural world.

"Got your attention, did I?" The stranger laughed.

This comment made no sense to Joshua at first. Then he connected the odd stranger to the vision of loveliness that had slowed their ride.

"I'm thinking about making this like one of them amusement park rides. You know, you ride through the forest and enter an enchanted kingdom, etc. etc."

"Enchanted?" Peter stared with his mouth half open and his brow clenched.

"Are you the spirit of the forest, then?" Joshua tried to play along. "A wood nymph, perhaps?"

The cowboy hat began to bob and the stranger snorted a laugh so unselfconscious that it infected both of the mortals standing over their bicycles.

Peter was just catching up. "Wait. So, are you a guy or a girl?"

This opened the throttle wider on that slurping and snorting laughter. The cowboy hat was off now, the skinny little man using it to smack his knees and flail the air.

"Well, I suppose that would matter if you was thinkin' about askin' me out on a date." The stranger snorted and guffawed some more. "But that ain't gonna be part of my amusement park ride."

Joshua had enough experience with the immortals to wonder what the real agenda was for this meeting. He knew that the citizens of Jerusalem were free to play around in the woods if they wanted. They could transform themselves into different shapes and sizes. But they generally did that on their own time, out of sight of mortals, as far as he knew.

"I'm thinkin' you're messing with us." Joshua felt some responsibility to translate for Peter.

Peter's blank eyes implied that he needed a translator, or perhaps a guide.

"Well, Joshua, my boy, you got an unfair advantage in breakin' up my game here. But I'll grant you that. It was Pete, here, that I was really trying to mess with."

"Me? Why me?"

The stranger almost looked serious for a moment, eying Peter as if sizing him for a team uniform. As he kept his focus on Peter, the stranger appeared to Joshua to be changing. It was subtle at first, but the stranger wasn't quite as skinny as he had been when he first sauntered out of the woods. From his stick-like legs to his rail-thin arms and beanstalk neck, the odd little man began to expand, to grow, to beef up. To Joshua, it seemed as if the stranger was morphing to look more like Peter.

To Peter, *nothing* seemed obvious about this encounter. "Hey, what are you doing? Are you changing again? What's this about?"

After a minute of gradual transformation, the big and buff stranger kept laughing. His laugh grew deeper, reverberating through his expansive chest.

"What is this?" Peter turned to Joshua now.

"What's your name?" Joshua asked the stranger.

"I am Leon." The man was now taller than Joshua and heftier than Peter.

"Leon as in Lion?"

Leon's handsome face grinned before he lifted his head to the sky and roared like a lion. It wasn't a man imitating a lion. Not even a very life-like imitation. It was the roar of a lion.

Though any of the immortals could perform all these tricks and illusions, Joshua felt now that he knew who this was standing in front of them—an immortal, but not just *any* immortal.

Joshua began to shake slightly, as soon as he realized who had interrupted their ride in the woods. Peter was quaking violently too, but he might not have understood why.

Leon began yet another transformation, converting to the form Joshua had seen before, the one most people expected to see of the King who reigned in glorious light. Joshua still suspected that this new form was more muscularly imposing than the way most people saw the King.

"Who ...?" Peter's shaking intensified, becoming more like a vibration, a vibration that dislodged something in his emotions. He began to weep. And these were not dainty tears, not subtle sobs, or gentle sniffles. Peter heaved and wailed and bawled.

Joshua hadn't yet witnessed any evidence that Peter understood what was happening. In his own shaken state, his intuitions seemed to be jammed by an overwhelming interference. That didn't stop Joshua's curiosity. But he knew when to give up and wait for further instructions.

As soon as he settled into that posture, Joshua could hear a familiar, gentle voice in his head. "Just relax and be available to Peter when all this is done. He will need you to explain and help him recover."

Joshua began to snicker, and then giggle and chuckle. Relaxing had become disassembling, his tighter parts becoming the looser, until not a single thought seemed possible to hold from beginning to end. He just laughed.

In that relaxed state, Joshua began to see a sort of mental movie of what was happening to Peter. Dumbstruck and nearing panic, his friend was searching for the meaning of this intrusion on his fun and carefree life. The feeling Joshua found first, when searching in Peter's soul, was betrayal. It was as if Peter and the King had a tacit agreement that they would not interfere with each other's lives.

The King stepped up to Peter now, taking hold of his bicycle, just as the stunned man lost his ability to stand, withering like a parched vine draped over his bike.

Joshua dropped his bike and lunged to catch Peter. The King hadn't asked for this assistance, but, as usual, Joshua felt free to act out of instinct. Like the rescued children from the walled cities, Peter would probably welcome a mortal touch in the face of infinite power.

Smiling at Joshua, the King said nothing, still waiting for something, it seemed.

Perhaps that something was the settling of the muscular young man onto the bike path, resting on his back and still bawling uncontrollably. At that point, Joshua sensed that Peter's feeling of betrayal had moved aside, returning him to the cathartic spin that had started him weeping.

The King addressed Peter, squatting next to him and looking at him as one might examine the first shoots sprouting in a vegetable garden. "You are welcome to stay in my world, Peter, to continue on as you have been. That is your choice. You have the right to that private path through your life. I just wanted to offer you more. You have told yourself that it is wise to take all the benefits of my kingdom, and not be like those rebels who wall themselves away. But that is not the only choice, not the end of choices."

Joshua could see a change in Peter's sobs. He had begun to breathe more evenly. Now Peter attempted another spoken question.

"Why ... what ... what am I crying about?"

The King nodded and sat down, his legs crossed and elbows resting on his knees. He was still wearing those floppy shorts and the too big tee shirt. But they fit him more closely now. They also made sitting on the rubbery pavement easy.

"My presence so close to you, in a way that you cannot ignore, has awakened a part of you that is full of feelings—feelings of all sorts. My appearance broke the dam on those emotions. You did not store them there consciously, and they came loose in the same way, without conscious effort."

"What are you gonna do to me?" His voice sounded squeezed in his throat, but his sobbing had stopped completely.

The King reached out a hand to help the big man to his feet. Joshua grabbed Peter's near arm.

"'*Do* to you?' What do you *want* me to do to you? That's why I'm here, to give you a chance to put some thought into that question."

Joshua shook his head at the consternation that clasped Peter's face. This would not all be settled in one encounter. As amazing as it was, seeing the King and feeling his hands lift him off the pavement was not enough to bring Peter into the kingdom. The possibility that he would continue on as a free-riding passenger seemed very real. From Joshua's personal life, this made absolutely no sense. From his experience with survivors from the world outside the Reign, it was predictable.

The King, however, wasn't finished unfolding the offer he had brought to Peter. Still holding Peter's hand, he leaned forward and began to whisper in his ear. Whether he still would have done that if Joshua wasn't there, Joshua could only guess. Certainly, it was an intimate way to communicate. What it stirred, as far as Joshua could sense, was a memory.

Peter's soul opened to a time early in life, when he was playing, he was free, perhaps in a grassy field. Whatever the specifics, Peter's memory of that time was full of joy and freedom, full of possibility and hope. He was probably alone, physically, but he felt something there—some*one* there. That feeling intrigued and enticed him. It was as if the pilot light inside his soul had been turned up to ignite his whole heart, to begin a burning expectation of the future.

Joshua followed that little boy into a time when he shared his experience of that loving presence with family members. There the flame was doused. Fear is what Peter got as a response from his family. Certainly, there would have been warnings from them about the dangers of entertaining such flights of fancy, yielding to emotions and dreams. Even if Peter doubted the truth of their warnings back then, years of growing up in the world would have reinforced that fear since.

The King was reminding Peter of that moment, explaining who it was that had whispered an offer to that boy. But he didn't push now for a life commitment from Peter. Peter wasn't being compelled to sign on the dotted line, or to make even a verbal vow. The invitation would remain open ... always ... as Joshua well knew.

Riding their bicycles again, back toward home, Joshua and Peter remained silent for a long time. They had abandoned their original plan, related to Peter's work. Now they pedaled pensively.

As they approached their neighborhood, still cruising at a leisurely pace, Peter finally asked Joshua a question. "You understand all that went on back there?" His voice had lost almost all the awestruck wonder and childlike submissiveness the encounter had inspired. But his tone was still vulnerable and intense. Something had changed for him.

Joshua answered briefly. "I think I do understand. And I'll be glad to work through it with you."

"This is the kinda stuff you do, isn't it?"

Joshua tipped his head to the side slightly, as Peter looked over at him. "It's not exactly what I do for work, but it is pretty familiar territory. I'm confident I can help you as much as you want it."

Another silence accompanied them for half the remaining distance home. Then Peter spoke again. "That's really it, isn't it? That's the question. How much do I want? How much am I willing to let myself change?"

"Yep. That's how it is for all of us. That's what true freedom is."

Peter shook his head and snorted. "I wouldn't trust people with so much freedom, if I was him."

Joshua laughed lightly. These words from Peter heartened Joshua. From them, he could tell that his friend really did understand what the King had offered him.

CHAPTER FORTY-NINE

"So, at what point did you figure out that Leon was really the Lion of Judah?" Natalie reclined against a chestnut tree overlooking a field of wild daisies.

Joshua answered without looking away from the scene of hundreds of white blossoms grooving with the wind. "I didn't really figure it out. It just popped out of my mouth without much warning." He turned his head toward her.

"Do you think he was waiting for *you* to reveal his identity? Or did you just shortcut the process?"

"There was a reason he appeared to Peter while I was there." He turned his whole upper body toward her now. "And I don't think it was just to play a good joke on me about all those transformations—beautiful wood nymph to roaring king. Though I could tell he was enjoying that."

Natalie laughed. She was skipping over a bit of envy at Joshua's description of that beautiful woman. She diverted herself to a more serious question.

"If I hang around with you, then, I'll get to hang out with the King?"

Again, her voice betrayed her a little. All his stories about seeing the King in various contexts had stirred another kind of envy in her. Though Joshua hadn't said anything about her limited experience seeing the Lord, she wanted him to. She wanted to know what he thought about that. Yet she was afraid to ask outright.

A long, gentle look from Joshua reminded her that he could feel more of her frustration than what she let slip into her tone of voice.

"Some people need him to appear to them. They won't believe unless he shows himself. Some people get totally strange about it, when it happens to them. It's not even a positive experience for them. But, with all that in mind, I'm confident he knows just the time and place to meet with you next."

Natalie looked away, considering the daisies and their dance music on the breeze.

He continued in a sedate tone. "Meeting with him in Jerusalem is a different experience for everyone, too." He paused until she renewed their eye contact. "I suspect your time with him there is more intimate than for others."

Natalie exhaled some of her tension. "Yes. I feel the truth of that when you say it. I'm just being the typical kid, longing for the toy the *other* kids have, and not genuinely appreciating what I've been given."

"You don't really feel like you're deprived, or that he's withholding something from you."

"That's right. I know you're right." Perhaps he could see her soul more clearly than she could, at least sometimes.

She relaxed back into enjoying those flowers and the leaves of the big tree.

"I don't even know where we are." It was an embarrassing admission.

Joshua laughed much louder and more freely than she expected. He turned bright red. "Neither do I." And he snorted before reining himself in.

For a moment, Natalie assumed he was just kidding, that he *did* know where they were, and was just teasing her. But the volume and duration of his laughter changed her mind on that. "Wait. You *really* don't know where we are?"

Joshua curbed his laughter. "I have a confession." He checked as if to judge how much trouble he was going to be in. "When you messaged me about where you were, I misunderstood. I thought you were saying you were leaving your office and were heading for home. So, when I transported to see you, I was aiming for your house." He paused to catch his breath.

Intrigued by this roundabout explanation, Natalie interrupted. "You popped over to my house before you met me."

Joshua was already shaking his head. "I went directly to your office, even though I was aiming at your house." He sat, nodding as Natalie tried to absorb this fact. "I checked the message again, when I landed in your office parking lot, and saw my mistake. But that made me wonder how I got redirected to the correct destination. I wasn't aiming to see your house, after all, I was transporting to see *you*. So I figure that's what happened, even though I didn't know where you were."

"Like a homing device?"

"Kind of romantic, don't you think?" He offered a sheepish grin this time.

He had never used the word "romantic" around her before. She wanted to camp there, but still needed the rest of the explanation about where they were.

Apparently, he saw her continued confusion. "So I checked with Theresa while I stood in the parking lot. And she explained that geography isn't nearly so important as it used to be. In the King's world, the people are more important than the places. We don't even have to know where we are in order to get to someone we want to see."

Natalie realized she had furrowed her brow tightly. She forced herself to soften her expression. She was still holding onto that comment about a romantic attraction.

He finally got to the answer to their mysterious whereabouts. "So, once I grasped what Theresa was saying, I just decided to take us to a beautiful field, under a shady tree. I didn't specify where."

Natalie nodded slowly. "Ooooohhhh. You didn't specify. Wow." She grinned at him. "That's really deep." She laughed at herself and then stared wide-eyed, first at Joshua and then at the beautiful scene to which they had been transported.

"I mean, it's not really me that's doing the transporting anyway. It's the King, right? So he can send us where he wants. It's like riding a wave, you just have to get on it and it'll take you on the ride you're looking for."

Her speechless surprise was clearly compelling Joshua to keep talking, trying to make sense of what he had done. But she didn't mind listening to him, even if he was trying to justify himself—and even if he didn't know where they were.

That drew out a serious thought from her. "Maybe I should just enjoy meeting the King right in the middle of my daily life, at times like this. I don't need a visit like Peter got."

Joshua tipped his head, apparently impressed. "That sounds right. He brought us here because he thought it was a beautiful place for us to sit. He's with us, at least in that way."

And the King was in her head. It was enough, for now.

CHAPTER FIFTY

The next day, back in Chicago, Joshua put in a request for a visit from Theresa. Though he was adjusting to not thinking of her as his mentor, and more of a partner, he still needed her counsel on important matters, especially matters of the heart. Theresa had learned things about Joshua that others would need to download from the throne. She had *experienced* his life with him, watched him grow. He respected what she had to say out of that reservoir of experience.

Joshua was walking along the lakefront when Theresa arrived.

She spoke over the sound of the wind. "You said it."

Joshua laughed. Reading each other's thoughts, to some extent, shortened the introductory matter in their conversations.

"Well, I didn't say *it*."

"You didn't say you were in love with her." Theresa tossed the hair off her face, allowing the lake breeze to comb it for her.

Joshua snickered. They had been over this territory before, when he was much younger.

Theresa responded to that echo from the past. "You've grown up now, become what you are supposed to be. Back then you were still longing to grow up and be like one of us."

Her assessment wasn't something Joshua would dispute. He saw no shame in wanting to be like one of the glorious ones, the ones who circled the throne every day and lived free of all cares and concerns.

"You made a commitment to celibacy, and renewed that commitment several times—sometimes informally, when offered something else by women you met along the way."

Joshua hadn't kept track of either formal or informal declarations of his intention to stay single. But he knew that Theresa's memory utilized her entire brain. And that brain was always logged into the mind of the King. She would remember everything that was relevant for any given moment. That was another good reason to consult her.

This time Theresa waited for Joshua to respond. They both understood the value of words, of making sound an ally in building resolve, and exercising authority over one's own life. Joshua was wondering whether he wanted to renew his commitment to celibacy. That was the reason for this conversation.

"She's a magnificent person." He swung his gaze toward Theresa. "You knew I would think so before we even met."

"That doesn't mean I knew how you would respond to that attraction. In the past you have used attraction to repel yourself." She looked down at the path and kicked at a pinecone that had strayed from the trees a few yards inland.

"Did you introduce me to her in order to offer me a chance to reconsider my commitment to life-long singleness?"

"I wasn't instructed to suggest that you change your commitment or told to persuade you to stick with it. And I'm not your temptress, my dear boy. I was only encouraged to offer you a choice. But it's not just for the exercise of choosing. You and Natalie are particularly matched." Theresa paused, standing still and crossing her hands in front of her. "And, of course, Natalie also has a choice."

Joshua was still laughing at the idea of Theresa as temptress. He set that aside, to stay on topic.

"I don't suppose you could tell me if Natalie is having this same conversation with Joanna." He tucked his hands in his pants pockets.

"I would not tell you that, even if you asked me very nicely." She hooked a hand around his near arm and chuckled.

"You do remember what it was like to be mortal, don't you?"

"Yes. But even that is not going to persuade me to violate Natalie's privacy on your behalf." She shook her head at him briefly. "You will just have to work on making a mind connection with Natalie the way you do with me when we're apart. You can use that when you have some pressing need for romantic reassurances."

He laughed from his belly for a few seconds. But the thought of being able to link to another mortal the way he could communicate with Theresa distracted him from almost everything else they had been talking about.

Almost.

CHAPTER FIFTY-ONE

For years, Natalie had been guided by a trinity of immortals, Joanna being one of them. And it had been over a decade since Joanna had stepped back from her shepherding role in Natalie's life. But Joanna knew her intimately and had seen how Natalie had gotten to where she was.

For Natalie, the commitment to singleness came only after a failed marriage and another broken relationship. By the time she was forty, she was finished with romance. Over the years that followed, she allowed her immortal friends to wash away the residue of those two lost loves. By the time she was in her fifties, she had taken on a sense of destiny and vocation in singleness.

Joanna lounged on a patio chair behind Natalie's house in the woods just south of Portland. The house was sixty years old but looked better than it did when brand new. Immortal craftsmen and women had worked on the house, as had mortals who had learned from them. Like most homes under the Reign, it was grand and sunny and breezy. But, of course, the breeze was even better on the porch, which was covered only by a grid of narrow beams intertwined with two types of vines that bloomed at alternate times of the year. Both species had been invented in recent decades, splicing vines found in the Amazon rain forest with others found in East Asia. This night, the purple blossoms of the caliper vine were closing, a process that gave the plant its name, the large petals bending toward each other like closing calipers.

Natalie arrived out of the kitchen, bearing a tray with glasses of iced tea, a mango and spice blend she knew Joanna preferred. She would never forget that because Joanna kept her supplied with it. Dressed in a light, flowing cotton gown, like the one Joanna wore, Natalie took the part of a lounging aristocrat from an earlier age, an earlier world.

Joanna thanked Natalie for the drink and continued to rest her head on the back of the chaise lounge, taking her time before answering the question that had prompted her visit. She seemed to like taking her time, but she certainly recognized the point at which this began to annoy Natalie.

"I was usually the one who was 'it' when we started games during my childhood. Whenever someone said 'one, two, three, not it,' my mouth simply refused to jump in with a quick reply. I got used to being 'it' before long." She smiled and sipped her tea.

Natalie chuckled. She was used to Joanna responding to an unspoken mood. Leaning back on her own cushy chair, pulling one leg up under her and allowing her other foot to dangle above the ground, Natalie allowed her old friend to take her time.

Joanna set down her glass and leaned forward, her eyes reaching out for Natalie's. "Do you want to be with him?"

"Of course, you know I want him." She was only admitting out loud what both of them recognized. "The question is whether I want him badly enough to mess up my whole life for him." She wasn't teasing or exaggerating. She was also not complaining.

"You know how much I love messes." Joanna closed her eyes and chuckled.

"That's because you are incapable of seeing it as chaotic and out of control."

Joanna stuck to the agenda. "You will not know whether it is worth it until *after* it happens."

As a politician, Natalie was very familiar with weighing costs and benefits, and even agreeing to test an idea, to see what might happen. Doing this with her own life seemed much less inviting than doing it with a new plan for landscaping around the capitol building, or distributing a new type of job among the mortals.

"You're not going to make this easy for me? Letting me know how this little experiment will turn out?"

Joanna smiled. She knew that Natalie was teasing about the prospect of a glimpse into the future. The immortals surely did this sort of thing all the time, but sharing it with the mortals was out of the question.

"I've told you many times. I can't see past the decisions you have not yet made."

Natalie sighed deeply. "So the question is whether I want to be with him badly enough to take the chance that this will be a mess that I don't like, and you can't clean up."

"And there is also the question of whether he wants the same, of course."

Natalie nodded, staring now into the darkness around her patio, where golden-green lights had begun rising from the thick grass. Like searchers fanning out into the night with tiny lanterns in their hands, the lightning bugs cast their glow and began their silent quest. They were, in fact, looking for the same thing as Natalie and Joshua. But would any of them find what they really, truly needed?

CHAPTER FIFTY-TWO

One Friday morning, Joshua landed at Natalie's house, greeted at the door with a surprisingly intense hug. They were expected at an important meeting, so he didn't stop to get an explanation about that intensity. He thought momentarily about that mind link Theresa had teased him with. But he stuck to their schedule, and launched them to Claire Moore's office in Missoula, Montana, as planned. The wind from the west was insistent when they landed in the parking lot, in front of a two-story house that had been converted to a handful of offices.

"Good thing we weren't flying. Would ha' been a tricky landing."

"You're always looking out for me." Natalie bowed in exaggerated gratitude.

Joshua had arranged to meet two other people who would assist in this mission. Zhongli was making her first trip to North America, and the immortal that monitored Grizzly settlement arrived with her. His name was Collin. He had been a musician in his first life, before he became a pastor of an edgy congregation north of London. Collin and Joshua had briefly met once before.

With four people now approaching the front door of Claire's office, the team was in place for the first stage of introducing a little girl to her new life. Her name was Violet, and she was seven years old. That was how much Joshua knew about her in advance. She was from an extreme rebel enclave calling itself Grizzly Settlement.

What he really needed to know couldn't be sent in an electronic message or summarized during a phone call.

Joshua followed Natalie, who stepped through the door of the well-maintained chalet and led the way to the back office. The congresswoman's name and title stood on the door, in gold letters, on a plaque with a black background. Inside that door, they encountered a receptionist's desk which was unoccupied. Claire emerged from her big corner office to meet the team.

"Hello, hello. Welcome, all of you." She shook hands as each person was introduced. When Natalie introduced Joshua, Claire hung on for a few seconds longer, evaluating the man of whom she had certainly heard a great deal.

"So you're the guy?" She nodded slightly. She seemed to approve. Claire was one of Natalie's closest colleagues in the congress, and a personal friend. She represented the district in which the small rebel community had formed. That was her connection to this rescue mission.

Though Joshua hadn't received any specific debriefing from Natalie, he had expected that Claire might have heard a few things about him. He returned the squeeze she gave his hand, along with a little grin.

The team loaded into a twelve-passenger van driven by one of Claire's staff. She had been dealing with complaints about the Grizzly Settlement for months. Now Natalie had talked her into accompanying her and Joshua to see some of what the rescuers do for refugee children.

They drove on immaculate roads to a safe house twenty minutes north of Missoula. Rolling into the unpaved yard of a little white farmhouse, the van bumped to a stop a few feet from the front porch.

Joshua had to break away from a conversation with the driver regarding the revival of baseball in Chicago, something Joshua knew little about, but with which the driver seemed deeply fascinated. The establishment of a free world with ample resources raised the possibility—and even the priority—of recreation. But people now had so many options in which they could *participate*, that spectator sports hadn't grown to what they were before the war.

More generously appointed, this farmhouse stood in stark contrast to the safe houses Joshua had known. This house had more the feel of a home than safe houses he had visited recently. There was even a dog lounging near a doghouse twenty yards from the porch.

Collin answered Joshua's observations. "We actually have a family living here. They serve as temporary hosts for our lost little ones. We haven't had many rescues in this part of the world." Collin led the way out of the van. "The ones we do have are mostly kids who get sick and are healed by my brothers or sisters. Violet is one of those."

He walked right in the front door, without knocking, or standing aside to allow only mortals to enter. Again, Collin answered Joshua's surprise. "This little one seems not at all perturbed by our presence here, as if she so thoroughly disbelieves that we immortals exist that, to her, we're not really here."

Joshua glanced at Collin as they pushed through the mudroom and into the front hall of the peaceful little house. Collin was a known jokester. This was no joke.

A woman with dark golden hair tied into a braid down her back came from the kitchen, preventing Joshua from investigating more of Collin's explanation.

"This is Marin." Claire extended a hand toward their hostess. Then she proceeded to introduce the three people Marin didn't know.

Joshua sensed two things from Marin when they shook hands. The first was a gentle probing that she ventured into *his* soul, much like what he did to others when he met them. It was similar to the feeling of meeting one of the immortals. The second insight was about early pain, deep wounds and old scars, that seemed to be old news, but familiar stories. And he could tell that Marin knew that he had glimpsed these secrets.

He then noticed a twinge of jealously in Natalie. She seemed to see something of the communication between Joshua and Marin, though he guessed that she didn't know all that they had communicated. She blushed when she realized that Joshua was apparently reading her jealousy. They exchanged a smile. Joshua hoped his was a reassuring smile. He was busy ignoring the significance of Natalie's jealously toward another woman. That was something for a later conversation.

Two girls passing the doorway into the kitchen, toward the rear of the house, drew Joshua back on task. Marin saw the eyes of her guests switch toward the movement behind her.

She glanced over her shoulder and explained. "My daughter, Rachel, is taking Violet out back, so you can see her there." She looked at Joshua.

Joshua was still checking for confirmation that he should do the initial interview with Violet. The King seemed to communicate a fairly urgent affirmative. But no reason for that urgency came across that connection. Joshua nodded to acknowledge Marin's arrangement and then followed her into the kitchen.

She offered drinks to everyone, even as Joshua headed for the back door. Marin seemed at ease with the process and made no comment about Joshua's quick pass through the kitchen.

A small pantry, shelves lined with Mason jars on both sides, led to a small mud room, and a screen door onto a concrete porch. Joshua pushed through the freshly-painted green door, his focus resting on the two girls at the swing set. The older was clearly Marin's daughter, her light pink face and small clouds of freckles giving her away.

Violet looked very different—small, slender, and dark-haired. Her nearly black eyes hinted of native American heritage perhaps. Her fine fingers promised a mature elegance in her future. But, of course, Joshua was intent on looking into Violet's heart. What he found there at first glance was surprising. She struck him as a content child who had been shocked only with a recent trauma. She didn't show signs of a life of abuse, only one recent devastation to a heart that had been relatively at peace.

She was like a strong, young sapling sheltered from storms until suddenly bent low by one very severe wind. She had bounced back up, but a trained eye could see the creases where that sudden trauma had nearly broken her.

Joshua wondered if Collin's characterization of her inability to see the immortals was less the point than her mental paralysis, which kept her from expressing what had happened to her. It wasn't just the immortals she was ignoring. She hadn't recovered her balance enough to deal with what had happened to her.

As Joshua walked toward the swing set, hoping some nonverbal communication with Rachel would smooth the way, he smiled at the two girls. "Mind if I join you?"

Rachel readily played along, though they hadn't been formally introduced. "Of course, there's a swing still open."

Joshua took the third swing, the one farthest from the house and on the opposite side of Rachel. Violet mutely watched him walk past, not responding with any particular emotion on her face, not even curiosity that this tall man would want to swing on a kids' swing set. She had a bit of a sleepwalker look to her when Joshua glanced her way. It seemed worth trying to wake her up.

"So, where are you girls from?"

Rachel hesitated a moment. "I live here."

Violet blinked rapidly for a few seconds and then relaxed back into her dulled state. "Yeah, I live here, too."

"Oh, how long *you* been here?"

Rachel looked at Violet. Violet seemed to notice the void and twitched her head self-consciously. She kicked her legs and launched the swing higher, rousing it from the diminishing pendulum she resembled until then.

"I just came here last night."

Joshua kicked off the ground, so he matched the motion of Violet's swing. Rachel stayed at a small back-and-forth, with her heels resting on the ground. This allowed an illusion that Joshua and Violet were together, just the two of them.

"Oh. Where did you live before last night?" He tried to sound as if he were just making polite conversation.

"In the woods."

Joshua coasted forward and then back, attempting to stay with Violet's pace.

"But you live here *now*?" Joshua asked it, as if the question had just occurred to him.

Violet nodded, perhaps less convinced of her earlier answer. She pumped her feet harder and rose higher in the shushing wind. The aspens around the house seemed to be advocating silence.

Prompted by a change in the emotional signals coming from Violet, Joshua focused more intensely on her posture. She was swinging high with her eyes closed, as if she wanted to fly away from the answers to simple questions, such as where she lived.

Joshua could tell that she was about to break. He stopped his swing and stood up quickly, placing himself in front of Violet's swing. Rachel stopped swinging entirely. She watched Joshua with wide eyes.

Violet began to cry and her body went limp, causing the swing to falter and wobble. On her next forward coast, Joshua stepped up and caught her out of the swing. She released the rubber-covered chains with one hand and clung to Joshua's neck, while still holding the other chain, the swing banging against her legs, for two beats before she let it go.

Cathartic tears gushed from Violet. Joshua could feel her flailing emotionally. He knew she wasn't entirely comfortable with him holding her. But she was beside herself. He only touched a child when he thought it very important to do so. Embracing a little one like this, when they had hardly been introduced, was extraordinary. But the explosion of Violet's emotions required an extreme response.

Rachel stood up, glancing toward the house. When she looked back at him, Joshua motioned with his head for her to come close. He nodded toward Violet's back, and Rachel began to stroke that little back. Joshua moved his hand to make a space.

As soon as he could feel Violet growing uncertain that she should be held by him, Joshua squatted to the ground so she could extricate herself as soon as she wanted space. She let go of Joshua's neck, pausing to look at the big wet spot she had left on his light blue shirt. But she didn't apologize. She stood sniffling, dizzy with emotions. Joshua kept a gentle hold on each of her arms as she steadied herself.

Violet reached up to take some tissues from Rachel's hand. Then she looked at Joshua. "I don't really live here." She shuddered a breath inward and then released it in more sobs.

Rachel wrapped her up, Violet's face buried in the older girl's green cotton shirt. The tears and sobs expanded again.

Joshua spoke gently to her. "I'm here with some good friends, Violet, to help find you a new home. You can stay here for a little while. You need to rest. Then we'll make sure that you have a place to live that you can be proud of." He knew her stretch of the truth about living in this house was to protect her shame at not knowing *where* she lived. He could also tell that she was confused about what she had done to lose the only home she had ever known. Apparently, she didn't know the immortals had intervened to heal her.

Signaling toward the house, Joshua beckoned Natalie and Zhongli to join them, a prearranged stage in helping Violet settle in. He could see, from the redness of her nose, that Natalie had been crying. Zhongli, more clinical in this context, appeared sedate as always.

Over the next half hour or so, Zhongli, Joshua and Natalie spoke sparse words to Violet, watching her release the last of her tears. After that time in the back yard, Joshua led them all inside, where food and drinks would further help the little orphan recover.

Claire and her driver left soon after Joshua and company returned to the house, leaving a quiet scene around the kitchen table. Violet devoured little sandwiches and guzzled limeade with Rachel. Joshua and Zhongli monitored her emotions, even as they engaged with the adults around the table.

CHAPTER FIFTY-THREE

Marin's husband, Rich, had come home during snack time and joined them around the large, rustic table. He and Joshua followed a predictable path of getting to know each other through question and answer, with Collin inserting a joke now and again. They laid a foundation of normalcy for Violet, allowing her to focus on filling her tummy and on letting go of any need to perform for the adults.

But that peace broke down with the sound of a vehicle crunching gravel in the driveway and doors slamming as soon as the vehicle stopped. Collin was the first to launch into action. He stood quietly and swiftly, heading for the front door.

Natalie looked a question at Joshua. He was calculating whether he would be needed more on the porch or with Violet. She seemed well covered, so Joshua decided to join Collin.

A strange scene greeted Joshua through the front door. Like a museum diorama from days before the war, something he had only seen on video, four figures stood motionless on the porch and the sidewalk. They were frozen in poses that witnessed to a hasty approach, before they became living wax figures. The only obvious sign of life was their eyes roving wildly. He had seen this tactic used by other immortals in similar situations. The attackers would feel no pain but couldn't move any more than Collin allowed them to. He had obviously frozen their mouths. Joshua wondered what they had been saying that required such a verbal lockdown.

"You have everything under control." Joshua offered it as a compliment to Collin.

Then he spoke to the three men and one woman posed before him. "Collin will release your mouths to speak, if you promise to behave yourselves. He can shut you down faster than you can say a single syllable." He looked for some sign in their blinking and glaring eyes. "Do we have a deal?"

A gentle blink by the woman seemed a good response to Joshua, who was monitoring emotions as well as eye movement. He nodded toward the woman and Collin released her mouth.

"Who are you, and what are you doing here?" Joshua asked, for starters.

"We're looking for my daughter."

"What makes you think she's here?"

"Some friends traced her to this house as of last night. Her name is Violet, and she doesn't belong here."

"Violet was abandoned by her parents in the woods."

"We ... he ... I was wrong, I ... might ... I shouldn't have agreed."

"Agreed with your husband?"

The woman hesitated. "Yes. He doesn't know I'm here."

Joshua had already detected that the entourage didn't include the woman's husband, Violet's father. He sensed that the men were her brothers, or brothers-in-law.

"So you didn't tell him you were coming here, but you think you can talk your husband into taking her back, now that you've found Violet in the company of immortals?" He refused to call Collin an alien, as much as he would like to tease him. This was deadly serious.

"I don't know. I guess ... I guess ... I can't take her back to him."

Joshua looked at Collin, who had already decided to let her go, only waiting to coordinate that with Joshua.

The woman nearly fell over when Collin released his hold on her. Joshua reached out a hand and helped her steady herself, her heavy boots scraping on the wooden porch.

Joshua introduced himself and the woman reciprocated.

"I'm Carrie Snyder." She shook Joshua's offered hand after a brief pause. She looked at him the way she might regard a stack of explosives that she needs for some vital purpose.

"I'm as mortal as you are." He answered her unspoken fear.

He could read Carrie's confusion. There wasn't anything he could do about the clash of worldviews that was thundering inside her head.

Joshua turned to the three men, who were watching uncomfortably from their action poses. "What are you gonna do if we let you loose?"

Collin made a hum deep in his throat that might have sounded threatening to the strangers. But, to Joshua, it sounded like a suppressed chuckle.

When Collin released their mouths so they could respond, what came out was two simultaneous profanities and one glob of spit. All the above were followed by apologies. Carrie cast a corrective look at her three co-conspirators.

Joshua let the gentlemen hang for a moment longer. "What was the plan? You can't do anything by force. It just won't stand. You must *know* that. Even if you still think these people are aliens from outer space, you have to deal with the fact that you can't overpower them. You can't outrun them. And you can't predict what they'll do next. What was the plan?" He truly felt sorry for these folks, after that summary.

He had pushed his voice toward a scolding sound, one that reminded him of his father, when Rodney had to deal with irrational rebels. Joshua felt pretty good about the effect he had achieved.

One of the men cleared his throat. But it was Carrie who answered. Her answer came in a torrent of tears. Apparently, Joshua's speculation covered how far the plan had been developed. Another curse fell from the mobile mouth of an immobile man, and Joshua returned to his more diplomatic and gentle tone.

"We never take kids away from parents who aren't harming them. We have no interest in destroying your family or messing up Violet's life. But we will always step in where a child is abused or abandoned. Violet was abandoned, so now we have an interest that won't go away just because you've changed your mind." He realized, when he finished, that he was still scolding, surprised at himself for how long he could wear that cop uniform his father had worn—the same invisible uniform Rodney had worn.

Joshua sighed and patted Violet's mother on the shoulder. She was beginning to rummage through her pockets as if looking for something to blow her nose on. Joshua pulled a cotton handkerchief from his pocket. In his line of work, it often came in handy—handy, that is, when his shirt wasn't used to catch the outpouring.

Collin made significant eye contact with each of the frozen men and seemed convinced that they would behave themselves. He released his hold. The one who had frozen while scaling the stairs, fell over when Collin let him go. A fairly sincere apology from Collin followed.

Though the cleanup was somewhat comical, and the crisis had settled into a standoff, Joshua had some serious decisions to make. He sent a question off to his divine advisor and got the go-ahead to allow Carrie into the house for a discussion. Her three bodyguards would drink limeade on the porch, in this next phase of the negotiations.

With Carrie sitting in the living room waiting, Joshua consulted with the adults around the kitchen sink. Violet was nearly asleep over her empty plate, hours yet until sundown. Knowing what to do next would have been easier if the girl were at the peak of her freshness. She was emotionally beat and another trauma was not an option. Marin and Zhongli ushered Violet out of the kitchen and up to the bedroom where she had been sleeping. She would go down for a nap of undetermined length.

When Violet was settled, Carrie joined the rest of the adults in the kitchen, along with her two brothers and her sister's husband—her three bodyguards. They crowded around while Rich pulled together a meal for everybody. Meal preparation at least gave one person something to do, something with which he was quite comfortable. The same couldn't be said for the majority of the people at the table.

With Collin as the enforcer, Joshua knew that nothing would transpire there that wasn't the best they could arrange for Violet. He wasn't confident that the outcome would also be the best for Carrie.

Having covered all the niceties and preliminaries, a conversation followed that resembled meeting a fiancée's hostile parents.

"So, with your other children at home, you're not gonna be able to just take Violet and disappear." Joshua spoke gently, the voice of reason in Carrie's head.

The bowed heads of her brothers seemed to concede Joshua's assessment. Carrie stared out the kitchen window at the sky turning deeper blue in the late afternoon sun.

Natalie tried to move them all toward a solution. "What if we could arrange a good home for Violet, and you could come—alone—to see her?"

Carrie furrowed her brow at Natalie. Joshua knew that his friend had just revealed her naivete about the culture of the resisters. Amicable cohabitation was beyond them. That was why they had scampered off into the woods to hide from the aliens. These particular exiles were so intolerant that they couldn't even coexist with most other rebels. Carrie wouldn't be allowed to visit her daughter, a captive to the alien horde, and then simply return home to cook dinner.

The mute response of everyone at the table surely revealed what Natalie hadn't recognized. She pursed her lips apologetically. Someone *had* to try to provide a working plan for a way forward. Natalie had sacrificed herself in the attempt, or at least sacrificed her optimism.

Joshua detected a strong emotional shift in the room, and then heard a little voice. Later he would wonder why no immortal intervened to prevent it. But Violet stood in the kitchen doorway looking confused.

"Mom? What are you doing here?"

All the adults froze. This time, Collin wasn't responsible for that statue-like display. But Joshua knew his immortal friend was ready to control the situation when the four visitors awoke from their shock. The only thing that had changed, however, was that Violet's heart would be more directly exposed to the impossible decision he had to make.

That she didn't simply run to her mother and beg to be taken back, signaled something for Joshua. Perhaps the raw instincts of a seven-year-old are wiser than the entangled problem-solving of a whole room full of adults. Perhaps she had done her own problem-solving and drawn the same conclusion with which Joshua and his team had begun this adventure. And, perhaps, she knew that clinging to her mother now would only make it hurt more.

Whatever process—mental or emotional—that Violet had used, she had accepted her separation from her family. She knew she couldn't go back. She knew it was wrong for her mother to be in this house.

"Mom? What are you doing here?"

Joshua winced at a very small sampling of what these words did to Carrie's heart. He simply couldn't stay connected to that much pain.

Later that night, after her family left, Violet didn't resist being transported and resettled in another location, to prevent another desperate rescue attempt.

Rachel and Zhongli went with Violet to provide some human continuity for a girl who still thought of the immortals as aliens. And Joshua and Natalie transported back to her house. Natalie's role had initially been to connect Joshua with a case that lay under Claire Moore's jurisdiction, from a political standpoint. But that political role had evaporated like spilled water on hot pavement in the face of emotional trauma and family conflict.

"Can you stay and talk for a while?" Natalie looked more vulnerable than Joshua had ever seen her.

He checked on the wisdom of the two of them being alone late in the evening and heard an assurance that they would *not* be alone. This was where having the immortals watching over him added the sort of accountability that people used to get with a chaperone.

Joshua nodded toward the front door and Natalie led the way. They settled onto the patio. There, temperatures had dropped just enough that hot tea seemed a perfect way to end the day.

Standing under the flowering vine, studying its unique twist and its tantalizing blossoms, Joshua let himself relax another notch, as Natalie returned with the tea on a tray—a tray that included homemade cookies.

"Wait, you never mentioned that you bake. Were you saving that as a secret weapon?"

"I do bake, but I don't think these cookies would constitute a weapon." She settled the tray on the glass-top table between the lounge chairs. "They're not *that* good, I would guess ... and they're not *that* bad either."

Joshua laughed. "You mean not so bad that you could literally use them as weapons?"

Natalie laughed in return, kicking off her shoes and selecting a lounge chair with deep cushions.

Joshua knew they still had a serious conversation waiting. "You feeling pretty beat up by what happened today?"

Natalie stopped sipping her tea and released a slow sigh. "I guess you're never prepared for something like that, if you haven't seen it before. My heart was just torn apart for Violet. What a horrid situation to experience at such a young age."

Joshua tested his tea and then responded in gentle, even tones. "It's perfectly understandable that you identify with her and that you feel her pain. That's natural and healthy. But I've had to learn to let it pass through, in the door to my soul and out toward the King."

During the pause after his last statement, he could tell that Natalie was probing, trying to measure his heart, to monitor his feelings. "Do you still feel the pain of these children?"

Joshua was chewing and swallowing a bite of a cookie, detecting pecans and some other crunchy bits.

"When you learn to listen to another person's heart, you learn to hear their pain. When you allow your heart to beat with theirs, you *feel* their pain. What I have to do at that point is not make it my *own* pain." He smirked a bit and took another bite, as he thought about what he did intuitively, in a way that he could explain it to an intelligent person. "This is why I've had to spend so much time getting my own issues addressed. If I still have unfinished business, then I get entangled pretty easily—my pain and their pain twisting together. I don't think any mortal can do it perfectly, of course. But I try to keep it all as clear as possible, so I don't get burned out."

"Have you known others who *did* get burned out?"

"Oh, I don't have to look to others. In fact, we're really the first generation doing this. No, I've struggled with emotional fatigue many times in the past. Usually it alerts me that I need to get something healed in myself. A really big issue was trying to be the savior of these kids. I can help, but only the King can save them." He squinted into the darkness around the patio, as the sunset faded. "I'm still working on it."

"Well, you know where I'm going with these questions, of course. I want to make sure that the reason you stayed single isn't that you've numbed your heart, and can't let anyone in." She looked at him over her teacup and the set it down. "I'm still recovering from failed connections in my past, my failed marriage, for one."

Joshua had heard about her marriage to an ambitious politician who lacked emotional depth and marital loyalty. He was still uncertain whether her singleness was a way to avoid repeating the pain of her ex-husband's infidelity. But he backed off that for now and focused on this one evening. This one moment.

He left his tea and cookies behind and sat at the end of the lounge chair where Natalie reclined. Lifting one foot into his lap he gently started to massage it, starting slowly and focusing on his work. He could feel a large balloon of emotion rise in her as he dug in.

For the next half hour, very few words passed between them. He massaged her feet and Natalie cried. For that evening, she embraced the role of a receiver. Joshua was glad to see that she could let go and trust him with such deep pain.

CHAPTER FIFTY-FOUR

Rodney was the grill man around the house these days. It hadn't been something he had relished all along. Grilling was a luxury that had to gradually evolve on the farm. When he and Emma first built this house, cooking was mostly utilitarian. Cooking over an open fire meant squatting over coals made from salvaged wood. It took them a while to go back to outdoor grilling with the same enjoyment Rodney had known before the final war.

When Joshua landed on the front porch for a brief visit that would include supper with Daniel and Tina, Rodney couldn't stop grinning. And it wasn't about the barbeque, of course. He could still remember beef steaks on a grill, but he didn't miss them as much as he used to. He did, however, miss having the kids around.

How long had it been since they had all been there? But not all of them were here this night. Where was Miranda?

He huffed at himself. More and more he found his mind wandering into a sort of dead end, getting lost down trails that led to no reasonable place. He knew where Miranda was. She was on the other side of the world. She didn't get over here more than once a year. And this wasn't one of those visits.

These stumbles weren't just happening in his head. He was glad that everyone was laughing at Daniel telling stories about his robot store clerks doing nutty things. No one seemed to notice the way Rodney kept fumbling the grill tools. What was that thing called? Pincers? Was that right?

This last falter Joshua might have noticed. He was watching Rodney when he picked up the fork and turned the moist protein pieces toward the cooler part of the grill. Rodney tried to fake his son out with a shrug and a little smile. But Joshua wasn't likely to fall for such an easy dodge.

Later, when Rodney headed for the kitchen to get the corn on the cob, he hesitated at the door. He didn't mean to overhear them. But he did overhear Joshua and Emma.

"Dad seems to have more trouble doing things these days."

"Umhmm. He's even agreed to turn that crazy robot back on." Emma did one of those unconvincing laughs.

He should interrupt them, Rodney knew. But he didn't.

"Did something happen?"

Emma let go of a carrot or something, letting it rumble into the sink. "I guess I shouldn't be surprised that you figured that out." She paused. "He had another visit from the King."

Rodney wanted to tell this part. He pulled the screen door open.

"I heard." He didn't want to deceive them.

Joshua nodded. But his eyebrows were still raised. He probably wanted to hear what the King had said.

It took Rodney a couple of beats to let loose of his story about seeing the King. He leaned on the counter near the sink.

"He just showed up by the barn this time. Didn't even take me anywhere. I guess this is the seventh visit. I'm always so grateful." He checked how Joshua was doing, wondering if he knew where he was going with this. "And we talked about a lot of the same things. But this time he didn't try to stop me from longing for what lies ahead. He didn't try to stop me from wanting to move on ... to immortality."

"Did he give you an idea when it would happen?"

Rodney shrugged. He was feeling pretty tired. But at least his thoughts were clear right now. "I don't know if he ever tells anyone when. I guess he cares more about how you think or feel about it than the exact date."

Joshua nodded. "That makes sense. But why did this visit seem to slow you down?"

"Slow me down? Well, I guess that really is what it did." He cocked his head back a little. "I guess it made me stop trying so hard to stay alert, to stay alive."

He could see Emma's face clouding up here. A harsh rebuke swelled up inside him. How could he be so selfish? He stepped next to his wife of eighty some years and put an arm around her waist.

"Part of me always wants to give up on *this* life." He stared hard into Emma's eyes. "The picture of my future with the King makes me long for a new start." For a moment, Rodney lost track of where he was going with that.

"We all have that same pull," Joshua said. "Of course, we want to be with the people we love. But, if the King has a better life for them, how can we resent them wanting it?"

Emma rested her head on Rodney's shoulder. "I guess part of me is still that scared single mom looking for a home, after the earthquakes and wars. I was so lucky to find you."

Rodney stood up straighter. "I'm not goin' anywhere just yet, old girl." He looked at Joshua with his head held higher. "I'll be glad for some of that healing you do, Joshua. I've been havin' a hard time controlling my hands lately, and a few other little issues too."

He expected that his son, who spent so much time with the glorified saints, could recognize the temptation to move on. But Joshua had also acquired the skills for keeping his father alive and alert for a little longer.

Standing there in the kitchen, in a mere two minutes, Joshua pulled a sort of veil off Rodney's mind. When it lifted, he could see that the King hadn't meant for him to give up living yet. He had just offered a picture of the future that was meant to reassure him that he would be going from one beautiful life to an even better one.

It would come, in due time.

CHAPTER FIFTY-FIVE

A week after their trip to Montana, Natalie sat in a restaurant watching candlelight play in eyes that shone deep blue in the low light. Something had changed between them, and Natalie was trying to discern exactly what it meant, even if she couldn't define it precisely. Joshua had told the story about his father, which moved Natalie to tears. Now she fought to restrain herself from asking a question that pressed hard against her throat.

When she paused to wonder how much of these internal gymnastics he could read, she started to chuckle.

"What?" Joshua spread an uncertain smile.

Natalie reached across the little table and took his hand. "I'm just laughing at myself for trying to find a way around you knowing what I'm feeling, while realizing what a treasure it is that you know, and still want to be with me."

Joshua's relieved laughter echoed Natalie's. "I get a strong sense of what you're feeling, but what you're thinking I can only guess, based on those feelings."

Sighing through her nose, even as she kept her smile on, Natalie faced the question. "I was wondering, of course, whether you would choose the same way your father did." She stopped short of the most vulnerable part of that question.

"If I had to choose between becoming an immortal and going on living as an old man with a beautiful wife, who has the whole world in her eyes and my heart thoroughly captivated by hers?"

Maybe reading someone's feelings was a good way to find just the right thing to say. She sat stunned, trying to replay the words he had just said. For a moment, she was too overwhelmed to even cry.

But Joshua let some of the air out of the moment. "Now, if I could only find such a woman ..."

She nearly spit when she started laughing at that. They were in a little Ethiopian/Indian restaurant in Seattle. Natalie looked around to see if anyone had seen her spew that laugh. She was grateful to not be in her own congressional district just then.

When they had finished their meals, Joshua made a serious declaration. "I'm officially ending my commitment to staying single." He was sitting back in his chair as if allowing room for the rich meal he had just eaten.

Natalie got some revenge for his last joke. "Is this so you can devote yourself to finding that woman with the whole world in her eye?"

He smiled big. "Yes. Then I can finally help her get the darn thing out. That must really hurt."

She laughed hard for a few seconds. She cleared her throat with a sip of wine. "So, I guess I really should respond to your declaration seriously."

Joshua nodded and waited with a more placid smile.

"I want to make the same declaration." She raised her eyebrows at him, then leaned forward a little. "And I want to explore this whole new adventure with you. We have something special between us, Joshua. And I know I will only benefit from getting to know you better. From here on, I plan to keep an open mind about the future."

"I like that," Joshua said. "Open-minded is good."

CHAPTER FIFTY-SIX

It was just a few days after the "dinner of the declarations," as they laughingly designated it, that Joshua met with Theresa. For once, they got together just to see each other, and to catch up, no new assignment, no critical agenda. Violet's move toward a long-term home had advanced one step further, and Joshua's role with her would end. He was preparing for his next meeting with Brice. But neither of these topics was likely to enter the conversation.

They sat in Joshua's living room, Theresa still the only woman he had entertained there unaccompanied. He sat on the couch, his right leg crossed over his left knee at the ankle. And Theresa sat on her favorite plush chaise. Gwendolyn lay asleep at her feet, worn out from purring so hard for so long.

"How's Osana doing?" Joshua asked this as a matter of polite interest and not any official responsibility.

"She's so different from you, but the process still reminds me of how it was when you were a teenager." Theresa sipped her latte and leveled a motherly grin at him, a look full of fond remembrance. "You remember that girl you were in love with, when you were nineteen?"

"Katie," Joshua said. "No, Cindi. Yeah, I remember Cindi. Was I really in love with her?"

Theresa allowed herself a rare eye-roll. "You didn't *really* forget her name?"

Joshua fixed a gaze on his friend. "You gotta remember who you're dealing with here." He dropped the serious tone and defensive look. "No, I didn't forget her name ... just a little hesitation. I think there's this defense mechanism that slows my brain when I see you digging up a dangerous memory."

Theresa grinned very slightly and stared at him under eyelids a quarter closed. This was Theresa's, "I love you, but I wonder how I put up with you," look. He knew it well. He still didn't believe it was a serious rebuke, after all these years.

"What's so dangerous about a girlfriend from eighty-two years ago?"

"Eighty-one."

"Who's counting?"

"You brought it up."

Theresa was slow to surrender that slightly superior tilt to her head.

Joshua scowled at her. "Why *did* you bring her up? Did you discover that she joined the resistance because I broke up with her?"

"No, she's the very happy mother of four kids and six grandkids. She still lives in Iowa."

"Why do I need to know this?"

"You don't. That's my point. She survived." Theresa paused to take another sip. "Natalie is a big girl. You'll both be fine."

"Wait, I thought this was just a friendly visit."

"It was. But while I was sitting here, headquarters requested I pass on the message."

"Headquarters?"

Now Theresa was laughing full-throated. She had to put her coffee down to avoid spilling it or having to do some kind of miracle to save the rug. "I have this new kid who's fascinated with pre-Reign spy movies and books."

"Can't you people destroy all those?"

"'You people?'"

"Okay. So you got the message to tell me to relax, 'cause I'm not likely to mess Natalie's life up by breaking up with her someday?"

Theresa sat in patient silence for five seconds. "Remember Natalie's notion of keeping an open mind about your future together? Well, you will find still more emotional elbow room when you also give up your vow to never hurt anyone ever again."

This bit of wisdom banged into Joshua's brain like a well-aimed brick. Joshua dropped his head onto the back of his sofa. He wanted to joke that she should warn a guy before hitting him like that, but he couldn't even form the words, let alone generate the comic timing.

"Wow." He took a few more purging breaths. "It feels good to let that go."

"Doesn't it though?" Of course, Theresa would have to recall her other life to really know firsthand, but she had been reading the hearts and minds of mortals for all these many decades, and certainly knew what they felt when they dropped a cast iron delusion that had been a bothersome weight for most of their lives.

"So, you really didn't know you were gonna hit me with that?"

"All these violent images. Have *you* been watching old movies, too?"

Joshua snickered and relaxed his head back onto the sofa, his hands resting at his sides. With Theresa, he had no need to be the host. She didn't need to be entertained. And he knew she wouldn't be annoyed at his pause to bask in his newfound freedom.

CHAPTER FIFTY-SEVEN

On a return trip from the Western Suburbs, riding on a local train, Joshua was checking his messages and thinking about something new to do with Natalie, when a message caught his attention. It was from David Adeyemi, the African man who had helped him learn to fly. Instantly, he envisioned Natalie and David meeting—a coalition of kindred spirits.

Though he had mastered travel through space, Joshua had yet to conquer the frontier of time. Finding the time when the three of them would all be free, was still the same old challenge.

Joshua had been testing going directly to the source for information about where someone else was and whether they were available for a visit. The King knew all of this. Joshua could hear the King talking to him, directly into his spirit. So he decided to try to arrange a meeting between himself, Natalie and David Adeyemi, without intervention by Theresa or one of her companions. Once again, he blazed a trail that only the immortals had walked before, as far as he knew.

He put in a request for an alert when Natalie and David were available, to be followed by a call to meet with him, and all of this without using the Internet or the immortal equivalent. With the immortals, all of this was second nature. They could tell in real time whether someone was available, and where to meet them, without any serious strain. Joshua put some strained thought into this, but he would have to rely on divine assistance—something that wouldn't be enhanced by strenuous effort.

For two days, Joshua waited for that message from within, a confirmation from the spirit of the King. But he was busy with meetings with his supervisor, with new parents of rescued children, and with two newly liberated kids. His request had been for the King to prompt him when *all three* of them were available, including himself. By the end of those two days, he was reconsidering his experiment. Perhaps he could just make an appointment, like everyone else.

At eight a.m. one Saturday, Joshua felt a strong prompt to go see Natalie. He checked whether he could just pop in for a visit but received a hesitant answer. He wondered how the King could be hesitant. Still in experimentation mode, he took five minutes to clean up his apartment and to change his shirt. Then he checked again and felt less of that hesitation. This time he decided to land on her sidewalk, in front of her house and do something conventional ... knock on her door.

A hairbrush in her hand, Natalie answered her door to his apologetic smile. At least she was dressed ... mostly. She didn't even speak, just rolling her eyes at him and smiling appreciatively. After striding to her bedroom, she came back with a light pink, long-sleeved shirt over her blue tee shirt.

"Is it okay that I just dropped in?" He was looking at photos in her living room.

"My dad was a shrimp farmer." She gestured toward the mantelpiece, and her array of family memorabilia. "He hated surprises. He said mostly they were bad news."

Joshua suspected he was being set up. "Good thing you're not a shrimp farmer." He stepped up to her and, for the first time, wrapped his arms around her for a full kiss on the lips.

When she slowly drew back from him, a different look on her face, he finished his thought. "I plan to always be full of surprises."

Resting a hand on his chest and looking up at his eyes, Natalie gently chuckled. "I love surprises."

Joshua had plans for their day, so he didn't let his mind drift toward forbidden territory. The King was arranging a meeting, so he knew it would be the best thing to do today.

"How about a trip to Jerusalem?" He knew this would rank high, as positive surprises go.

"Wow."

"A tongue-tied politician? This *is* the kingdom of God." He raised a hand to block the swat he expected.

Natalie just laughed.

"I want you to meet someone that I only met once before. I hear he is going to be in Jerusalem with some of his friends, and I wanted to crash their party."

"This just keeps getting better." Natalie tottered slightly, like a girl fresh off a carnival ride.

No need for further preliminaries, Joshua took her hand and launched himself along the King's superhighway, landing on the ground within a mile of the throne. His navigator found a rare patch of clear ground near where David Adeyemi was worshipping, with a few dozen friends.

Taking a moment to get reoriented, Joshua and Natalie stood holding hands amid a whirl of people--dancing, singing, clapping, twirling, wheeling and soaring. David flew past and then circled back hard, landing on the ground just in front of Joshua.

"My friend!" He shouted against the songs holding the air. "I thought I heard you were going to be here. How have you been? How is your flying?"

Joshua clasped David's outstretched hand and clapped him on the shoulder. "I want to introduce you to my new flight instructor." He shouted into David's ear and then gestured to Natalie, who stepped up for the introduction.

"I'm Natalie." She shouted as she leaned toward David.

Joshua realized his oversight, once they had exchanged names. "David is the guy that convinced me I could fly, and then transport."

Natalie nodded with big sweeps of her head. She looked at Joshua with uninhibited joy on her face.

He just laughed.

Then David seized the initiative. "Here are some of my friends."

Swooping toward the ground, a flock of people, who appeared to be from David's home country of Nigeria, whizzed past. A few landed in the shrinking clearing among the worshippers. The flow of the crowd had shifted. A veritable train of dancers now consumed that open space.

Instead of staying in that crazy crush on the ground, the flying mortals launched into the air just above the heads of the earthbound. Joshua, Natalie and David spun around each other, along with several others, who twirled above the ground. In the air, David pointed from his head to Joshua's and then Natalie's.

Then Joshua heard him in his head. "Your flying has improved ... a little." David laughed and spun up above Joshua and Natalie.

When he returned, Joshua defended himself. "I've become quite good at transporting. I'm nearly qualified to be an African." He hoped he was sending these thoughts to both David and Natalie.

He expected Natalie had done this with the immortals. He hoped her receiving equipment was good enough to make up for any lack in his sending apparatus. The smile on her face implied it was working.

"I've never done this with anyone before, besides the gods on Mount Olympus." She sent that into his head.

Joshua recognized her label for her immortal advisors and laughed. He turned his attention back to David.

"Are all these people mortals?" There were Nigerians of all ages spinning and flying around David. Some of the children were even playing tag in the air.

David nodded toward several as they swept past. "Yes, they are. My city has become more and more a place of flying people." He laughed at the joy of it, and at the surprise on Joshua's face.

Noting a bit of jealousy, Joshua wondered at himself. Was he so possessive of his own image as the trailblazing mortal that he would resent others who could do supernatural things? Just months ago he was feeling alone, before he met David and Natalie.

"You thought we were the only ones?" David spoke into his head, seeming to intuit Joshua's internal struggle.

Joshua glanced toward Natalie, expecting that David had included her in that "we." He nodded his acknowledgement, which was also an admission of guilt, regarding his envy that his special skills had suddenly become commonplace—at least, more commonplace than he had expected.

CHAPTER FIFTY-EIGHT

Natalie wasn't understanding some of the complex emotional changes happening in Joshua there near the throne. But she had become distracted by an invading thought about a visit with the King. She was trying to decipher the origin of that thought. She had met with the King here before, three times in her life. So she associated this proximity to the throne with meeting him face-to-face. But she chased the thought away, thinking she was here with Joshua and under Joshua's agenda.

She knew they had achieved his first goal, being introduced to David. Apparently, Joshua was now dealing with some confusion or envy at finding so many mortals who could fly on their own power. She could understand the feeling of losing some of his sense of uniqueness, even if she wasn't feeling the same. She watched as Joshua drifted toward the ground. Natalie followed him, even as David was caught up in singing and worshipping with an airborne choir.

Around the throne, human concerns and social mores blurred. While Natalie would have been concerned about Joshua's sudden change of mood if they were in Portland or Chicago, here in Jerusalem she was feeling an odd tug *away* from Joshua. She still fended off the feeling that the King was calling a meeting.

When she landed next to Joshua, standing shoulder-to-shoulder, she found his hand. But he now seemed as distracted as she was. The King had taken over the itinerary for this trip. Suddenly, Natalie knew she had to speak quickly. She leaned into Joshua's ear and nearly choked out the words.

"The King wants me. I'm going."

When Natalie left that spot where she had been holding Joshua's hand. She felt as if she had left her body, as if she were flying without the burden of flesh and bones to weigh her down. Then, as if the truth finally caught up with her, she knew that she was still in her mortal body, still alive, but hurtling toward the throne.

The speed with which she vanished from her concrete mortal reality was unfamiliar to Natalie. The intensity of the rush toward the King's presence was more urgent than any previous experience.

Linear logic seemed to be still functioning in Natalie's mind during parts of this rush toward the throne. In that left-brained mode, she expected the hot light of the glowing presence to deepen and sharpen. At first this seemed to be happening. But, as if there were a pocket of something else concealed in the glory bubble around the throne, the light changed. Suddenly she landed on the ground, cushioned by lush, green grass. Her landing ended in a tumble and roll that were painless, against all logic.

When she opened her eyes, a large, gray rabbit hunkered next to her, nibbling grass and regarding her with brown eyes that seemed a bit concerned. "Was the human all right?" Those eyes seemed to wonder.

Focused on these strange thoughts about the rabbit, Natalie didn't notice the approach of another person. A gentle wind moved the grass, and birds sang nearby, masking the fall of bare feet on the soft grass. Only the rabbit turning its attention toward the approaching person alerted Natalie. The rabbit turned playfully, with a small vertical hop, when it saw that other person. This piqued Natalie's interest regarding the identity of the rabbit's friend.

Lying on her side, grass obscuring most of her vision from her left eye, Natalie raised her head slightly to catch a clearer view of the new arrival. That she hadn't yet realized who it was, only testified to the extent to which her mind wasn't entirely under her control, her thoughts no longer going where she told them. That she wasn't surprised when she recognized the King, further confirmed her altered state.

It was like a meeting with an old friend, in a familiar spot, at a regularly appointed time. No part of her mind found this rendezvous unusual.

He nodded at her, familiar and content. "You resting?" He sat next to her head and began to stroke her hair.

"Yes. It's so peaceful here."

She noticed her hand lying in the grass, just then. At first, she wondered at the aqua-blue fingernail polish. Then her fingers seemed much shorter than she remembered. Or was that a mistake? It was odd, but not worrying. She decided to sit up and assess the rest of her body. She was wearing stretchy shorts and no shoes, a pink-and-yellow-striped tank top, and a little bit of her breakfast on the front of it. She was now eight years old. That realization came with the thought that she couldn't recall having a birthday and turning eight, as if eight came after ninety in this part of the world.

The smiling man sitting on the grass stopped stroking her hair so she could sit up. He looked pleased that she wanted to get up and play. She knew that this was what he was thinking, before she knew that she was, in fact, getting up to play.

He reached slowly toward her, as if he might start stroking her hair again, then he gently touched her shoulder and leapt to his feet. "You're it!" And off he raced.

As if her feet had agreed to this game before her head received the invitation, Natalie was off and running too. He dodged and she dodged. Her pursuit was constantly being hindered by her uncontrolled laughter. It was not *uncontrollable*, only uncontrolled. She liked it that way.

Of course, he slowed down, pretending to stub his toe on a mushroom or clover, and then she smacked him on the rear end.

"You're it!" She shouted before the giggles took over again.

And then *she* was off and running. This time her feet seemed to be made of wind and her legs flashed like lightning. She knew, then, that she could run as fast as she wanted. But she wanted him to catch her, so she slowed down. The world around her became more precise and less of a blur.

When she looked back once, she couldn't see him chasing her. She slowed down as she craned her neck. Then she ran into something which tumbled with her. Everywhere her head landed was soft, her elbows and knees only found easy places to bang and bounce.

He was mixed in with her. She couldn't tell where she ended and he began.

They finished the tumble in a heap under some lilac bushes, a salting of fallen petals all around them. That's when the tickling began. And it seemed to go on forever. Then, when he stopped, she couldn't wait for him to start again. Her own chirpy laughter made her laugh even harder.

Now she realized that, though she was still a twisting and chortling eight-year-old, she was enjoying herself with her adult mind. How was that possible?

The question of possibility clearly signaled the return of her grownup faculties. But her little-girl self didn't disappear. Her playmate stopped wrestling and plopped himself down on the thick grass, sitting cross-legged. Natalie rolled over and turned all her attention on his face. She had seen that face before. But it still felt new, like the newness of a child's dream about a birthday or Christmas.

Rising to her feet, Natalie sensed a sort of echo of herself, as if she were trailing part of her soul behind her. The height to which she rose clearly belonged to her adult self, and the person bouncing along behind was much smaller. The smiling man wasn't far away. But going to him while trailing that three-dimensional shadow, made joining him seem more complicated. She felt as if she should do something to change this, to get herself together, to make moving toward him more natural.

Natalie sat down next to the friendly man and turned to see her child-self join them. But the younger part seemed to vanish when she tried to see her, like trying to see her own back in a mirror. When the King began stroking her hair once more, Natalie was that little girl again. His stroking soothed something in her that she hadn't realized was tense and anxious.

When the sound of another person drew Natalie to turn away from the King, she gasped.

"Daddy?"

She bounced to her feet. She didn't rise to the full height of a grown woman this time. Instead, the grown part of her remained seated next to the King, watching her eight-year-old self run to her father. Her father looked well, much better than the adult Natalie could remember. He had no wrinkles on his face, and his hair was that chestnut brown which she had known as a child. He also seemed to be missing a burden of fear and guilt that had altered his gait during his life.

While the little girl hugged her father, Natalie—the adult—realized that she wanted to join them. As soon as she looked at the King for permission, he gestured and nodded toward her father, permission instantly granted. Her grown-up mind needed to check the propriety of this meeting.

She had been carrying a silent fear that her father wasn't with the King after his death. He hadn't been a resister, in a political or social sense, but she always knew that he was skeptical about the King. When Natalie had attached herself to the Reign of the King of Kings, her dad had softened his external doubts, but she knew he still kept his heart to himself.

But here he was with the King, in this wonderful place outside the mortal world.

The little girl was content to hug and then stare lovingly at her father, relieved to see him. She couldn't articulate the source of the relief, which was why her grown-up version came to help.

"Dad!" She opened her arms to join in the hug. "I'm so glad to see you here!"

Her father chuckled hard and long from deep in his belly, exuding more joy than she had seen during his life. "You were worried that I got sent to some other place, I know."

Natalie tipped her head and shrugged slightly, with a sheepish feeling of being caught at something she didn't want to admit. She had never really confronted her father about his lack of connection to the King, afraid of his gruff defensiveness.

"Some are saved as if plucked from the fire, plucked out just in time to keep them from looking like one of those marshmallows you used to hate on our camping trips." Her dad grinned at her.

Though he bubbled with enthusiasm now, Natalie expected that his reticence during life hadn't been without consequences.

He answered this thought. "The glorious ones that you have met in your life are ruling on the Earth, under the authority of the King. I, too, am under that authority. But I have a much humbler place in Heaven. I am content and grateful, nevertheless."

This explanation landed on Natalie like a very large dog jumping up into her face. She staggered back one step.

Her father had made it into the King's presence after he died. But he was one of the lowliest of servants in the kingdom. And here he was, that lowly servant, happy and thankful.

As she regained her balance, the eight-year-old reached up and took Natalie's adult hand. This was the first time she had made solid contact with that little one since she found herself split in two. The girl tugged her back toward the King.

Only the King could so easily draw a girl away from her long lost father. Both the woman and the girl swished their bare feet through the cool grass, to where the King was standing from his place on the ground. He bent slightly and lifted the eight-year-old in sturdy arms and pressed his cheek to hers. Grown-up Natalie felt a thrill go from her cheek into the rest of her body, even before the King touched her. She followed a pull into that dual embrace and wrapped her arms around the King's neck. She felt herself beginning to weep without feeling any pain that would cause such tears. Her anxiety evaporated more rapidly than the moisture in those tears.

That was the last time Natalie saw that eight-year-old version of herself. As soon as she pressed herself against that girl, held tightly in the arms of the King, she was one person again. And she was the most important person in the world, according to the look in his eyes.

As long as that was who she was in his eyes, that was enough.

CHAPTER FIFTY-NINE

A sort of stillness had settled in Joshua's head, even as the worshippers spun and whirled around him. Natalie was with the King. That made everything about this day more than worth it. He joked with himself about feeling obligated to stay around and wait for her. He was her ride, after all. What kind of guy takes a girl to Jerusalem and then just leaves her there with the King of Kings?

He was snorting at his own deliriousness when David landed with a flap of his arms and a panting smile on his sweaty face. "It seems you have found a woman who wants to spend time in the presence of the King, just like you and me."

Joshua shivered briefly, shaken out of his reverie. He could only smile. No words coalesced in his head. David smacked him hard on one shoulder. He laughed loud and then launched himself into a flock of flying worshippers.

For just one moment, a swarm of fears sped through Joshua. The chief fear was that he wouldn't be enough for Natalie. As he grasped this threat, he realized that it was true. Then he let go of his fear. He didn't have to be enough for her. She had the King. The King had her. And Joshua wasn't responsible for that relationship. Occasional chauffeur to Jerusalem, maybe. But the important part was up to Natalie and the King. He had growing confidence in her, and infinite confidence in the King.

"I wonder what they're doing."

Theresa landed next to him, as if in answer to his question. But when he looked at her, he knew she wasn't there to answer his curiosity. She had that locked-in focus in her eyes. She had brought him something. And the atmosphere around the throne had made his soul as porous as it could possibly be at this point in his life. A teachable moment.

She put a hand on his back and Joshua reeled. The world rocked. Joshua tipped forward and onto the ground. Strong hands softened the landing. He was back on the ground. On his face. A familiar posture around here.

Joshua lay with his hands up to his face, propping his cheeks off the ground and allowing his nose to breathe. Then came the peace. Wayward emotions evaporated. Curiosities collapsed. Rest settled on him.

In the deep space that enveloped him, Joshua heard a voice. Perhaps it was the King. But somehow that didn't seem to matter. It was the message that mattered.

"You are nowhere near the end of your course. Days are no longer counted as they were in the days of your father. He will pass soon. He is a remnant from the old order. You are the first generation of the new order. You will live on. And on."

He allowed some distracting thoughts about that voice. Who was it? It seemed certain that it wasn't the King. Did that matter? The King had many servants, many messengers.

Now he turned his attention to the sensation of someone stroking his back. That hand emanated intense supernatural energy that ignited his body. He flared into flame. Or so it seemed. But he couldn't feel the usual shaking he had experienced in these power encounters before. And his spirit seemed to soar more freely than it ever had.

There was the King. He was the sun around which Joshua orbited. He was the target into which Joshua was being fired. The King was in him. He was in the King.

After time undefined, he was back on his face, on the ground. He could hear the roar of worship all around him, even footsteps scuffing and stamping nearby. And that hand was still there. Stroking him. Theresa? Perhaps. He wasn't sure.

He still couldn't rise, not even to look at whoever sat next to him. He was planted. Face down.

Again, time couldn't be defined. It didn't matter. He had time. He apparently had a lot of time.

When Joshua could finally lift his head, he looked to his right. No one was there. The owner of that soothing hand had gone. He was alone. But not alone, of course.

It seemed time for him to rise to his feet. It happened in stages. By the time he stood, Bai Ming was there. She handed him a cool glass of water. He had to force himself not to release the hysterical laughter building inside him, so he could drink the needed liquid.

Perhaps someday he would no longer need water. Anything was possible, after all. Even for mortals. Mortals like him.

Then Natalie appeared right in front of him. She staggered and seemed to faint. Without time to think, Joshua stepped quickly to her and caught her before she was halfway to the ground. When he lifted her into his arms, she giggled as if she were drunk. The King had that effect on people sometimes.

As Joshua held her in his arms, the numbing intoxication he had been feeling had nearly faded. He was splashed awake by the cool refreshment he was reading in Natalie's soul. She clung to his neck and rested her head on his shoulder. He could tell that she knew he had her, and she knew he was reading her. And she raised no barriers against him.

What he read in her was mostly about her love for the King. And she was glad to let him see that, hear that and feel that with her. It was a new sort of openness in her, a new openness between them. It was as if some shutter had been pried open and nailed out of the way.

He lowered her to the ground and sat next to her, resting her head on one of his legs. They stayed that way for some minutes before he was interrupted by the drumbeat of feet landing on the ground nearby. David was back. He stood over him again. This time he was with an eleven- or twelve-year-old boy.

"Joshua, this is Anthony. He has news for you."

Anthony looked at David, as if checking for permission to proceed. David nodded once and the boy stepped forward and squatted in front of Joshua. That position seemed entirely comfortable for the boy, so Joshua remained on the ground.

"Mr. Joshua, I have a message for you, about your future." Anthony waited for Joshua to respond.

"Go ahead. What is it?"

"I see you living for many hundreds of years. I see you living above the Earth, as if you do not need a place to live, as if you do not need anything. And this is *really* living. This is not the life after life. This is a mortal life. And I see you as a leader of many people, a leader in the space above the Earth and on the Earth. And you are setting prisoners free, and those prisoners are setting other prisoners free. And you do this with very little effort, because you are so full of the power of the King that he can do *anything* through you. And people will come from all over the world to find out how you do it.

"You will be like the immortals and take assignments only from the King and train only the ones that the King gives to you. And this is far in the future, way beyond the life anyone we know has lived. That's what I see about your future, because the King has showed it to me."

Joshua stared at Anthony. The boy's oval face showed little emotion, but Joshua could tell that he was relieved to have delivered the message, glad to have fulfilled the weighty obligation.

Joshua snorted, the start of a laugh, the precursor for tears.

"Thank you, Anthony. You delivered that well. And I feel the truth of it. Bless you, young man."

The boy stood up, and Joshua reached up and shook his hand. Joshua looked at David, who was beaming. He, too, seemed a bit drunk, swaying where he stood, the prospect of falling down very real, it seemed.

Joshua heard a strange little sound that reminded him of the woman curled next to him on the ground. That sound was something between a giggle and a chirp. Natalie pressed a hand against his thigh, trying to sit up.

She pointed toward Anthony, who was preparing for takeoff. "That boy sure can see into the future."

Anthony laughed at her and then took off. David followed close behind the young prophet.

Natalie was sitting up now. Turning her head toward Joshua, she tried to steady herself. "You're gonna be great!" She laughed at herself and then rested her forehead on the point of Joshua's near shoulder. "That's what I know about it."

Joshua's eyes were blurry with tears now. He sniffled hard, the sound of it lost in the crowd of worshippers. He didn't know how to respond to her drunken commentary. Except to say one thing.

"Whatever happens to me, I hope you'll be there to see it."

She raised her head and quirked one side of her mouth at him. "You can count on that." And she rested her head back on his shoulder.

Joshua reached around her and leaned a bit forward to balance their weight. Natalie curled close against him and sighed.

Theresa had promised to introduce him to a woman who could fly. He had looked forward to meeting someone who held no obligation to old rules like gravity. But here he was, silently celebrating meeting a woman who was content to rest before the throne and even giggle once in a while, under the intoxication from the spirit of the one who gave them freedom to lift off the ground and hurtle through space.

And, apparently, Joshua had a long future ahead of him in which to share that rare air, and to revel in that freedom. Now, he was more certain than ever that he wouldn't be doing that alone.

Acknowledgements:

I'm grateful for the folks who read and enjoyed the first REIGN book, especially Nathan Ovitt and Joshua Jones, who motivated the writing of this next book with their enthusiasm.

Also, thanks to Laurie Visher for her extensive proofreading help.

Made in United States
Orlando, FL
09 March 2022

15579551R00162